Litty Mathew

THE MUSICIAN'S SECRET

A Novel

Third Floor Publishing
Glendale, California

Published by
Third Floor Publishing
Glendale, California 91205

Library of Congress Control Number: 2015900874

ISBN: 978-0-9864296-0-6

PRINTED IN THE UNITED STATES OF AMERICA

First Edition

Book and cover design by Judy Walker
www.JudyWalkerDesign.com

Front cover photo of duduk player by Sage Leitson
Back photo of duduk by Shea "Sheram" A. J. Comfort

FOR MY HUSBAND
MELKON KHOSROVIAN

CONTENTS

CHAPTER ONE

Seven months ago, I was eating a guava pastry, warm from the oven, edges caramelized where the filling had spilled out, when the need to piss came over me like a scratchy, stinging, insistent yellow waterfall. I excused myself from the café table so fast, I spilled my coffee.

It hurt to pee, so I didn't notice him enter the men's room. He stood at the urinal next to me.

The boy.

"I know who you are, old man," he whispered in Armenian, a language that is quite common in my town of Glendale, California.

"Of course you know who I am. Can't I take a leak in private, or do you want me to autograph toilet paper?" It was an idle offer because the bathroom had run out of toilet paper.

"Maestro," he said, baring his darkened· gums. *A smoker.* He rubbed his yellowed fingertips together. *Nail biter.* "How are things in Sis these days? Isn't that near your family's home?" He leaned in and whispered, "Someone I know is from there, too. She *recognize-ed* you." He said the word in English, as if it had five syllables.

I could only see his head and shoulders above the stainless steel divider that smelled of industrial cleaner disguised in lemon scent. His hair was so closely cropped, his lashes were longer. They fanned down in a lush curve onto his cheeks when he blinked his large, wide eyes. He would have looked innocent if his thick eyebrows didn't meet at the bridge of his long, straight nose. It was a face that could have appeared on an ancient cave wall, a gold coin or under a knight's visor.

I shook myself dry, zipped up my pants and walked toward the door.

1

"Aren't you going to wash your hands?" he asked.

"Are you the police?"

"It's good hygiene."

He seemed sincere, so I washed my hands. It was almost 4 P.M. and I had an appointment to keep. That was March 24, 1992. I'd been eating a very late lunch with my agent, Viktor.

"Rupen *jahn*, the public loves you. You're our most celebrated musician. An icon!" Viktor said when I came back from the bathroom, waving a sandwich in the air for effect. He'd helped himself to half my *medianoche*.

We sat by the window at the Cuban bakery. With the first flaky bite of chicken empanada, I'd felt guilty. I should've been down the street at Bakery Opera. The place with the red velvet curtains and the heavenly rosewater cookies. The one my friend owned.

In Glendale, switching bakeries is like changing a gang affiliation. Cross a baker here and you can kiss fresh bread goodbye. On both cheeks. And never ever ask for the family recipe for rosewater cookies. That can get your tires slashed. Or worse, no fresh bread.

I drowned my remorse in Tapatío hot sauce, holy water, which I shook onto the sweet-savory crusts of the pastry.

"If you spread any more butter on me, you must swear to roast me at 425 degrees and turn me every half hour," I said. Viktor got me to do many things with flattery.

We conversed in English because his Armenian sounded like Portuguese spoken while juggling toothpicks in his mouth. He'd been brought up in Brazil.

"How many people here can say that three hundred paying guests want to spend a couple hours with them on their eighty-fourth birthday?" Viktor moved his arm in an arc like he was the coming Messiah, and I let him put on his own song and dance for me. I might as well enjoy the production. As any pushy agent worth his percentage, mine was chasing me into the coop for a tribute concert. "Honestly, Rupen, you should be very proud." He tried to look hurt.

"Viktor, have you ever considered chewing with your mouth

closed?" I handed him a paper napkin.

Around me, people stockpiled dozens upon dozens of empanadas and guava pies packed in glossy yellow boxes as if they could smell approaching unrest and planned to build a defensive perimeter with pastry. Despite my ill-fated trip to the bathroom, I'd eaten two chicken empanadas. I stockpiled on the inside.

A few of the customers smiled at me. One even bowed slightly. I tipped my beret. If I didn't get the occasional glance in Glendale, I wouldn't get it anywhere else. I was famous in my hometown. This is funny to me now that I sit here in my music studio and reflect on my circumstances. My dull pencil floating above these words in a notebook I should have used to write my magnum opus long ago.

"Are you sure you're not going to eat the other half?" Viktor's fingers trembled at the rim of my black plastic plate, itching for the particular solace of *medianoche*. I didn't answer not because I cared for my sandwich, but because the boy from the bathroom crossed in front of our table and walked out the door to join his friends. Viktor didn't give up. "I don't want it to go to waste."

"Help yourself. I'm watching my figure."

We both laughed.

"You and Pavarotti," he said. "But seriously, you have lost a bit of weight. It's been years since I've seen you in that jacket."

"*Merci*. I'm trying." I brushed the arm of my old plaid Pierre Cardin blazer. Vintage, my granddaughter called it.

"Well, you'll have to play for a half hour or something." His voice trailed into the roasted pork for two sloppy bites. "But that's okay with you, right? You won't be too tired? I'll schedule some singers and dancers to fill up the rest of the program. You know how we are. We want our money's worth."

Outside, the pack of Armenian youths, dressed almost identically in black, their hair slicked back in defiance of their willful curls, leaned against a single Mercedes-Benz. A goddess of a car. Shiny black, and the car's gold-rimmed hubcaps matched the boys' abundant gold chains and crosses. The car stereo blared loud enough to reverberate in my gut. I recognized the song: *Kani Vur Janim* or in English, "As Long as I Am Alive," an eighteenth century melody.

It was set to a techno beat. The boys slunk into the refuge of the bakery when a squad car slowed down in front of them.

There he was again. The boy.

"They look like trouble." I motioned at the pack with my head. "Kids with nothing to do in the middle of the day give us a bad name with the Americans. What could they possibly be doing in here?"

"The guava pie," Viktor whispered, leaning closer. "It's the best." He was a frequent bakery cheater.

I looked at each one of them, scanning their recently de-pimpled faces. Did they even understand the poetry they were listening to? I caught the boy's eye. He didn't look away.

"So, we're okay for April 24, right?" Viktor asked, examining the contents of my coffee cup.

"Okay, Viktor *jahn*. Okay." I put my hands up like the prisoner I was.

"Bravo, Maestro. I'm glad to hear you say that. We already gave away some promo tickets to the concert last month."

"Why do I even bother with you?" I asked. "Come by the studio later and we can go over the details."

"What? I'm allowed back into the temple?" he asked, his right hand clutching his chest.

"As long as you don't try to auction my things again."

"*Merci*, Rupen *jahn*." Viktor took a sip of my second coffee. "Since it's also our Remembrance Day, it will be so special." His eyes filled for a second, then he blinked the wetness away. "Also, I forgot to tell you. There's a journalist from the *Times* who wants to interview you that evening."

"Good God! Why?"

"You're Rupen Najarian. The world's most famous duduk player."

* * *

A concert. The genocide remembrance. A journalist. Too much. But nothing like the boy. I couldn't shake him, and it wasn't for lack of trying.

The fool followed me after I said goodbye to Viktor outside the bakery. He left his friends eating guava pies on the hood of their shiny deity and jaywalked across Brand Boulevard, an orange backpack slung across his shoulder.

I walked briskly up Wilson Avenue, toward the park, and he kept on my heels without saying a word. I couldn't see him but he lit a cigarette, which I could smell in the breeze.

Now why did he mention Sis? It's true. That was close to my village, sixty miles north of the Mediterranean in a place and time so long ago it felt like a suitcase on an airport carousel. Black and familiar but probably not your own.

I walked faster and turned into the atrium of my apartment complex. He'd never dare to enter such a fancy building. But he did and he cornered me by the cacti. I've always found that garden feature to be dangerous.

"You can't run away," he said. "My grandmother told me about you. She knows you."

I tried to imagine what his *tatik* must have looked like in her youth. One of those girls with red hair and blue eyes? That's what Armenians were supposed to look like before the depredations of other cultures. Or did she have dark curls and the limpid eyes of a gazelle? No matter. I didn't permit memories of the village. My life started after the fire when no one who knew me was alive.

My palms were sweating. I blinked from the sun reflecting off his plastic sunglasses.

"What are you talking about?" I fantasized about stuffing his cheap Russian menthols down his throat and choking him with the leather belt he couldn't afford to replace. His sweat was as sweet and cloying as an overripe pineapple. "I'm very busy, young man. You'd better leave before I call security."

I put my hands on my hips and stepped forward even though he was taller, stronger and younger. I'd seen elephant bulls do that to scare their enemy on the Mutual of Omaha nature show. My heart thumped. What could he possibly mean?

"I know about you." He looked around for the security guard and took a step back. "I know your secret."

"What drugs are you on?"

He seemed unsure yet tempted to answer the question. We stood still, me in my pachydermic pose and he, the nuisance tiger cub. His phone rang to the tune of the Armenian national anthem. He didn't bother to turn it off. *Let it shine against the enemy.* The song seemed to brace him.

"You'd better leave now or I'll call the police." My voice steely, I made like the elephant again. So, this was how I'd be undone? *By a hoodlum.* But the boy wasn't just any hoodlum. He was going to be my personal hoodlum.

And just then, my neighbor, Captain Cooper of the Glendale Police Department, in his uniform, walked in. The boy walked out, postponing our inevitable collision.

Captain Cooper and I took the same elevator upstairs. My hand trembled as I pressed the button.

"You okay?" he asked, taking off his jacket.

"You know what convergent boundaries are?" I asked him.

"Come again?"

"Convergent boundaries. It's what the Caltech scientist used to describe the big earthquake in Turkey the other day."

"No kidding," he said. He was more comfortable with my non sequiturs than my family.

I nodded. "In that place they now call Erzincan—the same place we call Yerznka where the temple of the goddess Anahit once stood—the plates of our earth crashed into each other in a most destructive way. Five hundred people died. And they may have been the lucky ones."

"Sometimes it feels that way," Captain Cooper said, getting off the elevator. "Devastation is hard to clean up."

This is the year of earthquakes, major and minor. Convergent and divergent. This is the year of secrets buried so deep it took an earthquake to heave them to the surface.

CHAPTER TWO

There isn't a moment now that I don't think of the boy. I am obsessed with him. His plans. His scars. His palm-frond eyelashes. Does he think of me? I think, yes. I was on his mind long before our bathroom tête-à-tête. He had even seen me before then. It was Tuesday, a few weeks before we met, when I officially entered his world.

The boy and his grandmother sat by the bay window at Bakery Opera. It was a coveted spot and they were lucky to get it. Two ladies, who had just done their hair in identical blond coifs next door at Elegante Salon, had tried to elbow the boy and his *tatik* out with their Chanel handbags (also matching). He sent them his famous look of death, which he reserved for rich snobs, before he seated his grandmother. She wore a black acrylic sweater that was pilling at the elbows, but hidden in the tufts of her hair, as fine as cotton candy, she wore her most prized possession, a brilliant ruby pin. The wealth of a different time.

They were on a budget, so they shared a glass of tea and one rosewater cookie apiece. If Armineh, my best friend's widow who now owned the bakery with her daughters, was there, she'd refill the glass.

Things were looking up. He'd just gotten a ten-cent raise at work. His grandmother hadn't gotten lost in an entire week. They'd won two tickets to the tribute concert of the year. All good stuff. He felt almost cheerful.

"This is so good. Mmm, *Tatik*?" the boy said, checking his orange backpack for his wallet.

"The pistachios bring out the rosewater. I'll bake a big tray of them for you when we get back to the village," she said, caressing his cheek with a shriveled finger.

"*Tatik*, we don't live in the village. Have some tea." He blew on the glass before handing it to her.

"You're always joking. That's why I like you, handsome boy. My mother would be angry if she found us together." His grandmother batted her thin eyelashes.

"Don't worry, she'll understand." He covered her soft, mottled hand and let go, his cheeks turning pink.

"But if we don't live in the village, where do we live?" the old woman asked after she slurped the warm liquid. Her hand trembled slightly as she set the glass back on the table.

"In a big place called Los Angeles. You used to remember it." He covered her hand again.

"It's true." She looked sad. For a moment, she remembered that she didn't remember. "But I know him!" She sat up straight and pointed at me, the fat old man with the beret.

They watched me stroll up to the counter, shaking hands with the people who waited in line, then stopping to nibble sample cookies before winking at the lady behind the counter, as was my custom.

"That boy did a bad, bad thing," the old lady said to her grandson.

"What did he do, *Tatik*?"

"He told a very big lie."

CHAPTER THREE

"The results are in, Mr. Najarian, and they're not good." The Russian doctor's wet egret eyes blinked, one after the other. "Oh, Dr. Koslov, I was never good at taking tests," I said. I was at the hospital in early April, two weeks after I met the boy. I hadn't been feeling good for a while and it was time to find out why.

"Joking aside, my friend, you are of strong character and I want to be, how do you say, truthful, so you can settle your affairs," he said. "Not many people are so lucky." Dr. Koslov tried not to sigh.

Strong character. Sure. I nodded. "Go on. "

"At stage four, your prostate cancer is incurable. The cancer is now in your bones."

I sat still. The walls tilted in on the tiny examination room.

"We can try something else, but—" He took a big breath. "You're dying, my friend. There is simply no cure for that." Dr. Koslov and his wet eyes looked away.

Relief bled through my muscles. Such a great burden had been lifted. My heart soared as I leaned back in the cracked plastic chair, although that could've been the blood pressure medication. The chair pinched my buttocks every time I shifted, as if the universe was reminding me to stay in the moment.

The doctor assessed the smile that spread across my spotted face, revealing one coffee-stained tooth after another.

"I know this is difficult news, Mr. Najarian," he said. "And it might be shocking to hear right now." Dr. Koslov patted my arm with the back of his hand, as if death were contagious.

I looked at my Rolex Oyster Royal: 10:40 A.M., April 10.

"*Spasibo*, Dr. K."

"This isn't good news I'm giving you, my friend."

"Thank you just the same." If he knew what I'd accomplished in the last seventy-seven of my soon-to-be eighty-four years, he'd have understood. He would've thumped me on my back. High-fived me. Did the hip bump (my granddaughter taught me how to do that).

Not that I was pleased to die, mind you. The thought of lying in an airtight box! I'm a bit claustrophobic. Still, this felt tidy. My worries were over. The boy and his decrepit grandmother couldn't hurt me now.

"Mr. Najarian, I'm going to get the results of your cholesterol panel. Will you be okay for a few minutes?"

I was still smiling, my eyes slightly glazed, cult member–like. Maybe he was going to call a shrink.

He opened the door and I thought I saw *him*. The boy. Or rather, I saw his garish orange backpack. But I wasn't about to let that gnat take my sense of relief.

Outside, the sun shone directly overhead, a spotlight on my triumph. I picked up a back issue of *Asbarez*—the Armenian-American newspaper—from the wastebasket. *Turks Killed. Justice Served.* I read the first line.

"Witnesses say members of the Armenian Church of the Holy Cross in Ankara stoned the children of a Turkish merchant accused of fingering Armenians in 1915."

I squeezed the paper into a ball so tight my knuckles turned from pink to white, like a pork cutlet cooking in the oven. I threw it back in the trash.

"Have you been completely honest with me?" Dr. Koslov entered the room. He smelled of rubbing alcohol and dry, scaly skin.

"Why?" I asked, a sour feeling spreading from my gut to my chest.

"You agreed to watch your diet, but your LDL is out of control. Two clogged arteries could lead to a heart attack."

I raised an eyebrow.

"Well." He cleared his throat. "I suppose it's okay to enjoy life. That's what counts."

"Sure, Mr. Doctor. That's what counts."

CHAPTER FOUR

D o you know what a thrust is? It made me think of sex as I wrote it down just now. Maybe because this sex is lacking from my life. What? People in their eighties think of sex even if they don't often perform it. Fine. I won't ruin your appetite.

A thrust, in the study of earthquakes, is a violent pushing of one side of the fault upward relative to the other side. Sometimes, ancient history—old secrets—are dug up and brought to the surface while the present is buried. This is called superposition.

Mountains are created this way.

The day of the concert, my birthday, I stared at the chaparral-covered San Gabriels out the picture window of my penthouse. It was hot. The mountains hovered above Glendale in a trembling smog mirage. Some of its oldest stones are more than a billion years old. If you look carefully into its most intimate cracks, you might find a seashell. The 10,000-foot San Gabriels were once under water until they were pushed up by a force out of their control.

Living in a high-rise has its advantages. My family and I occupy the top floor of an eight-story building. It's no Manhattan skyscraper but the same rules apply: Those above get to judge those below. In fact, it's a requirement.

Two Armenian boys ran down the street, tossing a pack of cigarettes back and forth. They wore Armenian flags like capes. A third chased after them, swearing. He stopped briefly to key a brand-new silver Honda Accord before running after his Camels.

A young Armenian woman tottered out. How did I guess her ethnicity? None other contemplates three-inch heels and matching jewelry on a daily basis. My wife told me it didn't matter if you were herding goats or singing opera, the desire to make a fashion statement was carved into the Armenian female DNA. With a stiletto.

Glendale now has the second-largest population of Armenians outside of Yerevan, Armenia's capital. The first is right next door in Los Angeles. My downstairs neighbor, Captain Cooper, once asked why "The People"—that's how he refers to us—chose Glendale, where two valleys meet, as our epicenter. The city with its one downtown street of vague glass office buildings and fancy foothill neighborhoods of Spanish Revival houses; sedate on the surface but crisscrossed below with at least six earthquake faults. The city where the most colorful feature is its residents.

The truth is I've lived in this place for the longest, least turbulent period of my life and I don't know much about it. I try to imagine Glendale without the shitty mini malls where I get my haircut and buy coffee or the paved streets that cover the earth in anonymity. I imagine the brush-covered hills and ravines filled with oaks and sycamore. Eagles and hawks soaring above in a clear blue sky. Me, surviving like the Indians, on toasted acorns and manzanita berries. Making flutes from the wing bone of a wild turkey. The weather dry and hot. Dry and cold. Surrounded by mountains of snow and fire.

Captain Cooper had waited for me to answer.

"Captain *jahn*, I think it reminds us of Yerevan," I finally said. "The mountain gives us the illusion of leaning on something solid."

He seemed to like that answer.

The truth, I've come to learn from the accountant downstairs, is more boring. It was the Armenians from Iran who made Los Angeles home shortly after the Iranian Revolution in 1979. They were just following the Persian Jews, since they spoke Farsi and knew where to buy basmati rice by the sackful at wholesale prices. The rest of us, whether from Lebanon, Syria, Greece, or even Argentina or Brazil, and as far away as Ethiopia and Chad, followed as family and friends gathered. We know where to buy the big bag of rice, too. And Glendale has excellent freeway access although I've used it only once.

The Armenian exodus to Los Angeles sped up even as what remained of Armenia gained its independence from the Soviet Union in September 1991. Few wanted to stick around and fix that mess—a 6.9 magnitude earthquake that left 25,000 people dead, the war with Azerbaijan over the enclave of Nagorno-Karabakh. Such a party.

The desperate thrashing of wings revived my attention. The noise reminded me of something I'd seen long ago on the shore of a lake.

"What the fuck!" one of the hoodlum boys exclaimed, except with his accent it sounded like "Whatzefoook!" He pointed to the sky before snatching his renegade cigarettes from his pals. I looked up with them.

A hawk had harpooned a pigeon in midflight as it took off from a bus stop shelter. The pigeon fought for its life in front of a gathering crowd. It failed. As one does during a solar eclipse, I looked away at the brilliant millisecond before death. The hawk unfurled its wings in victory, the limp gray corpse between its claws, before taxiing onto a balcony across the street and tearing into the warm flesh, gnawing the bright white cartilage.

"Incredible," breathed the high-heeled woman who would soon discover her new car had been keyed. "Its wings must be bigger than me." At least her heels.

"*Papik*, it's time to get ready," said my seventeen-year-old granddaughter, Lucy. "What are you doing out here? It's too hot."

I hadn't realized I'd walked out onto our wraparound balcony. "That bird just caught a pigeon in the air. Put its claws right through its brain," I said.

"Oh," she said. "The city released a bunch of scary raptors to thin out the pigeons. This must be one of them."

"That seems a bit cruel."

"It's nature, Grandpa. It wouldn't survive if it didn't eat." She brushed her long dark hair off her face, sincerity in her beautiful brown eyes.

"You're right." *Whatzefoook.*

"*Tatik* used to say not to worry about things you can't control."

My wife didn't always take her own advice.

Lucy nudged me inside with her elbow. "You'll be late."

I hadn't noticed that she held a bouquet of white lilies under

13

her chin.

"What's this? Did someone die?" I still hadn't told my family I had a one-way ticket. Once you start keeping secrets, it becomes a habit.

"They're from your record company. I'll put them with the rest," she said, taking them to her bedroom.

"Did you start a flower shop?" I asked, following her as she looked for a place to set the vase. Bouquets and baskets covered her matching white dresser and study table. Sheet music covered her bed.

"I've put them everywhere, even in Ara's pigsty. *Dammit*, I did his laundry and he put it on the floor!" She shut her brother's bedroom door as we walked across the hall to my room. "Look at all these flowers! People love you. I want to be just like you someday," she said, stopping in front of my bedroom door.

"No, angel, you don't want to be anything like me," I said.

"I do. You make music sound like words."

"If you wanted to be just like me, you'd have to be fat and a little blind." The creaking bedroom door muffled her sigh.

I'd only kept one birthday arrangement in my room—poppies and purple larkspur, sprigs of white sage and wild fennel collected from Glenoaks Canyon that morning. It was from my best friend's widow, the bakery lady. She knew it would remind me of Armenia.

"You always look nice in lighter colors," Lucy said, flipping through my long-sleeved shirts with the ease of a blackjack dealer. Lucy had been my style consultant from the moment she could say "pretty." She wanted to be my protégée, but that just wasn't done. An Armenian man wasn't going to marry a woman who was more accomplished than he was. What would his mother think?

I stripped down to my shorts and socks in front of the mirror. How did I look now that my days were numbered? Same thick gray hair and reddish skin. High on my left hip, my boxers hid a blue stain, like a bruise. They call it a Mongolian spot. It was supposed to have faded, but mine was a bad guest. It had decided to stay past its welcome. I pulled up my shorts to make sure it was covered. My belly still obscured the view of my feet. I sucked in my gut. I could see my big toe, but only the left one. It had fungus.

Lucy pulled out a cotton shirt with a faint diamond pattern and the best black wool pants money could buy, Zegna. She reached for an embroidered vest. It was reminiscent of a Persian carpet but I put it on. The look paid my bills.

"What are you going to play, *Papik?*"

I didn't want to admit how much time I'd spent thinking about this. What do you play when it might be your last concert? I'd always given my students the advice to play as if their lives depended on it. Like it was their one phone call from prison and they had to say everything that was on their minds. Now it was my turn.

"Something you hear me practice but I've never performed."

"A riddle? You're sly, *Papik.*" She pulled a square box from under my bed. "But so am I. Happy birthday."

"And Happy Genocide Remembrance Day to you, young lady."

"*Papik*, you say that every year."

"You hid my present in my own room? That's confidence, young lady." I ripped off the fine gold paper and unfolded the tissue. It was a new beret.

"They call that color *bosque verde*. It's all the way from Spain," she said.

I wear a beret almost every day. Mostly, a black one. It's my signature and people recognized me by it. I think I have brought it back. Now, I see shopkeepers and even the accountant that shares my office building wearing one. When I was young, you could tell where a man came from by his hat. The texture. The shape. The smell.

"*Merci*, Lucy *jahn*. This is lovely. I'll wear it tomorrow." I hoped a green beret wouldn't make me look like a mercenary.

She left the room and I opened my old volume of Kuchak. Between the pages was a smooth gold medallion. I closed my eyes as my fingers read the engraving. I put it away when I heard the doorbell. More flowers.

CHAPTER FIVE

The marquee outside the Alex Theatre screamed a touch hyster-ically, *For One Night Only: Rupen Najarian!* and then *Geno-cide Remembrance Day!* My daughter, Keran, Lucy and Ara's mother, took a photo as I walked through the theater's Art Deco iron gates.

"Papa! Wait!" Keran reached into her black leather purse.

"Do I need a mint?" I asked, testing a warm puff of breath against my palm.

"No. The *achk*." She pinned a small blue-and-white bead to the inside of my vest, just as my wife used to do on special occasions.

"You think someone is going to give me the evil eye tonight?"

"Not really. But I like a little insurance." She patted the vest back in place.

"Fine. Just stay away from my *vor*." I put my hands on my buttocks and pretended to be scared.

"Oh, Pa, you can be so silly." She punched me lightly on the arm.

"I'm so confused," Lucy said, holding my duduk to her chest.

"The *achk* might be the best way to ward off envy, but it isn't the only way," Keran said with a wink. "Say you forget to pin the eye on a new baby. You just pinch his cute little bottom every time someone compliments him."

"That rule was made up by a perv who wanted to pinch some baby ass," said Ara, my eldest grandchild. My unwilling protégé, when he wasn't studying for his engineering degree.

"Manners, Ara," Keran said, narrowing her eyes. "Really, Papa. Doesn't your overlord have an ounce of shame, making you work on your birthday?" She looked around for Viktor as she smoothed the little curls at her temples that had escaped their French confinement. "And tonight of all nights. Is he still taking twenty-eight percent of your earnings? You just let me know when you want to sue him." She worked at the law firm of Carter, Cooper & Klein as a Russian and Armenian translator. "That man has the grace of a wild donkey."

"Mother, please don't insult the wild donkey," Ara said.

"Yeah," said Lucy. "Donkeys are hardworking and they never complain."

"I didn't know we had a donkey fan club," I said, looking at the two cubs. "Beloveds, don't blame Viktor. I wanted to do this. And he's working tonight as the emcee."

As much as I complained about Viktor, I admired the man. He had the courage to be just who he was. We planned to donate the proceeds, more than $20,000, to the Armenian Genocide Institute.

The courtyard, usually empty at this hour, was filled with police and private security, awkward in their ill-fitting jackets. Their presence sent a tingle through my bladder. A car backfired around the corner and they reached for their guns. I squeezed my gut.

"See, you get a uniformed escort tonight, Rupen." Viktor surprised us from behind. "Happy birthday," he said, squeezing my shoulders. Viktor wore a tuxedo just old enough to be back in style. Not on purpose, mind you. He was good with money, but certainly not with fashion. I tried to blow off the dandruff that had collected on his lapels. He wasn't alone. "Ms. Susan Hahn, may I introduce you to the great Rupen Najarian?"

The tall redhead next to him shook my hand. "It's an honor, Mr. Najarian. I'm a big fan," said the music journalist from the *Los Angeles Times*. She wore a dark green dress that set off her cinnamon hair. She looked nothing like my wife, but I thought of my goddess just the same.

"Really? I'm surprised you've heard of our humble instrument." I bowed slightly.

"It's hard to miss it. Lately, it's in all the movie scores," she said.

"To my advantage!" I chuckled.

My daughter lifted her eyebrows. *Are you flirting?*

17

"Do we really need all these cops?" Ara blew his breath out in a loud, irritated sigh. "It's Genocide Remembrance Day, not Bosnia."

"They're here for our safety," Keran said.

"Glendale? The most Nazi city in L.A.? They just want any excuse to bust us. Go home!" Ara aimed his voice toward the row of uniforms.

"Stop it!" Keran hissed, turning her attention to her towering child.

"You're such an ass," Lucy said.

"And you're ugly," Ara said.

"Apologize to your sister," Keran said. "Now."

"Ma, I can't help genetics," he said.

"In that case, you're a troll!" Lucy reached over to swat her brother.

"Way to go, Luce. Call mom a troll," Ara said.

"Ma!" Lucy said.

"It's the change in weather," I said to the journalist, leading her away by the elbow. "Makes the youngsters tense."

The theater was cool and empty, its faded red velvet chairs expectant and alert.

"Where are you from, my dear?" I asked the journalist as we walked backstage.

"Burbank."

"No. I mean where is your *family* from?"

"My father's folks came from Ireland. I think my mother's side has some Scottish."

"Celts! You know Armenians and Celts go far back. Some people say we traded thousands of years ago. We might even be related!"

"Really?" She surveyed the stocky, dark-haired people who parked their cars behind the theater.

"Art, music, circle dancing, red hair. We have so much in common."

"Hold that thought, Mr. Najarian. Please let me find my pen. I'm sorry. I'm usually not this disorganized." The journalist hung her purse on the branch of a prop tree from *Swan Lake* and sighed.

"I had a little fight with my husband this afternoon." She turned her back as she looked through her bag.

"It's terrible to fight with family. You should make up soon." She made a sound that said she wasn't so sure.

I poured two cups of tea from the thermos Lucy had packed. I didn't drink tea often, but I liked to have a few warm sips before a concert to keep my throat moist.

"Thank you. You're quite the host." She took the cup I handed her and continued to tunnel through her purse.

I opened my leather case and lifted out the duduk I'd carved from apricot wood when my eyes were still perfect. I stroked it up and down, feeling its smooth amber shaft between my fingers, until I was embarrassed.

"That's a beautiful instrument," she said softly.

"It's the best one I've ever made." I presented it to her on my forearm.

"It looks like a recorder." She reached for it, but I pulled back just a little. She put her hand down.

"Yes. They're like cousins but from a distant part of the family tree. Like Armenians and Celts." I winked, hoping my daughter wouldn't walk in.

"It's your birthday today *and* Armenian Genocide Remembrance Day." She brushed off the cobwebs and sat on a rickety theater chair, propping her notebook on her lap. Her skirt rose above her knees, showing off her pale, slender legs.

"I didn't coordinate it," I said lightly.

She smiled.

"So tell me about yourself," she said.

"There isn't much to tell," I said, feeling the callus imbedded into my index finger. Decades of playing the duduk. "My life is like any other." I took another sip of tea. It had gone cold in the ages she had taken to look for her pen.

"Okay, why don't you tell me a little about the duduk, then?" she said in a friendly manner, although she tapped her foot just like my wife did when she didn't believe me.

"Now that's something worth talking about," I said. "It has a range of just an octave—that's eight notes—but as you have probably heard, it can sound like a voice wailing." Or the wind howling across a mountaintop. Its tone fleshy and pulpy, deep and haunting.

She nodded.

The duduk is the human voice without the encumbrance of language. Traditionally, another duduk keeps a low drone, like a hive buzzing, a counterpoint to the melody, called a *dam*. Ara played the *dam* at my local concerts.

"Is it an Armenian instrument?"

"Of course! " I might have said this a little forcefully. "There is no question."

"How so?"

"The proof of its *Armenianness*," I explained, "is that historically it was most often carved from *Prunus armeniaca*. Do you know what that is?"

"Tell me."

"Guess. I'll give you a hint. It's a fruit tree that has grown in Armenian territory from very ancient times."

"A plum?"

"An apricot. Others have borrowed the duduk, making it from their native trees. But it doesn't have the quality of the human voice. That sound is what makes it Armenian."

"Who taught you to play?" she asked.

"My father," I said.

"Tell me about him."

"I don't remember much," I said. "He died in 1915." I didn't tell her it was exactly seventy-nine years ago. To the day.

"Tell me about Armenians," she said.

"Is that a roundabout way of asking about me?"

"Most people love talking about themselves."

"Do you?" I asked her.

"Not really. Sometimes."

The truth is I love talking about myself. Words come out of me like a fountain. Look at me now; sitting here writing all this. I wouldn't have discovered this desire without him. My boy.

But back to the beautiful journalist.

"You want to know about the Armenians?" I settled back in a

scarred old church pew and polished my duduk. "Shall I unleash every stereotype and cliché I can find?

"If it helps," she said with a smile.

"You think your people are Caucasian? I will correct you. *Armenians* are the original Caucasians. The Caucasus Mountains are home."

We'll remind you if you call us Middle Eastern—or worse, Arabs. But we're stumped if we have to choose between East and West. Noah and his ark found dry land on our Mount Ararat. That's the story and we're sticking to it. He didn't leave us giraffes or zebras, two by two. He left his great-great-grandson, our first ancestor, Hayk. We became the *Hayastansi.* You measure time before Christ and after Christ. We measure time before Noah and after him.

Before Noah, our ancestors lived and tended to the lands that are now Turkey, Syria, portions of Iran and Iraq and Georgia, Azerbaijan and even parts of Russia. After Noah, we struggle to keep what little God has left for us.

"So you're Christian?" she asked.

"You said no tough questions," I said with a smile I didn't feel. "Most Armenians are Orthodox Christians, like the Greeks, but we've disagreed with their methods since 451 AD."

Armenia is the world's oldest Christian nation. But before Noah, we were sun worshippers, then we dabbled in fire gods. I attend Catholic services because my friends do. And they make a nice coffee after the service.

But sometimes, I look at the sun till I'm blind.

The Armenian alphabet was created more than 1,600 years ago. We believe the first sentence written in Armenian was from the Book of Proverbs: *To know wisdom and instruction; to perceive the words of understanding.* I would have chosen *Jesus wept.* Before Noah, we used the Sumerian cuneiform.

Regardless of our religious affiliations, we like a good bargain. We bend the law on occasion . . . okay, whenever we think it may benefit us. We're quick to temper. But if you see two Armenians on a street corner waving their hands at each other, don't assume they're fighting. We just get excited.

Our women like to wear high heels. Our men appreciate this. They like short skirts, too.

We fear crosswinds. They give us the flu. If we get the flu, our mothers will apply a mustard poultice to our chests. Sweating irritates our stomach. So our mothers tell us to always wear an undershirt. We call this affliction a cold stomach, but non-Armenians don't seem to understand what that is. No matter; I have no clue what Jimmy legs are, but they seem to bother many of my neighbors. We're prone to Crohn's disease and Mediterranean fever. Our mothers have no remedies for these.

We consume large amounts of fruit. Apricots are a favorite. Some of us are crazy enough to argue that cucumbers are fruits. We like picnics, especially in places where the sign says *Keep Off.* We love a good barbecue, the kind with a real wood fire. Most Armenians drink cups and cups of coffee. Armenians from Iran and India drink tea. They don't know what they're missing. We eat olives for breakfast.

We prefer the company of our own kind and can seem standoffish, but scratch a little deeper and we'll smother you with generosity.

We're excellent tradespeople, having survived at the crossroads of many civilizations. We cling to our culture and traditions but wear Western clothes. Gucci is a favorite.

We've killed once or twice. We've lost track of how many times we've been invaded and killed. Scythians, Persians, Romans, Mongols, countless Turkic tribes.

"The last time was during World War I when the Turkish Ottoman Empire finished off 1.5 million souls. That was more than half of the community," I concluded, resting the duduk back in its velvet-lined case.

"Invaders seem to come and go, don't they?" the journalist asked. "One day it's you, the next it's someone else?"

"Sure," I said. "Ask the Jews how they feel."

"I'm sorry. I didn't mean to imply your suffering was somehow less important," she said. "It's terrible to be killed just for who you are."

"It's okay. Some are just better at getting the spotlight."
She looked up but didn't say anything. We sat like that for a
few minutes until we were both comfortable.

"You must have been a baby during this historical period."
The journalist slipped off her shoes. Delicate blue veins tattooed
the tops of her feet.

"Oh, I wasn't around during the time of Noah," I said.

She laughed.

How could I tell her about *Medz Yeghern*, the Great Crime?
Would she even understand? When did it start?

Treaties came and went. Ottoman Armenians died in multiple
massacres in the late 1800s. Then in 1908, the Young Turks—
army officers who revolted against an out-of-touch, fanned-by-
slaves, fed-peeled-grapes, dressed-in-silk Empire—came to power.
This was it.

Armenians supported the Young Turks, thinking they'd be
treated better than they were under the Empire. They enlisted in
the army, sent money, threw parties for the same people who gladly killed them a few years later.

In November 1914, when I was six, the winter I learned how
to play the duduk, was also the beginning of World War I for the
Ottoman Empire. Armenians lived on both sides of the conflict.
Eastern Armenians were forced to fight with the Triple Alliance.
Western Armenians, under Russian rule, fought with the Allied
Powers. The Tsar made a pretty speech, telling Armenians that if
Russia won, they would all be free. This didn't sit too well with
the Young Turks, especially the nationalists.

The Young Turks' war minister, Ismail Enver Pasha, tried and
failed to overthrow the Russian forces at the Eastern front. He
blamed his monumental loss on the Armenians within his army.
Enver demoted all Armenians serving in the Ottoman troops to
unarmed labor battalions. This became part of a master plan to
eliminate Armenians from Anatolia. Men who might have been
able to defend themselves no longer could.

April 24, 1915, was my seventh birthday. I was getting good
at the duduk. Not as good as my older brother was at seven. And
nowhere near the same galaxy as my father. It was a perfect spring

day and I was old enough to take care of the goats and eavesdrop on adult talk. We'd heard from our neighbors that Armenians were being rounded up.

"Again?" my mother asked my father that night as they sat in the courtyard. "That thing in Adana was just a few years ago. The year of the earthquake." She referred to the massacre in the big city near us the year I was born. I heard my father say it was all just the beginning.

And it was. Prison camps burned whole. Entire Armenian army battalions shot to death. Boatloads of children sailed out into the middle of the lake and drowned. Villagers injected with typhus. Families herded into the desert with nothing. It was tough work figuring out how to kill a million and half people.

"How awful," the journalist said.

"Yes."

"It's been almost, what? Eighty years?" she asked. "Have you come to terms with it?"

"The Turks have never admitted to the genocide," I said. "How can one get over not existing?"

"I guess you never had closure," she said, almost to herself.

"Closure is for Oprah's guests," I said.

She gave me a sympathetic look.

"Before the killings, people could trace their family history for centuries. After, mostly young children, like me, were left. I barely remembered my last name. It's unforgivable."

"I'm so sorry for your loss," she said.

I didn't say anything.

"So what else do I need to know about Armenians?" she asked as Ara gave me the ten-minute signal from the doorway.

"We know how to hold a grudge." I smiled, putting away the teacups.

"Well, I'll do my best not to cross you." She sat writing as I blew air through my duduk. Did she care about my troubles? Not that it was a requirement. I release all from the burden of the twentieth century's first genocide. I liberate you from knowing about an empire that almost erased an entire nation. I grant you the luxury of not having to live with it.

It's just a shame I can't do the same for myself.

*   *   *

I usually played famous compositions from Khachatur Avetisyan and Alexander Dolukhanian with a few folk songs of Sayat Nova, the great troubadour. Tunes that have stowed away with us as we've traveled the world looking for a new home.

I was stinking tired of playing all of them.

Instead, I pulled out a sheaf of yellowing paper. Written on top in the handwriting of a much younger man was *The Crane's Lament*. It was my own work. Before that evening, I'd never performed it. Why? Because it had taken me half a century to finish. Even then, I wasn't sure it was done but if I didn't play what I had, I probably never would.

"What made you write this piece?" the journalist asked from behind. She'd put down her pen and notebook and come to read the music over my shoulder.

"I can't remember," I lied to her. "I'd better go the bathroom." She nodded as I excused myself.

The music had revealed itself when I first moved to the crumb of Soviet Armenia in April of 1937. Newlyweds, my wife and I picnicked on the shores of Lake Arpi one Sunday, still tourists in our new country. On the edge of the lake was a white crane fringed with black. It flapped and whopped, thrashing at the reeds with such intensity, that it injured itself.

"It's horrible! Why is it making that frightening noise?" the goddess asked, clutching at my sweater.

A fisherman, repairing his nets on the remains of an ancient wall behind us, explained that the bird had lost its lifelong mate. The wind rushed through the reeds toward us, carrying the crane's lament.

The bird's cries echoed through the cove, bouncing off the hills, magnifying its grief. Its sorrow brought me close to confession on the cold gray shores.

My wife believed we knew everything about each other. I knew about her mother's depression. I cried with her when she told me how her sister had jumped into the void of a ravine with her baby in her arms so she wouldn't be defiled. I held my wife when she explained that she was raped in the barracks because she didn't have the nerve to jump. I wanted to tell Artemis who I really was. I wanted to tell her how I would feel without her. But I didn't, even as we watched the crane bash its head against the rocks.

"Won't you kill it?" she begged the fisherman. He shook his head.

"No. To live is to suffer." He whistled a village dance as he packed up his nets.

Such anguish. Such betrayal. Oh, the loneliness. I've been writing the piece ever since.

The ovation began even before I started to play. When they saw Ara in his cheery folk vest, the audience clapped even harder.

"Don't you love the applause?" I whispered, feeling it wash over me like scented bathwater.

He sighed. "Sure, *Papik*. But it's for you." He played the *dam* for a good ten seconds before I started the melody. Then I plunged into my soul for the music.

The earth shook. A murmur threaded its way through the audience. I thought it was the music, but when Ara stopped playing and the stage lights moved with the sultry sway of a belly dancer's hips, I conceded it was really an earthquake: Later I learned it had measured 5.5 on the Richter scale, centered in Palmdale. Just two days earlier was that terrible quake in Joshua Tree.

"The earth has merely acknowledged our Maestro's birthday," Viktor adlibbed from the corner. He motioned to the skittish in the audience to sit back down.

"Is the earthquake an omen, Grandpa?" Ara smirked, filled his lungs with life, and restarted the *dam*.

I had arranged the first movement in B major, which helped mimic the call of the crane. I imagined the birds flying from Africa to our lake, their wings whirring in the headwind. I started the second movement, but something broke my concentration. Someone. It was the boy.

Truthfully, I heard his *tatik* first. They sat in the fifth row, right behind the *Times* journalist. The seats reserved for contest win-

26

ners. The old lady's wispy gray hair was clipped with an elaborate red hairpin. She spoke to him in the whisper of a person going deaf. Insistently. Loudly. She stopped talking and stared, then pointed her finger at me. My stomach dropped as the boy pulled her hand down, his eyes never leaving my face. He chewed gum thoughtfully, as if analyzing the flavor of spearmint.

The journalist turned her head, but I wooed her back with the music. I felt very tired, like a sad old bird that needed to piss all the time.

And this was how I played the final movement, thrashing like a crane unable to accept its fate. There was silence when I finished playing. I heard someone weep and realized it was me. Ara held my hand as we took our bows.

The boy and his grandmother were in the courtyard when I came out after three ovations. I pulled my jacket tighter not because it was cold, but to protect myself from their stares. The pair stood by the wall, drinking small shots of Armenian coffee, watching me with my friends. He leaned close to his grandmother and asked her something.

"*Eench?*" she creaked loudly in Armenian. She rubbed a small mole above her lip. He repeated his question. She looked at me and nodded and started to wave like she was signaling to a far-sighted bus driver.

I didn't recognize the woman. Old people really do look alike: gray heads, spines curling into a protective shell, features melting together until they disappeared.

My heart pounded, and if another car had backfired I would have pissed and farted—parted, fissed. I ignored them as I introduced the journalist around.

"That was amazing!" Armineh said. She was the one who had picked birthday flowers for me that morning. Armineh held both my ears between her hands, her customary greeting for me. "Why didn't you ever play that before?"

The scalloped edges of her lace handkerchief, tucked into her bodice, caressed my chin as she pulled my face closer. It smelled of cloves and her breath, warm brandy. My closest circle of friends had dwindled down to three as my peers "vacationed at Forest

Lawn," as we half-joked when one of us died.

The security guard interrupted us. "Sorry, folks, we have to clear the premises." We walked toward the street together under his beady stare.

"Fascist," Ara said under his breath. "Ouch!" he yelled after his mother pinched him.

"Yes, Rupen. The piece was marvelous!" my friend Robert said. He pushed Hovannes in his wheelchair, who nodded in agreement, his eyes still dewy with tears. I suspected their emotion was not just for me.

"We'll see you at the park in the afternoon, then?" Robert asked.

"If we don't die tonight," Hovannes said.

"He's such an optimist. Let's eat lunch together tomorrow, shall we?" Armineh decided on my behalf.

"Ah, there you are, Rupen." It was Viktor. He nodded his hellos. "I forgot to mention you got an invitation from the Istanbul Center for the Arts. All expenses paid and a healthy *honorarium*." He emphasized the word honorarium, since he also got twenty-eight percent of that.

"Fucking murderers," Ara said.

This time his mother had nothing to say.

"Turkey invited you?" Hovannes spewed a large amount of saliva. "And today of all days?"

"Well, not the entire bloody country," Viktor said. "Just people who love the arts. And they are usually a nice, liberal bunch."

My friends and family stood silent, posed in a nationalistic mural. All except the journalist, whose pen made fast scratching sounds against her notebook.

"You can say no to them. I'll never set foot in that country." I tried my best to sound scornful.

"Bravo," Armineh said, patting me on the back. Robert nodded.

"Right on, Gramps," Lucy said, her small fist in a Black Panther salute.

Viktor sighed. "It's just music, Rupen. But your wish is my command." He melted into his Jaguar, financed by my success, no doubt.

"Happy birthday, Mr. Najarian," the journalist said as she closed her notebook.

* * *

At home, Ara turned on the TV while Keran and Lucy prepared a late supper of caviar and vodka. I'd acquired a taste for this combination when I played with the state orchestra for a season in Moscow. It didn't pair well with the 11 P.M. national news.

"Mama, can I have a little vodka?" Lucy asked over the TV.

"Hmmm. Just enough to toast *Papik*. Besides, you hate it. You said it tastes like nail polish remover, remember?" Keran freed two small wooden bowls of osetra and salmon caviar from the fridge.

"I don't know. Maybe I'll change my mind." Lucy sliced black bread and spread the slices heavily with unsalted butter.

"My child, that's too much fat!" I protested, although it was the correct amount to enjoy caviar.

She shrugged the way indestructible young people do and placed the buttered bread on a platter delectably lined with thin slices of red onion, lemon wedges and sprigs of baby dill.

The phone rang.

"I'll get it," Keran said as she and Lucy raced for the phone.

"It's work." Keran stretched the cord into the laundry room, our cone of silence.

Ara poured cold Stolichnaya into four shot glasses with one eye on the madness on the screen. "Another murder in South Central. It's the cops. I bet they did it."

"Why?" I asked him.

"Because poor people have this superpower, like an invisibility cloak." Ara handed me a shot of vodka. "But the cops like to yank it off when it serves them."

"We drink to your health, *Papik*," Lucy said as she and Ara touched their glasses to mine. Keran was still entombed in the hush of the laundry room.

"I come to you with hungritude," I said solemnly.

"That's not a real word, *Papik*," Lucy said.

"What do you mean? I'm hungry and grateful. Hungritude."

"Okay, you lush, Ma said only one sip," Ara said to his sister.
"You are not my boss," she said, holding her glass up high.
"I'm your older brother. That makes me your boss. You're
supposed to listen to what I say."
"Well, what you say is usually stupid," she said. "Jerk."
Ara tried to trip his sister with his foot.
"Cherubs," I sang out. "No fighting on Genocide Remembrance Day."
Ara plopped on the armchair and Lucy sat next to me.
The TV filled in the silence. Tac. Tac. Tac. Shots from an automatic rifle.
"Ara, please turn that off. Let's toast your grandfather properly." Keran hung up the phone, her face flushed. She hid behind a shot of vodka as Ara made a second toast.

CHAPTER SIX

W hen I woke up the next day, my insides had been removed by sly Egyptian embalmers and stuffed with cotton. Vodka is a younger man's drink. I met Armineh for lunch at our local Zankou Chicken anyway. We usually ate at her bakery on Verdugo Boulevard, Bakery Opera, with its infinite pastries and confections, where one of the daughters would make us hummus cucumber sandwiches, but her seven-year-old grandson, Michael, wanted pita bread slathered with the secret garlic sauce (the secret is a little mashed russet potato). Armineh wheedled both for free from the register girl. Her perfectly arched eyebrows arched even more as she read the *Times*. Although she was almost my age, she looked a decade younger. She leaned over to kiss my cheek as I sat down next to Michael, tickling his ribs as was expected of me.

"People are already dead," she said over Michael's giggles, her Emeraude perfume mingling with the fast-food rotisserie chicken into a garlicky jasmine. "Rioting. In a rich country? Goodness." She flipped the page. "Did you know a McDonald's just opened in China? Now that's something to riot about."

She looked up to examine my outfit. I was wearing my favorite pink-and-brown plaid in fine cotton, khaki pants and the beret Lucy had bought for my birthday.

"Aren't you hot under that hat?" Armineh asked.

"I'm hiding a bald spot," I replied as I drank a bottle of *tahn*, the salty yogurt a cool river down my throat.

She sniffed. I was the only one of her friends with a full head of hair. "Your hat is what my mother would have called 'putting on airs.'"

"You don't remember your mother," I said. But she was right.

I wore it for the others who recognized me by my headdress, a tribal dignitary of Armenian Glendale.

Armineh studied me for a minute, and not just my ensemble. "Something about you—you should get a beam ray machine," she said.

"Are you from outer space, Rupen *Papik*?" Armineh's Michael asked, eyes wide, pushing out chewed pita through his missing front tooth.

"I wish I were, so I could scare your *tatik*."

"She doesn't get scared very easily," he said with the authority of a zoologist who had tracked his subject for several seasons.

"That's your problem, Rupen," Armineh said. "You never take what I say seriously. I read the machine can cure so many diseases. Herpes, polio, tuberculosis—"

"—leprosy," I added.

"Humor me." She went up to the counter. The girl handed her another warm piece of bread without a word. "Rupen *jahn*, you look a little tired. Are you okay? Are you sure you don't want some chicken? It's free."

"It's not free, Armineh. They're terrified of you."

"Still."

Armineh sat back down and we played one of our favorite games: dissecting the people who stood in line to order chicken. At the front of the line was a Mexican couple trying to buy five whole chickens, three bags of pita and twenty garlic sauces.

"Big family," I said. "I think the man works at Masis Market."

"They buy cake at the bakery once a month," Armineh said. "I don't know their names."

Between the Armenian register girl's minimal English and the Mexican couple's minimal English, the right quantity of garlic sauce was in jeopardy until the man behind them stepped in. He spoke excellent Spanish.

"Handsome and worldly." Armineh sighed.

"Who? Karlen?" I straightened my shoulders. He was our local heavy. He only had one name, like Cher (half Armenian) or 2Pac (spiritually Armenian), but that was all he needed. Karlen was an intimidating 6'4" with his reddish-brown hair cut Caesar-style.

His eyes were a steely blue gray that made him look meaner than he really was. He must have been in his sixties, but it was hard to tell because he was fit and yes, handsome.

"I can speak French," I reminded her.

"Yes. Yes." Armineh dismissed me. "Those eyes remind me of my husband," she said.

"Of Levon? I thought he had brown eyes."

"*Barev*, Maestro." Karlen approached us, his chicken-to-go fuming in front of my nose. "Madame." He bowed slightly to Armineh, who tittered.

"I didn't know you spoke such good Spanish," I said.

"*Si, señor*. I grew up in Argentina. I thought you knew." He nodded his goodbyes.

Karlen walked through the door respectfully held open by a familiar figure. The boy. He had the strut of a black man, fierce but guarded. His orange backpack grazed Armineh on his way to the ATM machine near the restrooms. Young people can be impractical. Didn't he know he'd be charged $2 for that transaction? He stopped to read the fine print on the machine and proceeded to look through his backpack for loose change.

"What were we talking about?" Armineh asked, turning back to me.

"The ray gun!" Michael said.

"So this beam ray machine works on different vibrations," Armineh said as she handed a fresh pita to Michael. "You just set it to a certain number code, depending on your sickness, and press the button. Then you sit next to it. The drug companies keep trying to stop the beam ray company from selling the machine." Armineh leaned in closer. "They're afraid it would put them all out of business."

The boy sat a few yards away, facing me with his falafel, the cheapest item on the menu. He unwrapped the foil and pinched little pieces of burnt chickpeas with his fingers like he was picking at a scab.

I found his manner offensive. Who orders falafel at Zankou? You come here for the perfectly roasted chicken with its skin caramelized to sticky, crispy perfection.

He caught my eye and smirked.

"Let's get out of here," I said.

"See. I knew you're not okay. Susie has one of those beam ray machines," Armineh continued. "We should go over and sit under it."

"Does it have a setting for a tan?" I asked as we walked out the door.

Some old women can hit hard.

Armineh's son-in-law, Aram, picked us up in a Cadillac limousine. He worked as a chauffeur and often took us to afternoon mass. His children, having ridden only in limousines all their lives, thought everyone traveled this way.

"*Papik* Rupen, would you like some scotch?" Michael offered politely. It was tempting. "*Tatik*, I know how you like brandy."

"Michael!" His father barked more for my benefit. "Your grandmother doesn't drink in the middle of the day."

For a second, Michael wanted to disagree. Armineh winked at him and he put away the decanter.

Next to the Mobil gas station, St. Gregory's medieval form stood out like an ancient relative. A relic that didn't quite fit into California with its thick exterior and conical pointed domes.

I find it funny that stones, often the result of earthquakes that push destructive magma to the surface, can make something so holy. So cherished.

Most churches in Armenia, built by masters known widely for their skills in Christendom, were constructed from volcanic stone in shades ranging from fleshy pink to the darkest of black. As the building aged—glued together with stone mortar—something strange happened. It got stronger, digging in its heels for eternity. Until a foreign power razes it to the ground.

Our Glendale church was a movie-set rendition of our history. It could be knocked over with a sledgehammer. But it smelled nice and new and had a beautiful set of hand-carved wooden doors.

A service was in progress as Armineh and I arrived at St. Gregory's. Past the carved oak doors and cradled by the bare walls, the old priest's voice hung in the hollowness. It was the end of a funeral service. A large photograph of a smiling man stood on an easel next to the coffin. He couldn't have been older than twenty-five.

Armineh caught her breath. "So young."

"Remove from my life the darkness of despair, sadness and sin," the priest said.

"Amen," we responded, as the deceased's friends carried the casket outside.

Despite the heat, the dead man's mother wore a wool suit and a black silk scarf covered her hair. I bowed slowly to her as she looked at me, her eyes asking if I knew what grief really was. She passed us in a camphoric cloud of frankincense.

One day soon, I'll be in front of my final audience, dressed in my carpet vest. I sit here and think I should at least pick the music. Brahms played on the duduk. That would sound very good with the acoustics in St. Gregory's. Djivan Gasparian should play for the service. And Ara, if he were up to it. Lucy, if not. They should serve caviar afterward with lots of butter. *In nomine Patris.* Amen.

CHAPTER SEVEN

I know something is going on," Armineh said as we climbed into the limousine after Mass. "I can smell it, you old fool," she leaned in and whispered so her son-in-law couldn't hear. He drove us to Forest Lawn to visit Levon's grave.

"You do have the instinct of a bloodhound," I whispered back. I did what I did best in these situations. I changed the subject.

"Aram," I called out to the son-in-law. "You make me feel like a celebrity when you drive me around like this."

"You are a celebrity, Rupen *jahn*," he said as he crossed Glendale Boulevard, our river Styx, and through the cemetery's grand iron wrought gates.

The winding road up the lush green hill was punctuated with black-robed Orthodox priests, offering their direct line to God. For a small fee.

Armineh's attention turned away from me to the religious entrepreneurs. "Selling their souls, that's what they're doing," Armineh said. "They should be ashamed. God is free to all."

Aram stopped the limousine next to the statue of Mary and pretended to search for something.

"What are you looking for?" Armineh leaned out the car.

"A big rock. Biggest you can find," he said as he searched among the grave markers closest to the road.

"A rock? Why?" I asked.

"Let those without sin cast the first stone," he said in a stern voice before he jumped back in with a pebble.

Armineh laughed. "Not bad."

"Extra points for the biblical reference."

The rest of the visit wasn't so funny.

Even on a 98-degree day, the cemetery was a cool, green oasis nourished by the bodies of our loved ones. The freeway, on the other side of the thick bank of eucalyptus trees, rushed like a river in springtime. I love eucalyptus. Their leaves are covered in oil glands. On hot days, I've seen the vaporized oil from the leaves hover above the trees in a bluish haze. They're the only trees that can explode into fire without warning. Spontaneous combustion. Arborial pyromaniacs.

Levon's grave was under a small oak tree, which was expensive real estate. But Armineh splurged. She wanted him to have shade even in the afterlife.

"It gets hot in the summer and how he hated the heat," she said as we got out of the limo and Aram left to pick up a real celebrity, a movie star, at the airport. "Besides, it's useful for us when we visit." She leaned her bag against the oak's young trunk.

Her husband's stone was a reflection of him. The brief marker held just his name and the dates of his birth and death. He was never prone to embellishments other than on his cakes.

We recited the prayer for the dead together. I stumbled on the words "—that, we too may be made worthy to enter into thy heavenly Kingdom with those we love."

"Having a stroke?" Armineh asked, one eyebrow up.

I shook my head. I was having doubts about my heavenly place, or whether I wanted to go there anymore. Maybe heaven was more of a vacation destination. Club Dead.

I held Armineh's hand as we burned incense in a little bronze bowl.

The woman with the black silk scarf was burying her son halfway down the hill. We watched her walk to his plot, her heels sinking into the soft ground with each step, the earth wanting to take her, too. She knelt down to light the incense. A man played a hymn on the duduk. Not terrible. I didn't recognize him. The priest said the final prayer and opened the coffin so the mourners could take a last look at their beloved.

From our spot under the oak, we had a pretty good view of him, too. His face was drawn up like one of those dried apple–faced dolls my mother used to make for the neighborhood girls.

The makeup two shades too pink for his skin. He wore a gray suit, a blue tie and white gloves. The white gloves were a style choice made at the mortuary. You don't want to see the hands of the dead. He didn't look like his photo.

"Remember when Levon died, we propped the lid of the casket outside the front door by the rose bush?" Armineh asked. "And our American neighbors got crazy but were too polite to ask what we were doing?"

"Yes."

"The girls finally told them it was what we did to tell the world our bad news."

"What did you tell the neighbors when we walked around the house three times with his coffin before we went to the church?"

"That we lost a button," Armineh said.

"You are a silly girl." I tugged a lock of her hair.

"We just told them that's what Armenian Christians did."

Another half truth. Even before Noah, we did that to confuse the dead so they wouldn't find their way back home to haunt the living. But this wasn't a worry I had with Levon. He wasn't great with directions. It once took us a year to get to our destination.

Below us, a girl wearing a thin blue dress wailed, falling onto the woman in the scarf. The weight of grief pushed them both to the ground. They would be back on the seventh day after his death, the fortieth day and on his one-year death anniversary. Crying just a little bit less each time.

Armineh pulled out a flask from her purse and poured some brandy into the cap for me. We toasted the young man quietly in the Armenian custom, making sure only our toasting fingers touched and not the vessels.

We sat on the grass in the shade of Levon's tree. "Tell me," Armineh said. "What's wrong with you?"

"What makes you think anything's wrong with me?"

"I'm like one of those small animals you see on TV that feels an earthquake before it happens."

"Like a rat or a snake?"

"Your compliments aren't going to go to my head. *Tell me.*"

"Oh, Armineh."

"What? Is it something serious?"

"I have the cancer," I said, brushing a leaf off of Levon's grave. "But you have to keep it a secret. Not even Keran knows." Armineh drew in an audible breath, her face a mask as she figured out how to react. What to say. What to do.

"This is good news," I said. "Now you get my Charles Aznavour collection."

"Oh no, Rupen *jahn*. What kind of cancer is it? You know, people get better all the time."

"Not me, my dear. This is my grand finale." I made a sweeping gesture with my hand.

Her mask cracked. Her eyes filled involuntarily. Droplets, trapped in the wrinkles at the corners, refused to fall down her cheeks. She hated to cry because she thought it weakened the immune system.

"I'm not dying this week, and it won't be a bad way to go. Better than being tortured to death, eh?"

She gestured with her palms upward in agreement. "That'll only leave Hovannes and Robert. They're not as fun." She smiled, her lips trembling with the attempt.

Just as the little oak protected us from the heat, Armineh's arms sheltered me. We sat like that for a long time. So long that the funeral party in front of us had stumbled to their cars with their mud-caked heels.

"Thank you in advance for keeping this secret." It was my turn to put my arms around her. "In return, you can tell me anything you want, and no matter what I won't ever tell a soul."

Her eyes welled up again. It had to be something, because the tears rushed through the ravines of her face. She sighed and took her shoes off, wiggling her warped toes in the fluorescent grass.

"Oh, Rupen."

"I feel generous. Anything you want. Double the portion."

She sighed and massaged her big toe, trying to straighten it into a semblance of a digit. "I've never told anyone this story, although some people must know, I suppose."

I wonder now if people at the edge of death give off a signature, like Susie's beam ray machine. Some sort of vibration that invites people to confess their innermost thoughts. The universe must think, "Let's pour the burdened hearts of the living into the dying." Emptying trash. Not that I didn't ask for it. I wanted all of Armineh.

There, at the graveside, she pulled out an old photograph from her purse. It was tucked between the back pages of a leather-bound diary. The one that held addresses of long forgotten people in places like Syria and Ethiopia. The corners of the picture were bent, the scalloped edges frayed and the black and white swirling into pools of gray.

"I've been carrying this around for a long, long time," she said, handing me the picture.

It was hot the day they'd taken the photo in that famous Beirut studio run by a Frenchman and his Maronite wife. Bees hovered halfheartedly over the laundry water that collected at the entrance. The three subjects were arranged on an ornate French settee with a backdrop of an open window framing sunflowers and vineyards on a hillside. They looked like they were taking tea in the parlor of their country home.

Although the studio was stifling, the smiling young man with the bushy mustache wore his best suit, a trim black wool ensemble cut in London. His dark curly hair was slicked back and his steel gray eyes were warm and friendly. Not more than twenty, he held a little boy in his arms. The baby, with eyes like his father and his mother's red locks, was dressed in white christening lace. He looked at his mother, reaching for her with his fleshy hand, a cherub in an Italian museum painting.

His mother sat to the left of her handsome husband, her hands folded on her lap. Her hair was glossy, although you couldn't tell from the photograph. She was wearing a silk dress with a fur stole around one shoulder and a diamond brooch in the shape of a peacock.

"The dress was the color of olives crossed with grass," Armineh said. "And someone was burning cedar outside. It was like perfumed toast."

Funny the things you remember.

Just eighteen years old, the girl she showed me faced the camera, her eyes challenging it to find a more perfect life.

"*Vous êtes parfait*," the photographer had said. He blew them a kiss and admonished them not to move for the next thirty seconds. They giggled. How would they keep this child from moving for *one* second?

They left the studio an hour later to walk on the Corniche and cool down with the ocean breeze. The man in the photo bought a bag of roasted sunflower seeds and they took turns cracking them between their teeth and scooping out the tender flesh. They scattered the shells on the seawall and watched the gulls swoop down until the sun set, pink and orange, turning the waves of the Mediterranean into the overlapping iridescence of mother of pearl.

A week later, Armineh told me, when the photo was delivered in a shiny black box, the household might as well have been a set for a silent drama, except it had sound. It was September 5, 1928, and the man in the photograph had died the day before in a building fire. The girl had screamed at the photo, at her in-laws, at him. She tried to rip it between her teeth, but her mother-in-law saved it. No one was going to destroy the last image of her son.

The girl thought of her baby for the first time since the accident. He was named after his handsome father whose name meant "lightning bolt." The baby would have to be strong enough to weather the storm on his own.

"Armineh, why are you telling me a story about a pretty Lebanese girl? Someone you once knew?" I interrupted, putting my hand on her shoulder. "I have to go to the bathroom. I mean *really* go."

"You idiot," she said. "That red-headed girl was me."

I cursed my bad timing.

I'm sure the McAllister family would not appreciate that I pissed behind their aunt's headstone (loving daughter, adventurous sister and vivacious aunt). But given the right circumstances, we are capable of anything.

"God, I never knew you were married before. Why wouldn't Levon have told me? Or you?"

Armineh didn't answer.

Those first three months after Armineh's young husband,

Shant (the lightning bolt) died, she didn't get out of their bed, inhaling the linen coverlet for his scent, dreaming of him in the waking hours. She didn't even get up to go to the graveside on his fortieth day. Didn't burn the incense, didn't wear black, didn't go to the table even to eat from the bubbling pot of chicken and pelted wheat *harissa* they made for mourners. She refused to release him to heaven.

"I loved him so deeply," Armineh explained, biting her bottom lip. "Did you truly and honestly love Artemis?"

"Of course!" I said, but I wondered how that could have been true if my goddess hadn't known everything about me.

"Then you understand."

They left her to feed from the deep, scum-covered pool of grief, keeping her little Shant, who looked so much like his father, away. And it was true, she didn't complain.

As was tradition, Armineh lived with her husband's family in an old Armenian-style house with a carved wooden balcony. It was one of the finest houses in the neighborhood. Even if it weren't their custom, she didn't have anywhere else to go. Her parents, brothers, anyone who could vouch for her, had died in what was now Turkey.

"It's a tight rope to be young and widowed," Armineh said. "So uncertain." Girls, especially Armenian girls, couldn't strike out on their own in those days. Even now. Sure, the family was obliged to take care of her, but twelve months of mourning was apparently enough for everyone but her.

"The lone dove must fly," Armineh overheard her mother-in-law confide to a neighbor as they dried figs on the rooftop with its view of snow-capped Mount Sannine. Like many young Armenian women of that time, she had to remarry. It had been a little more than a decade since the genocide and the population wasn't going to rebuild itself without some frantic copulation.

On the one-year anniversary of her husband's death, she wore her green dress to the graveside. Her mother-in-law handed her two uneven pebbles of myrrh that she added to the pot by his carved marble headstone, the largest and most ornate in the graveyard to demonstrate the magnitude of their love for their son. Two columns of smoke uncoiled skyward. The black-robed priest, with his sorcerer's hat and waterfall beard, swayed and muttered unfathomable words, gazing at the cloudless heavens. There. He was gone. Shant was free of her, as was his family. My grumbling stomach interrupted Armineh.

"My God, it sounds like a lion is trapped in your belly."

"Sorry. I guess I'm a little hungry. I should have eaten some Zankou chicken."

"Try these. I made them this morning." She brought out apricot cookies wrapped in a white napkin from her bag and refilled my brandy from her flask. She fed me a cookie. I nipped her finger to lighten the mood.

It was a distant cousin on Armineh's mother's side who introduced her to Levon. In order for that to happen, Shant's mother's cousin had heard the news from Levon's neighbor and told Armineh's cousin. The baker was looking for a bride.

He was a few years older than Armineh. He baked bread—*lavash*, *matnakash*, pita and baguette—every day at 4 A.M. except Sundays. Levon did a brisk business and wasn't a bad-looking man. He was stocky with the strong, thick limbs of a wrestler, so different from her Shant. Neither the creeping vine of scar tissue on his neck nor his two missing fingers bothered her unless he touched her bare arm and she noticed their pulpy edges.

Levon was built out of hero material. The stuff of legends in Bourj Hammoud, where most Armenians lived in Beirut. The gossips in the neighborhood told Armineh he'd killed three Turkish soldiers with his two hands. Cut off their ears and gouged their eyes before setting their dead bodies on fire. That was how he got the scar. Of course, that wasn't true. He got that scar fighting a thin Bedouin, high on opium, in the desert.

Why was he interested in a young widow with another man's child? If the pool were a bit deeper, he would have picked someone else. And Armineh, too, if she had a choice. But these were the circumstances, plain and simple. Two people with working sex organs and a chance at a new future.

Levon visited her at a cousin's house on Cilicia Street every Sunday afternoon for a month. He came dressed in an ill-fitting white suit to drink coffee scented with cardamom. He sat with Armineh, who wore her green dress, on the terrace lined with pots of bougainvillea and laundry. Without fail, he brought a box of *malban* from Al Rifai wrapped with brown paper and string. But they never went out. They never walked on the Corniche at sunset or shopped for trinkets at the flea market on Maarad Street.

Levon agreed to marry Armineh. But he didn't want little Shant. The boy would have to stay with his father's family.

"No. That doesn't sound like Levon," I said.

Armineh shrugged.

"If my first-born had been a girl, things might have been different," Armineh sniffled. "But someone else's son was out of the question."

Levon didn't know then that he'd never have a son of his own to carry on the family name. Or that he'd have five daughters. Armineh to the fifth power.

It was just as well, Armineh conceded. Her former in-laws weren't eager to let her take their first-born's only son away. He belonged to them. It was she who had been on loan.

Their wedding ceremony was at the Armenian Church in Martyrs' Square on a late fall afternoon. The snow had already started to fall in the mountains. In the barren space of the sanctuary, they promised before Christ to be true to each other for life. The priest crowned them with an ornate circlet decorated with lapis and jade, the very same she had worn with Shant. He declared them king and queen of their home.

They had no best man to hold the cross over their heads, so Levon's assistant, a thin boy wearing a choir robe to cover his worn clothes, stood between them, trembling with the weight of the olive cross and his responsibility to look after them in troubled times. They drank from the goblet of wine, symbolizing the wedding at Cana where Christ turned water into that fine red beverage. *Et voilà*, they were married.

That night, she cooked the wedding dinner for three—Levon, herself and the boy.

"What did you cook?" I asked. "Sorry, I'm still hungry."

Armineh rolled her eyes. "I don't remember."

"Yes, you do."

"His neighbors had a coop where they kept sparrows," she said after a moment. "They gifted us a few."

"Did you fry them?"

She shook her head. "Raw."

"Really? I didn't know you could serve it that way."

She made a tartare out of the tender flesh of the little birds, mashing it to a paste between two flat stones and flavoring it with allspice, red pepper and marjoram. There was rice pilaf with stewed chicken, which they ate by candlelight because they didn't have electricity. Levon poured *arak* out of a clay jar, but he didn't propose a toast. She unwrapped a box of *malban*, a gift from her cousin, the nougat and pistachio sticking to her teeth, forcing her mouth shut. Armineh hated *malban*. She gave the rest to the boy when he left them alone to start their future. Armineh washed Levon's cracked dishes and remembered they were hers now.

They undressed quietly without the candles.

"Please, Armineh, I don't really want to hear anymore," I begged. "Let's go. There's a bus in ten minutes."

But she remained seated.

"What is it you don't want to hear? About our sex life, or that you didn't know who Levon was?"

"Please—" I pressed my hands together. "I can't take it anymore."

"I cried when his ruined fingers traced the path of my spine," she said, ignoring me. "His touch that first night gave me such chills I can't remember anything after."

"But you loved him, didn't you?"

"I didn't know if I could go on any longer until I met you and we became friends."

"Me?" But I knew what she meant. I remembered the day I met her, too.

"I'm tired of being strong," she said. "I can't do it anymore." She put her head in my lap and sobbed. She used my slacks as a handkerchief, rubbing her face back and forth against the rough fabric, leaving thin traces of mucus. I noted to presoak my pants when I got home.

Leaving Lebanon quickly made it easy for everyone. Not two weeks after she remarried, she left for Armenia with Levon. Stalin had threatened to carve up what remained of the country if 30,000 Armenians weren't present. Levon insisted they go to the homeland, not knowing the years he would spend in Siberia or at the front fighting Stalin's wars.

"I saw my baby boy for the last time on his third birthday, two days before the bus through Syria."

Armineh brought him a tin train set and helped put it together on the terrace, under a canopy of white bedsheets trying to dry before the evening mist set in. She watched Shant peer into the dining car windows at the little people sipping tea.

"Where are these people going, *Tatik*?" he asked his grandmother, who hovered behind the sheets like a phantom.

"On a very long journey, Shant *jahn*," she replied. "Like your mother."

Armineh left him with his father's people along with everything else she had. Every cent, all her jewelry, including the peacock brooch and even the sapphire cross, the only artifact that remained of her own mother whose face she could no longer remember. In return, her former mother-in-law gave her the photograph. They didn't blame her for leaving. In fact, they insisted. It was her duty.

"God, I don't remember much about the trip." Armineh sighed. "Except for Levon throwing up at each stop. Who knew he'd be so motion sick? That sour bile smell. I can't stand papayas because of that."

A bus full of Armenians driven through the desert is a quiet one. They stopped often since the rattling Crossley overheated easily. The convection heat inside drove them outside onto the sand.

Each person looked deep into the desert, deciphering its shifting landmarks and outposts with the skill of an oracle, wondering where in the shimmering gold and brown inferno mothers and sisters, aunts and uncles, cousins and friends breathed their last gritty breath.

"I looked into the sand for a sign," Armineh said. "But it just kept changing until I was lost in it."

A few years later, when I got to Armenia, Armineh and Levon were there already with three girls of their own. A neighbor teased them that a doo-wop band needed at least two more girls. Armineh never backed down from a challenge.

"So do you know what happened to your son?" I asked, rubbing the small hump on the back of her neck.

"Shant's family went to either Argentina or Brazil a few years after I left, but that's all I know."

"Why did they go to South America?"

"It had the word 'America' in it." Turned out they thought they were traveling to New York, and figured any ship heading for America would get them there.

"I take it your father-in-law didn't have a map."

Armineh smiled.

"Levon would have been furious if I had tried to look for my baby. I thought I did the right thing," she said after a minute.

"Do you still think so?"

She didn't say anything.

"Maybe Karlen knows someone there."

The wind rustled through the fine leaves of Levon's oak tree. I wondered if it was him. I was miffed he hadn't confided in me. I felt angry at him for being cruel. Then I was glad he was out of the picture. Maybe this was a new chapter for Armineh and me.

"Well, you asked for it." She got up and brushed the grass off her pants, put her shoes back on and started to walk toward the bus stop with her large purse and flask. "You know everything."

47

CHAPTER EIGHT

Like most old guys, I loved my routine. Before my exile, I got up early to supervise the kids. I made sure Lucy didn't drink coffee and Ara took his vitamins. I watched them from the balcony, ready to wave if they looked up. Then, I'd go back inside to look at my wife's photo and tell her about the weather. It helped me figure out what to wear. Next, I sipped a cup of hot lemon water, letting the liquid work itself through the system before I cooked my breakfast.

The smell of browning butter is why I made an omelet everyday—yes, every day—cholesterol be dammed. I devoured it with the bitterest of olives and *lavash* spread with rose petal jam that Robert's wife makes. Only hers or that of the monks on the island of St. Lazarus would do. And two cups of coffee. Then I walked to my studio and worked for a few hours.

In the afternoons, I liked to sit at the park across the street from the building where I lived with Keran and the kids. I met my friends there most days. Keran's husband, Hovsep, died five years ago and she still refused to "move on," as her American coworkers urged. Although it wasn't for a lack of suitors. I'd seen how the lawyers stared at her from behind their open Louis Vuitton briefcases, straightening up their spines and holding in their stomachs as she walked by in her shapely suits. She looks a lot like her mother, with her luminous skin and ballerina figure. My two sons, Tigran and Movses, who live in Armenia, offered to send her a strapping mail-order husband.

"Please, boys," she'd told them over the phone. "Birthing a two-headed gorgon who's birthing its own two-headed creature is easier than an Armenian husband." She plugged her ears against their strong protests. Still, I wanted her settled in the matters of love and money before I died.

At the park, everything revolved around large quantities of coffee.

"Put it straight in my IV," Hovannes liked to joke, patting his flaccid, veinless arm.

I'd also surrendered to my addiction to Armenian coffee. (To call it "Turkish" in Glendale is a *faux pas*. "Arabic" is somewhat acceptable.) I made my first cup of the afternoon at home in a bronze *jezveh* with a long wooden handle—one heaping teaspoon of coffee and a half teaspoon sugar for a two-ounce cup. I like my coffee powdered to the texture of fine sand. The final effect, thick and sweet, the grit slipping between my molars like bad oil on old gears. That sensation grounds me.

I watched it very carefully because Armenian coffee can boil over without a sound. Only a new bride spills coffee, we say. And I am no new bride. I poured it into a cup and nursed it across the street. The aroma has the same reviving effect on me as smelling salts.

I tried not to miss a day at the park even though the space was a rounding error for nature. A ragged bite of green between a rash of new high-rise buildings, one fancier than the other. I lived in one of them, so I wasn't grumbling. It was convenient, even. I could run to the bathroom on the hour.

The sun, an unblinking cosmic spotlight, bared all defects in the early afternoon. But on its journey home, it slowly arced behind the buildings, turning their metal skins shades of fish-scale pink and purple, beautifying flaws as it disappeared over the horizon.

I'd never complained about this patch with its reluctant syca-more branches borrowed from a neighboring yard. This was *my* kingdom. I was known, even famous, among Los Angeles Arme-nians as Maestro with a capital M. The duduk had made my life comfortable. More than most of my friends at the park. This is where I held court.

Thirty or so people were already sitting at various concrete tables when I got there around 5 P.M., hours after Armineh and I had caught the Beeline home from the cemetery. I was greeted with light applause. I went around and thanked them all individually so as not to slight anyone. Feuds have started on lesser grounds. "What a moving piece that was, Maestro," someone said. "Yes. Better than the tribute itself," another added. "Everyone was wonderful last night," I said diplomatically, but I knew what they said was true. I was the best.

The warm greetings had only briefly interrupted the main topic of conversation. I heard the discussion resume before I got to my favorite bench.

We say one person is enough for an argument, and maybe not even two are needed to start a fight. It usually had to do with something printed in our newspaper, *Asbarez*. A blurry photo of the supposed Noah's Ark still lodged in Mount Ararat. A bribery scandal in Parliament. And lately, the blockade in Karabakh. And then, the story that never goes away: the Armenian Genocide. It happened in 1915 but as I told the journalist, don't ask us to get over it.

"Did you see the paper, Rupen?" Hovannes asked from his wheelchair. He held up the April 24 edition.

Ah, yes. How could I forget? One day a year just for me to remember what I did. April 24, 1915—Red Sunday—because 5,000 Armenians, too poor to get the hell out of Istanbul (it was called Constantinople then), were killed in the streets. *Damn Turks.*

"No. Sorry," I said. "Damn Turks."

"Just when we think the U.S. will pressure them into admitting they slaughtered us . . ." Hovannes' voice trailed off. The man was thinking of his twelve-year-old self burying his mother in the desert, her body wrapped in the delicate tablecloth she'd crocheted the year of her marriage. He told me the story every time he drank too much brandy.

I was numb from his constant recollecting, but I nodded.

"It'll happen next year," Robert said. "One step at a time. Let's be happy we finally got our independence." Seven months and counting.

It won't happen next year either, I thought. It won't happen because we will look away from the truth when we want something other than justice.

"You can say that so easily," Hovannes snapped at Robert.
"Life was a picnic for you."

"It's not my fault my family moved to Fresno." Robert's cheeks
turned pink. His parents had moved to the San Joaquin Valley in
1890 to grow apricots, bringing many of their relatives over before the turn of the century—one of the few Armenian families
untouched by the horror.

"It's not like your time-share in Palm Springs. You can't buy
into our suffering," Hovannes said, spit forming at the corners of
his mouth.

Susie, of the beam ray machine, who was knitting a potholder
but really eavesdropping, gasped.

It's true, Robert was one of the biggest individual donors to
the All-Armenia Fund. His best friend never let him forget it.

Hovannes wheeled himself to the table, turning his back on
Robert.

"That's enough, Hovannes." Armineh refereed from the corner, where the limo had just dropped her off. "Robert's one of us."

"What the hell does that mean?" Robert ignored Armineh and
swung Hovannes' wheelchair around with both hands. "Come
out and say it!"

"Calm down, Robert. Have a cookie. Look, it's still warm,"
Armineh said.

"I'll take a cookie," I offered. I started breathing again.

"There, someone with some common sense. They're pistachio
and rosewater." She smiled gratefully and wedged herself between
Hovannes and Robert. "Come on. Have a cookie. Everyone's
looking at you."

Robert loosened his grip on the wheelchair and sat down on
the concrete bench. We ate our cookies while the unsaid belched
and gurgled among us.

I got up to visit the bathroom. I may still have been able to
control my bladder, but my mind was incontinent. No matter
what its churchgoers think, the greatest Christian country would
gladly side with the Muslims who killed fellow Christians. For
military bases. I almost admire the egalitarianism. However, that
means the first mass murder of the twentieth century will never

be called genocide. Not in my lifetime. But I'm cheating. I'm dying soon.

Hell, at least we weren't as bad off as the Palestinians. We still had a crumb to call our nation.

In one of the Armenian creation myths, God divided up the earth for all the people he'd created. When it was the Armenians' turn, all that was left was a small, stony plot. But we forgave God for his thoughtlessness. Never mind, we said, give it to us, Oh Great One, and we'll manage. The Creator gave us the runt land and the Armenians have had to make their destiny off of it ever since. Sometimes, the kingdom has stretched beyond our wildest dreams. Other times, it has disappeared like a sinking island. Now, it's a rocky speck that once we considered negligible backwaters.

I turned the corner toward my home thinking I'd better hurry or I'd have to piss over the cactus when I saw an orange backpack resting on the bus stand bench. I crossed the street back to the park.

"Back so soon? Why's your hand shaking, Rupen *jahn?*" Armineh asked when I returned to our table, her grandchildren tethered two to each hand. She shooed them toward the swings.

"Everything okay?" she whispered before saying out loud, "Afraid I'll beat you at backgammon?" She had purple lipstick on her teeth. "You know old Benzatyan the lawyer, not the high school principal, was diagnosed with Parkinson's last month." Armineh flicked her head as if her hair was still long and auburn.

"Did you tell him about the ray gun?" I asked.

"It's called a beam ray, Rupen. And it could help you, especially now."

"Where's Robert?" I asked. Armineh motioned with a jerk of her head what I already knew: He'd left, angry he wasn't Armenian enough.

Robert had owned Masis Market on Colorado Boulevard until a couple of years ago. Once he retired, he channeled his frustration into igniting Armenia's lost carpet-weaving tradition. About a year ago, Robert convinced fifty friends to sponsor a sheep each. He arranged for a flock of Pomeranians—the sheep, not the dogs—from Estonia to be sent to Armenia. After a week's train ride through scenic territory, the sheep got to their home in the mountains, 15 kilometers from Yerevan.

The next year, Robert, per his promise to the cultural minster's attaché, hired a professional sheep shearer from New Zealand. When the Kiwi got to the village, the flock was nowhere to be found. Two villages had sustained themselves on mutton for the better part of six months.

But Robert didn't give up. He held another fundraiser and we sponsored another flock of sheep. The Kiwi was supposed to go back this year.

"Ha!" Hovannes laughed out loud.

"Is something really funny, or are you finally going crazy?" Armineh asked.

"Listen to this," he read from the paper. "Several traffic lights have been altered in Glendale."

"We drove past the one by the freeway exit." Armineh chuckled. "God, how did they do it?"

"What?" I asked.

"Someone pasted color filters on the lights so they're red, orange, and blue, like the Armenian flag," Armineh said. "They're still up."

"That's defacing government property. That's against the law," I said.

"Oh, lighten up," Armineh said. "Get it? I made a funny."

Happy Genocide Remembrance Day.

* * *

We drank more coffee from an anonymous selection of thermoses. Armineh and Susie poured it into chipped demitasses, remnants of someone's anniversary gift. Armineh embellished her cup with the contents of her bottomless purse flask. We slipped into an aromatic silence filled with half sentences and fractured thoughts.

Hovannes continued his page-by-page analysis of *Asbarez*. Next was an article on new satellite photos of Mount Ararat. "If only we could send a team up to verify the evidence!" He slapped the page with the back of his mottled hand. But that wouldn't happen, either. Ararat, Armenia's most famous symbol, the birthplace of our forefather, Noah, our snow-capped soaring icon, was actually now Turkish.

"Can you believe they're calling Khojaly a massacre?" Hovannes said in a huff. He referred to the February shootings in the Armenian enclave of Karabakh in Azerbaijan. "The Azeri soldiers hid in the crowd and shot at us first! What were we to do?"

I am so tired.

One. Two. Three. Four. That was all the gulps it took to finish my third coffee. My Lucy accuses me of slurping, which is probably true since I like to drink it very hot. If the heat doesn't sear my lips, why bother? I flipped my cup upside down. Something I'd done since my very first coffee.

Armineh picked up my cup and divined my future from its muddy depths. "Michael!" she bellowed. "Stop biting your sister! Do you want to make the Turks happy with your bad behavior?"

"Oh, you're not so bad, Michael," I assured him. He often hid behind my back when his grandmother scolded him. "No Turk is happy today."

Michael was only a momentary distraction. Armineh turned back to the cup with the concentration of a hawk, my future hooked to her fashionably painted talon.

"I see good things in your future," she said with conviction. "Look." She pointed to a rectangle in the middle of the cup. "You will get an important letter soon, Rupen *jahn*."

I told her I knew not to trust any envelope that claimed its importance ever since I fell for the Publishers' Clearinghouse scam. I'd tried to cancel *TV Guide* four times.

She looked deeper into the veins the sludge had left on its meandering exit. "Ah, I see an arrow pointing up. It means you are honest and true."

"That's not a prediction," I said.

"Take what you can get." She stacked my cup with the others she'd already read.

Telling someone you're dying is the elastic waistband of

secrets. It gives you room for the sins you might have committed, the untruths you might have told.

The boy with the orange backpack was about to snap that waistband.

CHAPTER NINE

Two years ago, there was a revolution at Masis Market, the place where I usually buy my coffee. Blame it on the dried chickpeas. My friend Robert, the owner at the time, always displayed them next to the tomato paste. The problem was, his two sons-in-law felt dry legumes should be shelved together so customers could easily find ingredients. But Robert was like Mount Ararat. He wouldn't budge.

"This is how I like it. You always need tomato paste when you cook chickpeas!" he told Armineh when he visited her at the bakery during this period. "Where were those punks when I opened the store thirty years ago? Telling me what to do."

Armineh didn't have the heart to tell them the "punks" probably hadn't been born yet.

"When they put up the money to buy the store, then they can change the rules." Robert's hand shook as he drank Armineh's fine cinnamon tea.

Armineh cleared her throat so she didn't have to respond as she refilled Robert's cup. She didn't want to speak too loudly. After all, it wasn't her idea to renovate Bakery Opera into the spectacle it is today. But Armineh knew how to pick her battles.

Robert's young sons in-law weren't about to buy him out. They wanted him to step aside. In their minds, they deserved the business after bowing to his crazy ways for nearly a decade. They gnawed at him like he was a well-cooked lamb shank, pointing out every mistake he made. They urged customers to complain. They bribed employees to side with their cause.

"We'll give you flex time," the younger son-in-law promised the crew. "And a ping-pong table in the warehouse."

"You can vote on the store hours," the elder one added.

"You'll be treated as equals."

The mostly Latin American employees were excited. Could their lives get better? Surely, a change would be good after working for the *viejo loco.*

"*Viva la Revolución!*" they said, except for Junior, the old man who worked in the warehouse. His sighs reverberated in the walk-in freezer as he stacked illicit, homemade beef *manti* behind the ice cream just in case the health inspector stopped by. He'd seen this story play out back in El Salvador.

The young in-laws' campaign created such a vortex of energy, especially in the back of the store where the dried chickpeas were moved next to the lentils one hour and moved back to the tomato paste the next.

Finally, after two months of aisle warfare, Robert, with tennis elbow from slogging bags of dried goods, stepped aside. He didn't say a word to anyone, but gave a nod to old Junior. Robert left the keys on the manager's desk and went home.

"We did it!" The boys opened a ten-year-old bottle of Ararat Armenia Brandy and they all drank it out of little plastic cups used for take-out tahini sauce. They went home happy, dreaming of a bright new future.

The next day, when the employees came to work, they were fired. The elder son-in-law stood in front of the locked automatic door.

"Listen, thank you for your support," he said, the sun blazing into the eyes of the workers. "But after how you treated our father-in-law, we're not sure we can trust you. Maybe Jons down the street is hiring."

"*Patrón*, we need this job. We have nowhere else to go," they begged in unison, sweat and tears forming on their faces. "We believed in you!"

The boys called Karlen to send in some security. The workers got the message when they saw the black vans and started walking toward Jons. Thirsty.

CHAPTER TEN

Irecently found out what a blind fault is. Some phrases look like they should mean something else but don't. Like "blind fault." I would define it this way: You do something wrong because you think it's right.

I would be wrong.

Maybe it's because my English is not the best. My Russian is better. My Italian so-so. My Armenian? Better every day.

A blind fault is an unknown break in the earth's crust deep underground where an earthquake can occur. It usually happens under a volcano causing not just an earthquake but an eruption.

I like my definition better.

I felt the boy before I saw him. He stood next to the swings a few days later right at 4 P.M., smoking a cigarette. I had to pass him to get to my table.

"*Barev*, Maestro. Shall we sit with your friends?" Even his nod in their direction was sarcastic. He was dressed in hospital scrubs, a green shade fit to be modeled only for the blind. Hovannes was in mid-rejoicing over something, most likely the Armenian capture of Shusha in Karabakh. Probably not the launch of the Endeavor. Armineh and Robert were already engaged in a heated backgammon tournament. They looked up to see why I lingered in the sandbox.

"A fan," I mouthed to them. I motioned for him to follow me farther away from my friends.

"Didn't you get what you wanted? I don't have more money!" The boy snorted. "Nice shoes."

"These are from 1985. Not that I have anything to explain to the likes of you," I said. "In fact, are you sure you want to make your allegations?"

"Allegations? How fancy of you. But my grandmother's never lied to me," he said. "Besides, you wouldn't be talking to me right now if you didn't have something to hide, would you?"

"Maybe I just feel sorry for you. I mean, look at you."

He clenched his jaw.

I didn't even know him, but I knew where to stick the dagger. He turned slightly as if to walk back toward my friends.

"Wait," I said loud enough to scare pigeons into flight. "Boys like you disappear all the time." I said it the way they do in the Russian gangster movies. "Do you want your parents to suffer?" I thought of the handsome Karlen, who ran a string of banquet halls as a cover for his other activities. Once, when I played a last-minute event as a favor, he'd told me to call him if I ever needed "assistance."

The boy paused. He knew the fluidity of the Soviet disappearing act. It could be arranged, especially in Glendale.

"It would cost you less if you paid me," he said. The boy was practical. "Besides, I already wrote a letter for my friends to find if something happens to me. You don't want the Kemal Arikan treatment, do you?" He was referring to the 1982 Turkish consul general who'd been gunned down at the intersection of Wilshire and Comstock in Westwood by a nineteen-year-old Armenian Youth Federation member. I remembered that. I remembered my heart beating and my palms sweating. A pressure on my chest so heavy my wife thought I was dying. I was. On the inside.

"Or I could stop bothering you very quickly if we could come to some understanding." He rubbed his fingertips together.

"You're blackmailing me?" I couldn't stop clenching my fists. "You're just a kid. You don't know anything yet." I said this in Armenian.

He stiffened when I put my hand on his arm. My fingers were cold even in the middle of a hot afternoon. Bad circulation.

"*Baron!*" That's how we refer to each other when we want to flatter. The boy called this out to a man walking his poodle. "You want to hear something very interesting about Maestro Rupen?" The man recognized me and waved.

"Shut up, you peasant," I hissed. He'd called my bluff. "How much?" The corner of Wilson Avenue and Glendale Boulevard had become my souk.

"Twenty-five K." He ignored my insult.

"Twenty-five thousand dollars! I'm a musician, not a movie star!"

He shrugged, his shoulders saying "suit yourself."

We stood still for a small eternity. A swarm of gnats flew by en route to their own prey.

"I'm not going to pay you," I said. This was money for Keran and the kids when I was gone.

"Yes, you are. You don't want your family to know."

By the slump of my shoulders, he knew he was the bull elephant. I had lived my life for this moment with fingernails bitten to the rosy flesh, waiting for someone to find out about me, and all I'd ever accomplished would turn to ash. The fight that had gotten me this far fled with the gnats, depositing me in this boy's outstretched arms.

"I want the money tomorrow." He smiled. He hadn't expected such a quick victory after all. After relaying a few instructions, he turned around and dissolved back into the mire.

I limped back to the park. Armineh and Robert sat still on the concrete bench. Susie stood behind them, knitting needles in hand. Something extraordinary had taken place for them to suspend their game 3:1.

Under the shade of the sycamores, a young Korean family had spread a blanket on the dry grass and proceeded to barbeque thin cuts of garlicky beef on a charcoal brazier. The father used his chopsticks to turn the meat.

"How do they eat with those twigs?" Susie whispered.

"It smells good. Just like *horovats*," Robert said, referring to the meats we like to grill over wood charcoal.

"Better than those awful hamburgers white people eat," Armineh conceded, suddenly unaware her skin was the shade of polished alabaster.

"I don't want to smell like Chinese food." Susie fanned herself with a paper bag.

"Don't they know this is our park?" Hovannes asked loudly.

"They must be new," Robert said.

I barely said goodbye, walking home in my internal barbecue. "*Qué pasa*, Señor Rupen?" the atrium gardener called as I walked into the building. He held out a broken piece of aloe vera. "For Señorita Lucy. Good for pretty skin."

CHAPTER ELEVEN

Early the next day, I waited for the boy in front of the looming central post office. The white stone glistened in the morning sun, a tomb for our mail.

A postal worker sat on the bus bench scanning the paper. His head moved back and forth with his eyes as they followed each line. I read over his shoulder to calm my mind. Sarajevo going from bad to worse. The siege was in its fourth week. The man gave me the evil eye when I asked him to turn the page. I should have worn my *achk*.

The boy showed up twenty minutes later. It must have been a long walk because a barrier of sweat had formed on his neck, a dark noose on his gray shirt. I didn't have anything to say to my extorter. What should I have said? That I barely slept all night? The Kemal Arikan treatment! I kept quiet. Wanted to keep him guessing what was going through my mind.

"You came." He didn't shake my hand. Blackmailing protocol didn't require that pleasantry.

"You'd know where to find me if I didn't," I said.

We walked toward the Glendale Federal Bank. Sure, I wanted to torture this boy but this was a calculated move. My quest for peace of mind was stronger than my desire to punish him. The easiest way was to pay him off. Get him to crawl back into his hole. This was an investment. An expensive one. I was doing the right thing. At least that was what I told myself.

As we turned onto Brand Boulevard, we met Hovannes and Robert. They were back to being friends and on their way to the bookstore to read magazines they would never buy.

"*Bari luis*, Rupen, you're up and around early," Robert said.

"*Eench pes ek?*" I greeted them. My head felt light and my

vision was a merry-go-round.

"Aren't you practicing this morning?" Robert asked as he kissed me on both cheeks. I cringed at the distaste that moved up the boy's spine. *How could he kiss someone like me?* They looked at him, then at me. Hovannes cleared his throat.

"Oh, this is one of my new students," I said after a few seconds. "His name is—"

"Haik."

And that was how I learned my blackmailer's name. I hadn't thought to ask before. Maybe I didn't want to know. Thankfully, my friends weren't in a questioning mood. They'd eventually remember I'd never stoop to teach a beginner.

"Haik, like in the old stories." Robert made conversation. "*King* Haik. The great grandson of Noah of the Ark. Bravo! Maybe one day you'll be as great as our Maestro Rupen." He patted Haik on his shoulder.

Haik's face showed no expression.

"More of you youngsters should learn our instruments."

"What'll it take? Michael Jackson to play the *zurna?*" Hovannes joked in his raspy, post surgical voice. They cackled and coughed their way across the street.

Only one other customer was in the bank. We waited in the lobby, looking at our dull reflections in the polished marble floor. People could mistake us for many things: grandfather and grandson, teacher and student. Employer and employee. Never victim and blackmailer.

"Mr. Najarian, so nice to see you," said the bank manager, a Filipina woman I'd known for years but whose name I could never remember. "I heard from Arax that you gave a wonderful concert." She pointed to the slim dark-haired teller with the pomegranate-red lipstick. "Happy birthday!" she said, handing me a free duffle bag with the bank logo.

Arax, the bank teller, motioned for us to approach the counter. "*Bari luis*, Maestro," she said. "*Sh'norhavor.* I hope your eighty-fourth year is your best ever." Her gaze shifted to Haik, estimating whether he had any dating potential. She took in his sweaty T-shirt, scuffed work shoes and defiance.

He looked into her liquid eyes briefly and then back to the floor. He was aware she had dismissed him. He pretended not to care.

"So what can I help you with today?"

"I'd like to withdraw $25,000." I felt Haik shift next to me. She hesitated only for a moment. "Of course, Maestro Rupen. Would you like traveler's checks?"

"No. A cashier's check, please."

It's amazing how quickly you can rid yourself of so much money. I counted 45 seconds before she handed me the rectangular piece of pale blue paper countersigned by the bank manager.

"Be careful not to lose it. We can't replace it."

"*Merci, akchik jahn*," I said as we walked away.

The bank had a height scale notched on its door, the kind you use to measure a robber on his way out. I'd shrunk to 5'6". The hot air repelled me, then drove me onto the sidewalk to complete our financial transaction.

"You have what you want," I told him. "Now you must promise never to talk about me." I enunciated each word, puffing out my chest.

"What do you mean?" he sneered. "I can't tell people what an asset Maestro Rupen is to our community?"

"Not even that. I no longer exist in your world."

"Okay. Give me the money, then." Haik held out his palm.

I handed him the check, hoping this would buy my peace of mind.

He held the paper for a second, then folded it into thirds before putting it in his front pocket. He nodded and walked away without looking back.

CHAPTER TWELVE

Months later, when it was clear he wouldn't leave me alone, I asked Haik how he came up with the blackmail amount: $25,000. Why not $10,000 or $50,000?

He told me it was the winning prize on *Jeopardy!* And way more money than he could imagine. He never pictured that one day he would be paid more than that for his true talent. Blackmailing was not it. But that story comes later.

Haik lived with his twin sisters, mother, father and grandmother in a sagging two-bedroom bungalow on Maple Street. I visited the house once. It was painted warm beige with a pale blue trim, as if it belonged near the beach. They joked that it was the termites and paint that held the house up.

It was a family of insomniacs. They regularly stayed up past midnight to play Blot with a creased pack of cards that was missing an ace. Even the twins, who were still in high school. They had a talent for card counting.

"Why are there helicopters over our house?" Haik's mother, Hasmik, asked the night before Haik approached me in the park, as she strung freshly shelled walnuts on white sewing thread to dip in grape molasses. She opened and closed the kitchen window, the helicopters her lunar pull.

"I don't know. What evil have you done, my wife?" His father busied himself fashioning an ace card from the back of a cereal box.

"Ma! You ask the same question every night!" Haik's sister Gohar whined from the bathroom where she sat on the closed toilet seat.

"And you say the exact same thing every night, Pa," Gayaneh, the other twin said, as she straightened her sister's long, curly hair.

"Has anyone seen *Tatik*?" Haik's mother got up with a start. "Make sure she didn't go outside again."

Haik wasn't around to hear this nightly loop because he worked the graveyard shift as an orderly at Glendale General, wheeling patients from their rooms to the lab, to surgery, to ICU and eventually the morgue. Although he was classified as a part-time, temporary employee, Haik had been working there for more than two years, clocking in sixty hours a week. The $1,500 a month he made lifting, pushing, stacking and wiping kept the creaky roof over their heads. He was the family's only provider.

Haik walked home from the hospital every morning around six. The family car, an old Ford Fairmont, sat in the driveway. A $600 repair would set it right, but they never had that kind of money. His mother still washed it every week to keep up appearances.

Most mornings, he'd find his grandmother rifling through the neighbor's garden. The morning before my blackmail was no exception.

"What's up, *Tatik*?" he asked.

"Oh, I was just picking berries with my friends. I don't know where those girls went!"

No one was sure how old *Tatik* Ruby, his mother's mother, was. Most of her family had died during the genocide, the stragglers at the end of World War I. They celebrated her birthday on the first of every January. Ruby was at least eighty-eight years old and had raised the white flag to dementia. The present might have faded, but the past. That she remembered in panoramic detail. She lived in the bygone with an intensity she'd never experienced when she had lived it the first time. That day when she sat by the window at Bakery Opera with Haik, the warm fog of steam from the cup of tea worked like one of those camera tricks that dissolved into a flashback. It rewound all those years back to the little village outside of Sis. There, they—Armenians, a few Turks and a couple of Kurds who had lost their way—modest people all, lived in relative harmony if not friendship. She remembered the wild garnet-colored berries she picked with the neighborhood girls in the summer and the way they stained the flesh around her fingernails. Her four boy cousins who chased them through the olive groves, their bare feet thumping against the baked earth. The precise, sharp tang of her aunt's famous sheep's milk cheese. The dense feel of the bright wool carpets they spread out in the meadow for picnics. And the little boy with the high cheekbones who played the duduk with his father, the carpenter. It was like it had all happened yesterday.

"My *jahn*, did you see the girls?" Ruby asked Haik. "I don't want the soldiers to find them."

"Don't worry, *Tatik*. I give you my word they're fine. Let's go home and get some sleep." Haik yawned, hoping it would entice his grandmother to give up her search.

"The birds!" Ruby said in wonder.

"What birds?"

"The green ones with the red tails. There." She pointed to the maple tree on the corner.

"Parrots? *Tatik*, they don't live in California," Haik said, rubbing sleep from his eyes as a noisy flock flew eastward against the light.

"These do."

"Okay, *Tatik*." Haik looked up to an empty sky.

The family was still asleep when he took off his shoes on the porch. He shepherded his grandmother to her room before washing the hospital stink off his skin. It never really went away. Rather, it smelled like Irish Spring and stink.

Although he was exhausted, he didn't go to bed. In the darkened house, Haik consolidated cold coffee from the little cups left over from the family's late night and drank it just in front of the door, watching the advancing brightness bleach the grass. Eventually, he slept on the couch rolled up in a green-and-tangerine blanket his mother had crocheted from leftover wool. He hadn't had his own bed in years.

When Haik went to sleep, he dreamt the same dream: dancing droplets of red and orange that beckoned him into a dark pine forest. He felt their heat on his cheeks. And as he moved closer, a girl with tiger's eyes materialized behind the flames, holding a bright yellow bouquet in her arms. He stretched out his hand to touch the petals, but they singed his fingertips. Jittery, warm and tangy, little bits caramelized into syrup before floating upward to the heavens. The girl drifted further into the darkness. And just as he began to follow her, Haik fell weightlessly.

He woke up sad the girl had gone away. And with a raging hard-on that saluted through the afghan.

He told me later that was the moment he decided to blackmail me. Hard-ons can do that.

CHAPTER THIRTEEN

I did something I thought would make me feel better after Haik took my money. I ate. There's a small fridge in my studio where I keep life's necessities—cheese and olives. There's also some chocolate and coffee, but I keep those on top of the fridge. You shouldn't refrigerate or freeze coffee the way I've seen some Americans do. It never tastes the same after such a big change. Same for chocolate. It loses its life.

My studio is upstairs from an accountant's office. The CPA, an Armenian man in his sixties from Isfahan, chain-smokes tobacco. When you spy on him from the window outside his office, it looks like he's deep in thought, his eyes cast downward and his thick, tobacco-darkened lips pursed. But I know his secret. He spends his spare time rolling cigarettes in special brown paper. He can do it with his eyes closed.

He keeps parakeets, thinking they help him relax during tax season. It's a good thing they're caged. They'd be an *amuse-bouche* for the hawks circling Glendale. Or they could fall in love and fly away with Haik's *tatik's* parrots.

That day, after the bank, I held my breath as I took the stairs up through the nicotine haze to the third floor. I wondered if birds could get lung cancer.

For years, the owners couldn't rent out this beautiful building. It'd been the headquarters of the American Nazi Party. The printing press for their newspaper used to stand where the accountant now kept his commercial shredder. The 210-volt outlets left over from the press were powerful enough to obliterate even the most sensitive of tax returns.

My corner studio had housed a small but notable Hitler

museum. I once found a torn military patch stuck in the back of a drawer. It was of a snake climbing a staff, but only the tail portion remained. The rental agent didn't tell me any of this when I moved in. She just said it was originally a hotel built in the 1920s and aren't the walnut built-ins beautiful? They are.

I have an amazing view of the mountains. Almost as good as from my penthouse balcony. A window at each side of the corner goes up to the decorated crown moulding that looks like cake icing. The ceilings soar, making my 500 square feet airy, almost Parisian. The room has great acoustics, which a musician doesn't take lightly.

An old cracked mirror hangs on the wall by the door. Cracked mirrors are supposed to be bad luck, and I guess it finally caught up with me. An oddly shaped closet once held a bed, or so the agent had told me.

"Who sleeps in a closet?" Armineh asked when I first moved in.

I told her it was a Murphy bed. Like a Bedouin tent, I explained, you put it away when you don't need it.

"How strange. Well, every Bedouin tent needs a coffeepot." She produced a hot plate from one of her bags, a small *jezveh* and a set of coffee cups and saucers decorated with the disciples. All but Judas. I think people judge him unfairly but on the other hand, you can't have thirteen cups and saucers in a set.

A two hundred-year-old Persian carpet hides the warped wooden floor. The blues and reds as vivid as they must have been those hundreds of years ago. I bought the carpet when I received my first big check. Both Armenians and Turks used to eat sitting on the floor. A carpet was a sign of wealth. But just like in one of those Darwin-inspired bumper stickers, we hoisted ourselves onto low stools and then chairs and table at the turn of the nineteenth century. I missed sitting on the floor with my family. Intellectually, that is. My knees are like gnawed chicken bones, and just a few months ago, my belly was the size of a mid-sized toaster oven. When I sat on the floor, it was a long-term commitment.

There's also an enormous worktable that I built from one olive tree. It died of old age in front of a Spanish Mission–style house on Mountain Avenue. They were going to mulch it. Better to be a table than fertilizer, I assured the wood, as Aram tied it to the top of his limousine.

This studio is my real home.

I put my beret on the table and slipped off my shoes and socks. I hugged the deformed wooden planks with my toes, feeling its knots against my arches as I made my way to the fridge. In the icy white cave was a pint of yogurt souring by the day. I wondered what to do with it. I remembered my wife's favorite dish, *sron*. Her people were from Van and they could do a hundred things with yogurt.

I beat the yogurt with a little water and salt and warmed it carefully in a saucepan over the hot plate. Then I melted butter in my *jezveh* and added minced garlic and dry mint. I soaked the pot in a little bleach to get the garlic smell out.

There's a moment right before the yogurt starts to curdle from the heat. That's when to take it off the fire and mix in the fragrant butter. I poured this over a bowl of coiled up rosettes of day-old *lavash* and covered it for a few minutes to let the bread soak. When I could wait no longer, I opened the dish and dug in. I rolled the celestial combination of cream and herb from cheek to cheek. Each salty bite consoled me until I had no more bread and yogurt to fill the emptiness. Then I threw it all up in the rust-stained porcelain toilet.

I mourned the loss of my appetite, sitting on the floor with my back resting on the cold subway tile. I sat there until I heard the mailman shuffle and complain about the smoke. I made the calculations to get up from the floor, putting my chest on the closed toilet and using the edge of the sink to get to my feet.

"Maestro, is that you?" the CPA called out as I walked downstairs in socks.

"Yes, Vahan. I meant to stop by earlier." The cigarette fumes filled my lungs. I imagined it ruining my duduk playing. Then I took a deep breath, letting the smoke swirl in my chest. My lungs would surely outlive the rest of me.

"Did you see the paper?"

"Armenian or Angeleno?"

There was a pause as he contemplated which one he meant. I

left him to his quandary.

Whether it was the loss of my hard-earned money or relief that my secret was still safe, something startled me into action. I decided to finish making a duduk that had sat on my table for months. Maybe a year. I had a waiting list of musicians and collectors who wanted to buy my instruments, but I made no promises. They were ready when they were ready.

I picked up the unfinished piece of wood, wondering what it would become. I smoothed it with the edge of a piece of sandpaper, resting my elbows on the windowsill, feeling the shaft for rough spots every so often. Nothing is worse than that electric jolt when a splinter launches under your nail. In the time of Noah, they made a duduk-like instrument from animal bone.

I'd made most of this one by hand, using a hand drill to form the cylinder. It took forty-two additional steps to finish the instrument, from drilling the finger holes to lathing it. That was after almost eighteen months to cure the green apricot wood to give it the specific timbre, the voice and strength that would express every emotion. And it has to be apricot wood. Everything else sounds nasally.

I learned to make the duduk from my father. He was also my first music teacher. He was a carpenter with artistic fingers and a love of music. My mother said it wasn't blood that ran through his veins, but notes. When she said that I'd pick up his arm and put it to my ear. When I chose Najarian as my last name, I merely translated his ancestral profession into my new family name.

My father used to sit under a gnarled olive tree too old to bear fruit, carving finger holes into a smooth cylinder of wood. It was usually a Friday because he found it meditative to carve before prayers.

One day, as I perched on the wall by his shoulder, he handed me a rough coil of wood, a twist of green that had turned brown snaking through its core. I was smitten as if it were a red-headed girl.

"You are old enough to speak to the wood." He would repeat these words every time I faltered in his workshop. I still remember the toasted tang of hot shavings mixed with his sweat and his soft voice when he sang our village songs. I refuse to remember his face. I started making the duduk long before I was allowed to play one. I was forbidden to touch my father's instrument but he played the notes for me often and with such ease, like wind whispering through the cypress.

"We'll see," he said every time I begged to play it. How I longed to be showered with the admiration the village gave him. How I wanted to be like him. But he didn't let me. It was almost as if I was unworthy of the duduk's voice until I proved that I could coax it from my own stick of wood and a few holes.

A few months later, I'd finally made a duduk. It looked nothing like his instrument but I was proud of it. With the impatience of a child, I told him I was ready to play it. He nodded and invited me to make my debut. But I insisted on gathering an audience, my little brothers and cousins, the girls from the carpet makers and the boys that chased after them. They sat in a semi circle in the courtyard, chatting and throwing leaves at each other. I shushed them and took a sweeping bow. Impressed, they settled down. My parents gave each other a look but I didn't care. I took a deep breath and attempted the scale I'd often heard my father play. I heard geese honking as I blew into the mouthpiece. The kids laughed, rolling on the courtyard floor mimicking the bleating noises of my duduk.

I burst into tears. My father shooed my audience away and helped me fix the finger holes, showing me how big to make them to get the proper notes. I learned and before the year was out, I was playing a duduk with my father. But how I wished I had his instrument.

The accountant whistled to his birds while I sanded the unfinished duduk once more and moisturized it with tung oil. Then I gazed at the San Gabriels, lost to time until one of my students came for a lesson.

It was Ara.

Teaching your flesh and blood your best skill is a necessity. How else would cavemen have survived? But teaching your grandson to follow in your footsteps is like walking on a goat path. You could fall off . . . and so could the goat.

Ara was not the most talented duduk player among my five grandchildren. That would be his sister, Lucy. But someone needed to be the next Rupen Najarian. Since none of my own children were musically inclined, my son-in-law, Hovsep, pushed Ara to be my successor when he was just a child. I should have said no. I should have said that we must each pick our own path so we can hold others blameless for our mistakes.

"Hey *Papik?*" he said, going to the worktable. "You started working on the duduk again."

"Hi, Ara *jahn*. Yes. What do you think?"

His brown hair was getting too long and he smelled like cigarettes. "Not bad. That last hole might not be big enough."

I drifted back to the mountains, stark against the clear sky.

"What's up, Grandpa? Everything okay?" He fixed his curly hair in the cracked mirror.

"What? Nothing. You're probably right about the last hole."

Ara might be just a passable musician, but he was a wonder in the workshop. Just like the great grandfather he'd never heard about.

"Why does it smell like garlic in here?"

"I don't know." I opened a window.

Fridays were group days, when all my students were invited to "jam" with their duduks. Only Brian showed up a few minutes later.

"Where's Zorab and Christopher?" Brian asked, looking around the empty room. He was a Hollywood composer drawn to ethnic instruments. He took sitar lessons. He played the taiko drums in Little Tokyo. Every two weeks, he came for duduk lessons.

"The duduk is the antidote to desensitization. We're living in tough times, man. Everyone should be here," he said, running his hands through his sun-bleached hippy hair. "Who fights when you hear the duduk?"

Tragedy was what drew people to play the duduk.

"Maybe we should go play *Knir im Balik* for the rioters in South Central." Ara nudged him with an elbow.

"The lullaby? Good thinking, kiddo. I'm right behind you, at least in spirit." Brian fingered the virgin duduk. "Bet you guys didn't know it's the one instrument that still can't be synthesized." "So the duduk can't be faked?" I asked. "Not yet, at least." He sat in a straight-backed wooden chair and opened his case. "Shall we?" I asked. "We shall," Ara said.

* * *

Brian gave us a ride home after our session and I started to feel better. But it was the first day in months I didn't go to the park. I watched my friends from the penthouse. They looked like a flock of pigeons in their grays and blues, warbling their daily news. I could predict the gist of their conversation. It was always the same anyway but with different details:

Robert: My hot water isn't working at home again.
Hovannes: It's probably the damn Turks.
Robert: Please! The building is owned by Jews.
Hovannes: You know *they* sided with the Turks to save their own skin.
Armineh: Can we please talk about something other than plumbing? Michael! Stop screaming. You want the Turks to be happy?
Michael: *Tatik*, are you from outer space?

The telephone rang. I answered the call of the refrigerator instead. I was always good in the kitchen, but my goddess thought it was unseemly for an Armenian husband to wear an apron.

"No kitchen work, Rupen *jahn*. People will think you're henpecked," she said on more than one occasion.

"I *am* henpecked," was my standard response. We both knew my cooking was tastier.

A fresh cut of filet mignon lay on the top shelf. Keran must have bought it at Masis Market. The meat, damp with blood, had stained the paper a rusty brown. I flipped the meat onto a wooden board and placed it on the counter. My hands found the spiked metal mallet and started to beat the flesh. A sliver fell on my top lip and I licked it. Bloody.

"Yo *Papik*!" It was Ara, who had emerged from his room.

"Huh?"

"What's up? The cow's already dead." He took the mallet from my hand.

"It's nothing. I was just thinking of something."

"More like someone. Is it 'cause I couldn't hit the F sharp today?" he asked as I scraped the meat paste into a bowl. "I'm trying."

"Of course you are, Ara *jahn*. You'll get it next time."

* * *

That night, I surprised them with a feast.

"Papa," Keran protested with a big smile on her face. She'd been working late almost every day for the last month. "I would have made dinner. You must be tired after your big concert."

"Ma, don't argue," Ara said. "He cooks better than you." He expertly ducked the towel she threw at him.

"Who chipped this platter?" Keran pointed her question at Ara.

"Don't look at me," he said. "*Papik* was at Round Five with the steak. *Papik* won." He winked at me.

"Yes, go ahead and blame the old man," I said. But how I deserved it, and more.

I'd already made *imam bayildi*—eggplant, peppers and tomatoes swimming in olive oil. That was the key to the dish. If it looks only slightly oily, add another half cup of the most flavorful olive oil you can find and it will be perfect. (What else would you soak the bread in?) And the raw beef *chi kufta* beaten to an inch of its life with just the right amount of bulgur, Aleppo red pepper, and a touch of fresh marjoram. I even baked a *gata* for dessert. I wasn't hungry.

"Wow. This is the best eggplant ever!" Lucy said.

"Pa, it's too much oil," Keran protested. "I'm watching my figure." She blushed and I wondered who else was watching it.

They passed the dishes in the punctual military rotation of people who had skipped lunch.

"Pa, did you hear about Armineh's Alice?" Keran asked.

"What has she done now?" I felt the tips of my ears turn pink. I ate a slice of cucumber.

"She's moving back to Armenia with her husband."

"Really? Armineh didn't mention it."

"I ran into her at the DMV." Keran swirled a crust of bread in the savory oil. "She wants to start a bakery there and whatshisname is running for some political office."

"That's crazy!" I catapulted *chi kufta*, Ara's favorite, onto his plate. He grunted his thanks. "Fantasies are always better than the real thing."

"*Papik*, aren't you hungry?" Lucy asked, looking at my empty plate.

"You don't look when my plate is full," I said, spooning *imam bayildi* onto her plate. The tangy smell of cooked vegetables made me nauseated.

"I don't know. Maybe we should go back. It's our country," Ara said with his mouth full of meat.

"Your *Keri* Tigran said there's no electricity," Keran said. "Remember our last trip? You were ten. You hated the village and never wanted to go back." She referred to the cinderblock Soviet-style settlement on the outskirts of Yerevan where my wife's family had settled. Their homestead, a large country house surrounded by an apricot orchard, had been confiscated by the Communist government and divided into four units that were assigned to four families.

"The bathtub in the kitchen freaked me out," Lucy said.

"Uncle Tigran exaggerates everything," Ara said. "It's better today than it was back then. They moved into that cool apartment on Boulevard Mashtots. They go to the opera. They plant trees in the park."

"Yeah, but who cut down the trees in the first place?" Lucy asked.

The girls were right. Electricity was rationed in the brave new Armenia. They were lucky to get water once a day. And deep in its soaring basalt mountains, under its fruitful orchards, skirting its wild-flower meadows, crooks were rubbing their hands together in glee, looking for a way to sell off its pristine spring water to the Italians, its brandy factory to the French and its telecommunications to the Greeks.

"It's like we're our own worst enemies," Lucy said.

"Shut up," Ara said.

"Enough," Keran said. "You can argue after we eat the *gata*."

CHAPTER FOURTEEN

I asked Armineh about her daughter a few days later when I saw her at the park.

"I can't stop her." Armineh shrugged. She picked through a bag of green apricots, the size of gumballs, that Robert bought from Jons. We dipped the sour fruit into the sea salt he poured onto our paper plates before eating them.

"But it might be dangerous!" I said. "You must try to talk her out of it."

Armineh looked at me for a second too long. I didn't think she knew. At least, I hope she didn't.

"It's a good thing what your daughter is doing," Hovannes said, sitting up straighter. "Are you thinking of going, too?"

"I did it the first time around," Armineh retorted. "They'll learn, soon enough."

"What's that supposed to mean?" Hovannes clutched the arms of his chair, ready for a fight.

"It means they'll go. They'll put their money into the country. They'll see how hard life is. They'll work harder. Put more money in. Then someone will steal it all."

"That's unpatriotic!" Hovannes' voice rose to a pitch more sour than the fruit.

"Shut up and eat," Armineh said, flicking an apricot into his protesting mouth.

Food is the ultimate peace offering. In fact, there's a dish called "shut up and eat." *Ker u sus*, a hearty stew of tender beef loin sautéed with onions, tomatoes and fried potatoes. It's best served in a chipped enamel pot.

We laughed like children when the tangy green apricot snack made our old cheeks pucker.

"Oh, my sister and I used to eat them right under the apricot trees," Hovannes said. "Nothing could taste better than those. How could they! How could they take all that away from us?" he beseeched the universe's unknown force.

"Shut up! Shut up!" I shouted twice. I left my body and watched my madman counterpart rant.

"What's gotten into you, Rupen *jahn?*" Armineh asked, putting her hand on my arm.

I shrugged it off.

"Don't stress yourself," she said.

Susie got up from the adjoining table and stood behind Armineh. She loved a good show.

I agreed fully with Armineh. I should have sat down but my alter ego had other plans.

"Holy Christ, that was almost eighty years ago! Could you stop blaming your unhappiness on some Turk who's long turned to dust?" I heard Robert take a breath, but I couldn't stop myself. "Your flabby chest must be bruised from all that beating." I stood up, knocking over the pile of fruit as I beat my chest like Tarzan.

"Now look what you've done," Armineh said, her voice quavering as she picked the fruit up from the grass. "That's not right, Rupen. You're not right."

"I'm so sorry," I said, coming to my senses. "I don't feel good today." The salt and wet fruit had soaked right through my plate and onto my pants, leaving a wet stain on my crotch. I stumbled back to the apartment.

I didn't go back the next day. But Haik did. He sat on the swings next to Michael for half an hour, waiting for me. I'm not sure if it was impulse, greed or our innate nature to kick someone weak that led the boy so easily back to me. I still don't know the answer. Maybe it doesn't matter.

I was on probation two days after my outburst, so I tried to make amends. I brought them my homemade *gata* on a silver plate and was sure to serve Hovannes first. For his part, he put his lamentations aside.

"You were always an excellent baker," Armineh said.

Since my eyesight was the best in the group, I read the *Times* out loud, stopping to add my own commentary. A billion dollars of post-riot property damage in Los Angeles. Nothing in Glendale, I added. Barcelona scrambling toward the Summer Olympics. Johnny Carson was about to perform his grand finale. Retirement, not death.

"Rupen, isn't that your student? He was here yesterday, too." Robert peeked over the top of the paper. He motioned to a gray BMW across the street.

"Are his parents from Lebanon?" Susie asked.

"No."

"From Iran?" Armineh asked.

"No. They're from Armenia," I said.

"Oh." Susie returned to circling bed sheets on the Macy's sale page.

The window was rolled down about an inch and a serpentine twist of smoke escaped through the crack. Haik got out of the car and waved slightly. I felt my bladder twinge.

"Yes. He missed the last lesson," I said. "He must be here to apologize."

"At least he has manners. Not all those boys are considerate. Brought up by inconsiderate parents —" Robert continued as I got up from the table. I risked the $80 jay-walking ticket—Glendale police are manic about illegal street crossings.

"What are you doing here? I thought we agreed never to meet again," I growled.

"I know." There was a long pause.

"So? This is your car?"

"Yes. It's new."

"You bought it with the money I gave you?" Typical, I thought.

He nodded and crushed out his cigarette. He picked up the butt and threw it in the trash can on the corner.

"Why would you spend it all on a car?"

He didn't say anything.

"I know this car. It costs more than $25,000. I'll be offended if you've been blackmailing others."

"I bought it at the auction downtown. It was in the impound lot," Haik said.

"Bravo. At least you stretched the money. But why are

you here?"

"I need you to do something for me." He leaned back against his new car.

"No." I could feel my undershorts dampening. I had to go home. I walked away from the car and toward the apartment.

"I'll tell if you don't do what I say." He raised his voice.

"Go away." I set off at a brisk pace. I didn't make it to the bathroom in time.

When I came out of my room, I heard the duduk. It stopped and started, soft at first, then like a gust of wind through the trees. It was Lucy. I listened at her door, holding my soiled clothes. She played *Chinar Es*, an old folk lullaby about being like a tall unbending plane tree. I didn't knock.

I burst into tears the very first time I played a song from start to finish. My mother ran out of the kitchen to find my father patting me on the back, laughing, as if I'd accomplished some confusing rite of passage.

"You know," he had said, "you know what it feels like to play." He looked up at my mother, his eyes shining.

It was *Chinar Es*.

I was doing laundry when Lucy emerged from her room a half hour later, a halo of notes dancing around her head.

"Why are you washing your clothes? I'll do it on the weekend," Lucy said, getting a glass of water.

"Oh, I just wanted to wear my checked shirt again so I thought I'd do everything." I added soap and closed the washing machine.

"But you're awful at laundry."

"I'm awful at a lot of stuff, my *jahn*."

"*Papik*, is everything okay?" she asked over the machine's peculiar arrhythmia.

"Of course, darling." I tapped the washer to adjust the balance. "I heard you play."

"What did you think?" She seemed shy.

"It was good. Komitas gathered a good body of work." I didn't tell her he went crazy after the genocide and never wrote again.

"Are you sure you're okay? You look so tired."

"You're right. I should rest a little." I went to my room and closed the door. I sat on the bed, facing the mountains, and looked at the phone. Before I knew it, I had dialed Karlen's number.

"Banquet services," a non-celebratory voice said over the line. "It's Rupen Najarian."

"How can I help you, Maestro," Karlen said in a low voice.

"Are you planning an event?"

Something like that.

"Hello? Are you still there?"

"Yes, Karlen. I might need help convincing someone of something at some point."

"Oh. I see. Are you sure?"

I heard the duduk sigh in Lucy's room.

"No."

"Call me only when you are sure."

* * *

Earthquakes make music. No, really. It's called a harmonic tremor, a long slow release of energy measured in hertz (not to be confused with the car rental company). It's a quick series of small earthquakes that make sounds like instruments do but so low we can't hear it. I imagine it like holding a buzzing, vibrating note on the duduk for as long as you can.

That night, with all the lights out, I thought about middle C. It's supremely well balanced. A brand new set of BMW tires balanced. When you play it on a good piano, middle C's resonance fills your body. Its vibration is at a pleasing 261.626 hertz. Its frequency ratio an even 1:1. I thought middle C is was what I'd aimed for all my life. But it's not true. Middle C is beautiful but not noticeable. I want to be noticed.

The thing with a harmonic tremor is it happens deep underground, usually under a volcano that is about to push magma and volcanic gases to the surface in the most destructive of ways. It often happens on a blind fault.

The question at this point was whether Haik was a harmonic tremor, or was it me?

CHAPTER FIFTEEN

I had a fever and didn't leave the house for a week after I ran into Haik. I read this would happen as my body produced more white blood cells that would try their best to fight the invading cancer. But Armenians believe fever can be brought on not only by the body but also by the soul.

"If your mind is at ease, it's probably the *Skvasnia*," Hovannes diagnosed over the phone, referring to the perpendicular crosswinds we fear. He was the resident expert at identifying fevers. "Have Keran put cabbage leaves in your socks at bedtime. That should do it."

Cruciferous or not, it was just a matter of time until I got better and had to leave the house. Never mind Haik, I just had to know who his grandmother was. I dialed Armenian 411: Armineh.

"Bakery Opera, are you craving rosewater cookies today?" she answered.

"How did you know it was me?" I sat on the living room couch facing the balcony. Two gray rock doves perched next to each other on the railing, cooing. It was late in the season for courting, let alone mating.

"I didn't, you old fool. Everyone likes those. So are you feeling better?" She yelled over the metal baking sheets that clanged like cymbals behind her.

"So-so. Hey, have you seen a woman, maybe three or four years older than you? Hard of hearing. Wears black."

"Rupen *jahn*, you're describing every female in that age group."

"She has a mole."

"*Merci*, Rupen. You've narrowed it down by three percent."

"Woman, don't be difficult. The mole is above her lip like

Cindy Crawford. She wears a hairpin with a sparkling red gemstone."

"Ruby."

"Is that her name?"

"No, It was probably a ruby stone in the clip. Does she crochet?"

"I don't know."

"Could be anyone."

"Give me something. Take a guess."

"Let's see, an Armenian woman in her late eighties living here in 1992. She was probably orphaned by the time she was ten. Didn't have enough to eat. Never went to school. Can't remember what her mother looked like. Might have been kidnapped, raped, sold into slavery or any combination of the three. That was before she was married off in her teens. She's probably lost a child. Maybe two. She kept house for a dozen of her in-laws who were just as shell-shocked. She planted a garden so they wouldn't starve. She couldn't wait till one of her sons married so she'd have some help around the house. She tried to forget the past. If that didn't work, she drank brandy."

I didn't say anything. I mean, what was I supposed to say? The pans clanged behind her.

"So are you still there?" she asked.

"Where else would I be?"

"Are you in love with an older woman? How European of you."

"Don't be silly!"

"You might want to try Garni," she said. It was the most popular Armenian adult day care center in the greater Los Angeles area.

"I hate going by there," I said. "Who thought it was a good idea to put a senior center next to a coffin showroom?"

"It's cruelly efficient."

"Or efficiently cruel."

* * *

In spite of my reluctance, I took two Tylenol and asked Armineh's son-in-law to drop me off at Garni, which was named after the first-century Hellenic temple to the god Mihr high above the Azat River. I crossed right in front of Rest in Peace Coffins. The bronze Prometheus model with royal blue velvet lining was on sale, but I didn't linger. I had to convince this woman to withdraw her accusation.

Garni, the day care center, was a cavernous square room lit by fluorescent tubes. Long folding tables covered in cheery but unmatched tablecloths ran along the length of one wall. Most of the tables were set up for chess or card games. Someone had painted, in garish tones, the ancient ruins of the Garni temple on the wall facing the tables. Today's ancient ruins played chess and backgammon, one drifting off to sleep, just to wake up to find his opponent cheating.

The activities director recognized me. "Maestro, are you thinking of joining our facility?" She took me by the arm. "Look everyone, Maestro Najarian wants to join."

"I'm just looking for a friend," I said.

"I'll be your friend," said the man who had woken up to his game.

"*Merci, Baron*, but I'm looking for a woman."

"Oh," they murmured, eyebrows raised. A woman in a red scarf beckoned from the refreshment table.

"Oh no, not like that. I'm afraid my wife would find out," I said.

"They have their grip on us even from beyond the grave," the man said, returning to his napping game.

"Have you seen a woman who wears a ruby hairpin? She must be almost ninety." I turned to the activities director.

"There was a woman who came many years ago," she said, pouring me a cup of coffee. "Who knows if she's the same person? What do you want with her?" The activities director wasn't being nosy. She was being Armenian.

"I'm not sure," I said. "Maybe we were friends a long time ago." I gave her my phone number just in case "Ruby" returned.

CHAPTER SIXTEEN

It seems that if there were a proper Armenian god of earthquakes, he or she is lost to history. However, there are demons called Torx that live underground and cause all sorts of trouble. There are dragons that live beneath volcanoes. They, too, have been attributed for shaking up the earth. Then there are the mobsters.

As a group, it is my opinion that Armenians have a strong sense of nuance when it comes to rules. The cleverness and can-do spirit of our criminals is almost a matter of pride. The upstanding in the community may object to my sweeping remarks, and I was one of them not long ago, but now it seems I prefer to admire such skill.

My favorite scam, our bards should immortalize in song, was when a group of Armenians, not too long ago, bought a totaled city bus at a county auction. They studied the L.A. transit system with the resolve of NASA scientists and determined which bus route was the most profitable. They fixed up their auction item, painting and numbering it identically to their mark. They ran their bus five minutes before the real bus. They did this for years. In legend, they may have expanded to two busses, even three in some versions of the story. Meanwhile, when a transit bureaucrat analyzed travel patterns and noticed the route in question had fallen dramatically in use, he canceled it. The scam was only discovered much later when, sitting at a red light, he noticed the bus go by. Full of paying commuters.

Haik wasn't a criminal like that. I want to make the case that criminality is a state of mind. Although he slit my belly, pulled out my entrails and held them up to the gods, I have trouble thinking of him as a crook. He has denied this furiously, pointing to his blackmail as his badge of evil. But he's a good boy.

Still, it was a jolt when Haik yanked me from the safety of the banks of good society and coerced me into crime. He's what liberal art lovers call an "assemblage artist." He likes taking things from their original location and putting them somewhere they don't quite fit. But in shifting their presence, somehow they make sense. They belong, even just for that moment. He was the illegal Christo of Glendale and for a spell, I became his reluctant Jeanne-Claude.

* * *

As I expected, Haik was waiting for me in the gray beast when I finally went back to work.

"Feeling okay, Maestro?" He followed me at a mile an hour in the BMW as I walked to my studio one morning. A procession of cars followed him, honking and swearing.

"I've been better. What do you want?" I blew my nose for effect.

"I need you to help me with something." He placed a cigarette between his lips and lit it with the car lighter.

"Can't you ask any of your friends?"

"I need someone above suspicion. An upstanding member of society like you." He laughed a raspy chuckle that ended in a cough. He knew I had been a liar all my life.

I was about to say "to hell with you, you poor excuse for a smokestack" when Ara walked by. No one from my family had seen the boy. And I'd made sure Haik had not seen my humans up close.

"*Vonts es, Papik?* Are you well enough to go to the studio today?" Haik looked at Ara with interest disguised as boredom as Ara assessed Haik's friend-or-foe capacity.

"Yes. I'm fine. I'll see you at home later." I tried to dismiss him, but it was difficult to do with someone as stubborn as Ara. He was his namesake, a god of war.

"I'm going the same way, Grandpa. Over to RadioShack," he said, still looking at Haik. "Hey, man." He greeted Haik with that blank look and nod kids use in lieu of proper greetings, "Nice car. A 750?"

Of course it's nice. My 25K went into it.

"*Merci,*" Haik responded and parked the car next to the curb.

"Yeah, it has a twelve-cylinder though." In other circumstances, maybe they could have been friends. I'd never let them.

I climbed into the car to get away from Ara. "I'll see you at home later tonight. It's time for Haik's lesson." We left him on the corner of Colorado Boulevard, squinting his eyes. Ara knew I rarely took new students. And Haik didn't look like the kind of boy who got private music lessons.

"Where are we going?" I asked, settling into the soft cream leather.

"To the donut shop." He sped past my studio and made a left turn onto Glendale Avenue.

"I'm trying to give up sweets."

He snorted, glancing at my belly through the corner of his right eye.

"Well, I'm working on it."

"That was your grandson, huh? He played with you at the concert."

"He's very talented."

"How hard is it to play one note?" He sped through a yellow light.

"Playing the *dam* is like the rope a tightrope walker balances on," I said. "You can't play the duduk without the *dam.*" We drove up toward the hills in silence.

"So, you've been sick, huh?"

"Just the flu."

"I thought you might be scared of me."

"I've seen more frightening things in my life," I said. "Since you're driving, can we stop at St. Gregory's first? I told them I'd drop off some sheet music. I like to keep my word."

"Whatever." He swerved into the parking lot.

"Do you want to come in?" I asked, thinking a religious setting might influence him. "It might take a few minutes."

"No." He lit another cigarette.

When I came out fifteen minutes later, he was sitting on his powerful haunches examining the carved doors. It was the story of the Great Flood. Haik traced the voluptuous edge of Noah's face, the cigarette between his fingers lost to ash.

CHAPTER SEVENTEEN

Haik told me during one of our more friendlier moments that he and his family had come to Los Angeles five years earlier straight from Soviet Armenia. Refugees on grounds of religious persecution. Except they were devout atheists. Haik's father, Gevork, had been a Communist party enthusiast, eventually giving up his job at the lumberyard to be a regional official.

Gevork wholly believed in its principles of equality ever since his father told him a Turkish military commander had confiscated their family's orchards back in Malatya and hanged his grandfather from one of his prized apricot trees. That Turkish family still held Gevork's ancestral land.

Communism, Gevork instructed his son, "was the only way to live in peace." Peace sounded boring to a twelve-year-old boy.

"But what about the Turk who killed your *papik*?" young Haik asked. "Would you be friends with him if he were a Communist?

"No. Never. You can't be friends with murderers."

"How about his grandson? He's probably around your age, Pa."

"No, Haik. We can't be friends with those people. Ever," Gevork said through a clenched jaw.

"I don't think we can be Communists, Pa."

Haik's prediction came true soon enough when Gevork requested a visa to take his wife to Germany. He wanted to surprise her with a cruise on the Danube for their fifteenth anniversary. He'd never asked anything of the Party, so he never anticipated they would deny his request.

When the regional boss informed him of the rejection, the shock made him choke on the cigarette he was smoking. As he spat out the saliva-slimed butt, it dawned on him that perhaps the

Party didn't care about him the way he cared about it.

Even as they packed their dozen suitcases and headed to Moscow, Gevork had second thoughts. Maybe their present life was better than anything the United States had to offer, but time was running out on the amnesty program.

They stayed in a creaky detention cell for almost forty-eight hours while officials interrogated them, searched their bags, even cut the lining of the suitcases. Finally, the supervisor came in for the exit interview. He examined the small amount of "non-allowed items"—Hasmik's diamond ring, Ruby's gold bracelet, Gevork's grandfather's Swiss watch—and was about to confiscate them when Gevork bribed the officer with one hundred rubles. The man took the money and still kept the jewelry, but approved the family's paperwork.

Gevork thought this shouldn't happen in Communism. He shouldn't want to take the bribe. That man shouldn't steal our things. Gevork was finally convinced it was time to leave, one hour before the flight, and nearly penniless.

Always resourceful, Ruby tucked her precious hairpin that she believed was her grandmother's into her elaborate hairdo. Damned if anyone was going to take that away from her. With a nail file, she separated the gold coins from her mother's dowry belt—a fashion and status must when women wore pantaloons and kaftans. She sewed the coins into her girdle in the form of a brace.

"It's a special ladies' item for female arthritis," she told the security guard who patted her down. Between the words 'ladies' and 'female' and the fart Ruby summoned up for good measure, the guard let her be.

As the plane climbed up the unseen ladder, Communism got smaller and smaller, farther and farther away. Haik, a teenager and relegated to the middle seat, leaned over Ruby's comfortable bosom to see his past disappear beneath the clouds.

"Your future is in front of you, Haik *jahn*," Gevork, next to him on the aisle, said. "Don't let anything stop you."

"God willing," Ruby said.

"God nothing," Gevork replied.

Being a nonbeliever, though, didn't stop Haik's father from

carving the Great Flood on the grand oak doors of St. Gregory's once they reached Glendale. He didn't turn religious even when the chisel he used to form Noah's weather-beaten face slipped and severed the tendon in his right hand. Gevork hadn't worked since.

Haik dropped out of high school.

CHAPTER EIGHTEEN

Haik drove me to twenty different donut shops in Glendale, Burbank and Pasadena and made me ask for their old donuts. I must have pissed in twenty different bathrooms. We went to oily places with names like Crazy Donut, Big Jim's Donuts (we know why he's big) and Donut Star. I told them it was to feed the ducks at the retirement home. Haik was right. No one liked to refuse an old man. By the end of the evening, we had forty boxes of raised, crullers, jelly, cakes and twists, the perfume of sugar blurring my vision. I imagined their crusty crackle and the spongy release of sweet dough beneath my teeth. I stopped visualizing and slipped a chocolate cake donut out of the box on my lap.

"Don't eat any more. They're for later," Haik said, grabbing the box from my lap and throwing it on the backseat.

"What do you mean later? Aren't we done? My family is going to wonder where I am." I licked the crusting sugar from the dry corners of my mouth.

"We're done for now. But meet me at midnight. I'll pick you up right here." He pulled to the corner closest to the park.

"Suppose I don't show up?" I asked

"You'd prefer I rang the doorbell?" With that, he squealed away.

* * *

Sneaking out of your own home is a strange feeling. I was, after all, the patriarch of the Najarian family. I answered to no one (except my granddaughter). I could come and go as I pleased. But how would I explain leaving the house at midnight at my age, unless it was in an ambulance?

Luckily, the ladies had gone to bed and Ara had not come home yet. I hoped I wouldn't run into him while I was with Haik. I was ashamed to hope Ara wouldn't come home at all that night. Haik waited on the corner by the park as threatened. The aroma of frying oil and vanilla overwhelmed the car.

"You'll never get that smell out of the leather," I said as I closed the passenger door.

"It's worth it." He had a prim smile on his face. He screeched around the corner.

"Holy Ararat! Why do you drive so fast?" I clutched the floor mat with my toes, but I already knew the answer.

I blame it on the Hittites, our ancestors in antiquity with the need for speed—the twelve-cylinder BMW owners of that day.

A Bronze Age tin mine lies behind my village near Sis (the city Turks now call Kozan), past the heat and vineyards and olive trees, through the cypress groves and red pine trees in the heart of the snowy Taurus Mountains where my father was born. There's something on a cave wall if you go deep enough. Drawn with red and yellow ochre and charcoal, two men ride a chariot, their stick figures leaning forward and if the eyes of a seven-year-old squint just right, locks of black hair fly past behind them. Algae on the wall makes it look like they're smiling.

The Hittites, so far back in the folds of history that maybe a drop of their blood is in both Haik and me, were renowned chariot makers and charioteers, fiddling with their design until they made the fastest vehicles, or so they thought. Their upper hand changed at the Battle of Kadesh, which was fought just a couple hundred miles from Sis around 1275 BC. With at least 5,000 chariots, it was the largest chariot battle ever fought. Being the best charioteers of their time, they should have won definitively against the attacking Egyptians. But they didn't. The Egyptians had their own snazzy chariot model.

Despite the heavy chariot losses, the Hittites didn't lose the battle. It was that unsatisfying middle ground where both sides could claim victory. The event did give us the first surviving peace treaty between sworn enemies. And the Hittites went back to figuring out how to make their chariots even better.

Haik, poised for unnamed battle, veered around the next corner. I girded my loins as the wheels embraced the asphalt.

"Where are we going?" I asked.

"131 North Isabel."

"Is that near the police station?" I held onto the armrest.

It actually was the police station. For the next twenty minutes, he stood across the street, smoking and directing me as I covered the grass and the concrete stand that held the station sign with donuts. He even had me hang crullers from the branches of the maple trees. They were maple crullers.

"Not bad, *Baron*," he said.

"If you like breaking the law." The sugar glaze glistened under the streetlights.

"Come look at it from here. Looks like Christmas. And there is no law that says you can't hang donuts on trees."

"I believe it's called littering."

"Don't worry. They won't send you to jail."

A police car drove out of the garage, then backed up to the front entrance. Two officers got out, examining the donuts before pulling out their radios. We ducked low inside the car.

"They're radioing for coffee," Haik snickered. We dipped lower as a silver Mercedes-Benz drove by. It was Keran. I wondered why she was out this late, but was in no position to ask.

But I had questions for Haik. "So why did you make me hang 'Installation Donut' at 131 Isabel?" I asked as we drove away from the scene.

"None of your business." He pulled onto Glendale Avenue, handing me a stray chocolate cake donut.

"I don't really care. Just take me home." I took a bite and threw the rest out the window.

Haik's artistic streak seemed to ebb and flow with his emotions, and I was caught in his wave

"We're not done yet." He pulled into the Rite-Aid parking lot and reached for a plastic shopping bag from the backseat. It had a pair of scissors and five pages of heavy cardboard-like paper with one letter, *K*, printed on each of them in Helvetica. "Cut these out and I'll take you home. Do it carefully!"

"Why? What are these for? A KKKKK meeting?" I snorted at
my own joke.

"Just do it."

"Fine," I said, leaning toward the window so I could see better
from the streetlight. "I'm bored. You could at least entertain me.
Tell me about the donuts."

He didn't say anything. He rolled down the window and lit a
cigarette. When he was halfway done with his smoke, he said, "It's
this girl I like."

"Which girl?" I asked.

"You don't need to know."

"Okay! Go on." I started on K number two.

"The day after I got the BMW, I went to see her."

"Figures you'd be a show-off."

He ignored me. "She said she needed to concentrate on her
studies. Man, she didn't even come see the car." He said this as if
his new chariot might convince her he was worthy of her affection,
or at the very least, interest.

"I was pissed, but I wasn't driving that fast down Mountain
Avenue when that fat bitch pulled me over."

"What fat bitch?" I asked, saying words I'd never dared say
before.

"The cop." He dragged on his cigarette.

"So what happened then?"

"She said 'Sir, do you know why I stopped you?'" Anger boiled
in his ancient veins as the plump lady officer leaned over to look
inside the car, disbelief on her moon-shaped face that he could
afford to drive such a beautiful vehicle. "And then I said, 'Because
you needed some donut money, honey?' Then I waved a ten-dollar
bill at her. Man, she and that Alexander Hamilton were looking
eye to eye. That sow twisted my shoulder before she stuck me
in her cruiser. I should have claimed police brutality," Haik said,
cracking his knuckles.

She hauled him in the back of her car to 131 North Isabel and
booked him for bribery. The charge was dropped when his parents
bribed the woman's partner. They had to "redeem" Ruby's last
gold coin to get him out.

"My parents didn't say a word to me on the way home. I was driving them in a fucking BMW!" Haik said.

"Well, hadn't they seen the car before?" I stopped cutting the letters.

"No. I always parked it on another street."

Only Ruby had admired the fine vehicle on her early morning berry-picking forays. His parents didn't ask right away where he got it not because they didn't want to know. The question hung in the leather-scented air for minutes because they were afraid of what other crimes he'd committed and certainly of upsetting their sole provider. Finally, his father cleared his throat to the sound of "The car is . . ."

"A friend's," Haik finished the sentence. "My duduk teacher let me borrow it." They were relieved with the answer and surprised he was taking music lessons. The things we're willing to believe.

Haik opened the door and stamped out his cigarette butt as if it were a roach. He sighed and picked it up and threw it in the trashcan.

"What is it you like about this girl?" I asked.

"I don't know. What is it you liked about your wife?"

"She was beautiful."

"Yeah."

"Here are your Ks." I handed him the stack of letters when he eased back into the BMW. "Are we done? Can we go home now?"

But how, when I was further entrenched in his life? I could go days without seeing him and think my life and my secrets were mine again. That I could respectably get to the end of my life. Then he'd show up and the truth, my truth, would stare me in the face through his angry brown eyes. While others watched the total solar eclipse or the Barcelona Olympics, I spent my last summer: duduk master extraordinaire by day and petty criminal by night.

CHAPTER NINETEEN

Later in the week of the donuts, I asked Ara to drive me to a rehearsal at Universal Studios. Brian had recommended me for a new movie score—Romans pillaging a random Mediterranean countryside. I could play that with my eyes closed.

"You're in a good mood," Ara said as he opened the car door for me.

"What makes you say that?" I asked.

"You hum like you're one of the dwarves going to work in *Snow White*."

"I do not!" I stopped humming.

"Yes, you do. Like one of the jolly fat ones, you know, hi-ho, hi-ho."

"Stop teasing your *papik*. I'm excited about the score."

We pulled out of the garage in the red Nissan Sentra I bought him when he graduated high school.

"You still like this car?" I asked.

"Yeah," he said.

"We can look for a new one if you like," I said as he turned onto Wilson toward the 134 Freeway.

"Mom would kill you. It's only two years old. But it would be nice to torture Lucy."

"Be nice to your sister. You'll have to count on each other someday." I closed my eyes and pretended I was some far-off troubadour like Sayat Nova, unraveling the essence of things, a fine thread on a red silk scarf. It was my pre-practice ritual.

"*Papik*, what do you hear?" Ara cut through the music in my head.

"Did I hum out loud?" I asked opening my eyes just in case he thought I was going deaf.

"Nah. I just meant . . . forget it." We waited at the red light on Harvey Drive.

"You mean music? Well, it's like talking." I had no idea what he meant to ask, but I tried to explain it anyway. "When I play, I feel like it's a conversation between three good friends. There's me. There's the music that someone wrote to share something very important, and then there is the duduk. When it really works, it means that we three speak only the truth to each other."

"Does it always work?" he asked, in his voice the same hopeful sadness as when he inquired what happened to his childhood goldfish.

"No. Not always."

"It's never happened to me, *Papik*. Ever."

I should've said something, but the moment passed. We followed the curve of the road and waited to get on the freeway.

"Motherfucker!" Ara said.

"What's wrong?" I jumped in my seat. I hoped I hadn't driven him over the edge. "Don't let your mother hear you speak like that. She brought you up with class."

"Shoot, sorry, *Papik*," He said but he started to laugh. "Cool!"

"What so funny?"

"Look at the street sign."

"Which one?" I glanced about.

"The white 'No Right Turn' sign by the freeway entrance. Someone covered the N with a *K*!" The sign had been changed to read 'No Right Turk.' With one of my hand-cut Ks. "Now that's talking some truth." Ara cheered up.

Motherfucker. I turned on the radio to drown out Haik's presence.

CHAPTER TWENTY

"Maestro, we have something to do tonight." Haik found me buying coffee powder one morning at Masis Market. I shopped there even after the new owners had done Robert wrong. Keran went to school with one of them.

By now, Haik knew my routine. I preferred he find me here than at the park when I visited my friends.

I shushed him because I was engrossed with the butcher and his activities. He was trying his best to avoid selling lamb's tongue to an American lady and she was trying her best to buy it.

"How long do I have to braise it?" she asked.

"This woman is impossible," the butcher said in Armenian, embarrassed his English wasn't good enough help her. "I wish she'd just go away."

"Soak it for four hours in cold water," I said in English.

"Then boil it for fifteen minutes, but throw that water away," Haik added, to my surprise. "What? I've watched my mom make it," he said, his voice cracking.

"What he said is true," I told the woman as she wrote down the instructions on the brown paper that held her fresh bread. "Then add more cold water and boil it for a good hour. After that you can peel the skin off and slice it and use it however you like. Lebanese style with garlic and lemon juice is very tasty."

"Thank you. I love Arabic food," she said.

"We're not Arabs," Haik said. "At least, not all of us," he whispered so only I could hear.

"I'm not an Arab either," I whispered back. "Moron."

"Oh, you know what I mean." She waved goodbye with the tips of her fingers as we turned to the next counter where the coffee lady was grinding my Colombian beans.

"You didn't have to bother, Maestro," the butcher mumbled as he handed her two pounds of lamb's tongue. "She's not one of us." He wiped his bloody hands on his apron.

"So I'll see you at 3 A.M." Haik looked at his Casio.

"You aren't working tonight?" I asked.

"Just be ready," he said.

"Should I wear black again?" At two hundred pounds, blending in wasn't my strong point.

"Don't bother." He walked toward the entrance.

"Why not? You always wear black." I paid for the coffee.

"No one's going to look at you. You're old."

I followed him outside, resigned to my fate as his serf, free only when allowed and invisible at all times. I mopped the day's first sweat from my face with my handkerchief.

"Jeez. Don't look so hurt. Wear black, if you like."

I walked to the parking lot behind Haik, wondering what excuse to conjure for sneaking out of the house. I could always pretend to leave my blood pressure pills at the studio. I noticed we were all in the habit of slipping out. With the kids, it was normal, but their mother? I didn't worry about her right then.

"Your coffee, Maestro Rupen," the pretty dimpled clerk sang out as I walked with my uneven shadow. We waited for her to catch up. "Don't forget it!" She smiled at Haik, who displayed the BMW keys like a badge.

"*Merci*, Miss." She pulled her soft white hands from my grip, leaving only my groceries behind. I willed her to rescue me from my new prison, but she ignored me and winked at Haik.

* * *

The car was already filled with traffic cones when he picked me up in the early morning.

We dropped them off behind the bushes at the side entrance of City Hall. Then we drove down every major street, looking for the scattered dollops of bright orange that kept our city's residents at bay.

"Why are we gathering these? What did plastic ever do to you?"

"It's not about the cones, Maestro." He blew out an angry, smoke-tinged puff of air. "You wouldn't care anyway. You've already made it."

"What does that mean?" I asked. "The recession's been hard on everyone." But that's not what he really meant. He assumed I didn't know many Armenians had trouble getting business permits as the city struggled to figure out its changing demographic. Gone were the Woolworths, the shoe-shine stand and the five-cent movie theater. Itching to take their place were the kebab restaurants, Korean grocers and *zapaterías*. Those applications were stalled in the flux of bureaucracy and changing cultures.

"Nothing. It means absolutely nothing." He stuffed another cone in the car.

"You think you've figured it all out?" I asked.

He straightened up and raised his chin.

"Yes. You've figured life out at twenty. That's why you're out here doing stupid things." I picked up a cone.

"What I do is not stupid."

"You think you're an *artiste*?"

"I have something to say," he said throwing a cone in the trunk.

"Maybe but you don't know what to say yet," I said handing him a cone.

He looked at me, his eyebrows lifted in challenge.

I put my hand up to stop him. "It's normal. I thought I was such a good musician when I was twenty. Then I heard Margar Margaryan's uncle play. Kid, at some point you're going to have to decide what kind of man you want to be."

He snorted. "I guess you picked being a liar."

"I don't lie when I play music." It was the first true thing I'd ever said.

His gaze dropped to the cone he'd reached for. "This orange is the same color as the Armenian flag," It was a cone of a different hue of orange, bent at the top, as if it'd been run over several times. Not so flashy as the others.

"Do you know what the color represents?" I asked.

"Creativity," he said.

"I was going to say apricots."

Haik smiled. It was clear we shared an obsession for stone fruit.

An hour later, we'd gathered fifty cones, then a hundred. We drove behind Masis Market. They had four in front of the dumpster.

"Hey, why do you think Armenians name their businesses after natural monuments?" I asked.

"What are you talking about?" Haik said. "Just pick up the damn cones."

"Well, Masis Market is named after the mountain peak next to Ararat. Then there's Ararat Retirement Home, Ararat Auto, Ararat Oriental Rugs. Zankou Chicken is named after the river. Sevan Meat Market is named for the lake."

"How else will we remember they belong to us?" he asked with a shrug.

* * *

My spine cracked like a fighter's knuckles with the constant up and down as we climbed in and out of the car, reaching and stretching for the elusive orange deep from construction sites and freeway ramps.

"Aha!" Satisfaction emanated from Haik's pores. He fished a sign from the back of a gas company truck: *Access Denied.* He stuffed the sign in the trunk and jumped into the driver's seat. He backed into the truck with a thump.

"Shit," he said, getting out to examine the damage.

I joined him. "Look what you did." The license plate was crumpled and the back bumper dented.

"It's no big deal," he said.

"Of course. It's not your money."

"It is my money," he said. "And I can do what I want."

We drove back to City Hall, blocking off every possible entrance and road to the building. We went back for more cones.

"Hey, I need to go to the bathroom," I said after our fourth trip.

"Just go over there behind that tree."

"That's the Scientology Reading Room."

"Even better. It will be your extra contribution."

"In case you forgot, I'm an old man. I need to rest." I shuffled toward the car.

"Fine. Hold this between your legs." He opened the door and shoved a cone in after me.

He drove me to Bob's Big Boy, a holdover that seemed to have weathered the changes. The giant fiberglass Big Boy statue, dressed in red-and-white checkered overalls holding a hamburger of preposterous proportions, welcomed us into the parking lot. Haik parked far away from the other cars, on the dark side of the restaurant.

The only waitress, a deeply tanned woman with brassy blond hair in a sprayed-stiff formal updo, seated us in a corner booth.

"Isn't it too late for you to be out, honey?" she asked me.

"I have insomnia," I said.

"So do I," Haik added.

"Yeah, coffee is great for that," she said, pouring Haik a cup.

He drank his coffee while I took care of business. A little blood in the urine. It wasn't the first time. I knew I should see the doctor but why? Thoughts of a warm brownie with ice cream and hot fudge—a great Western invention—were preferable. Melting chocolate could make you forget almost anything.

"Did you wash your hands?" Haik asked when I stuffed myself across from him.

"Yes, Madame," I said, signaling for the brownie. "I saw what you did with the letter K," I said after a couple of bites.

"Did you like that?" He looked me straight in the eye. "I did that just for you."

"Don't do me any more favors." I made a dent on top of the ice cream with the back of the spoon and filled it with extra cherries.

Haik sighed. I slid the plate of cake to his side of the table. "What's the matter with you now? Didn't get enough cones?"

He exhaled and weighed whether he should reveal something.

"What now? Still thinking of that girl?"
"I can't get her out of my mind."
"You idiot," I said knowingly.

CHAPTER TWENTY-ONE

Haik leaned back in the booth and used his spoon to cut a piece of brownie, then smashed it into the melted ice cream, soaking up the liquid. He scraped it off the plate and ate it.

"Yeah," he said, not looking me in the eye. "But I don't want to talk about it."

"Sure," I said.

He'd been wheeling bodies from the emergency room to the morgue for almost a year when he first spotted her: white coat, stethoscope, big breasts, surrounded by a pack of stick-up-the-ass residents.

She wore a halo of gold for hair. This girl had an entourage and not just because a blond Armenian was rare unless Clairol was involved every five weeks. Haik ate her up with his eyes every time she swung her hips through triage.

One morning, after a double shift, he got up the nerve to talk to her. He sat at her table in the basement cafeteria and asked if he could borrow the Tabasco for the dill omelet his mother had packed in a piece of tin foil. It was just after six in the morning and the sky looked foggy through the rectangular strip of windows near the ceiling. Like you were shipboard, floating on the ocean and not in a smoggy L.A. valley hospital.

"Sure," she said. Her voice was breathy like she was about to say dirty things but she didn't even look up from the six-month-old *Reader's Digest*. "I like my breakfast spicy, too."

"Thanks. I promise I won't hog it," Haik said, trying hard to control his accent. He placed the hot sauce back on her side of the table.

The lovely young woman looked up when she saw Haik's long fingers breach her air space. She was surprised to see it wasn't one of the junior residents, but an orderly with big brown eyes. She tried not to look past those long fringes into those dark eyes as she piled her hair into a bun, showing off a delectable beauty spot. She played with her hair like that when she was unnerved.

"Hi. I'm Haik. I work in the ER," he said. His voice cracked as if he was in sixth grade.

She didn't acknowledge his introduction. She just looked outside at the gray, which now had an orange tint, and said, "I think there's a fire up in Angeles Crest again."

With a name like Haik, she knew that most likely he was *Hayastansi*—the people from Soviet Armenia. She did that mental slotting we do to everyone we meet. He was classified as possible town drunk or village idiot. Haik understood (but disagreed) that he was at the bottom of an unspoken hierarchy among people who should be equals.

Haik was proud of his name. He didn't believe in God, but he sure believed in Noah and his great-great-grandson, his namesake, who was supposed to be Armenia's founding father. Haik, the name, held some weight.

"So what's your name?" Haik asked.

She still didn't say anything. Instead, she turned over her ID badge. Dr. Christine H.

They sat for a minute, quiet as the mice in the cafeteria kitchen, nibbling their perfectly spiced breakfasts. She was the first to break the silence.

"I think I can smell the fire. I know it's bad but I love the way it smells. Like wood melting into sugar," she confessed.

Her words made Haik's fingers tingle. Haik loved fire, too. Armenians. Internal pyromaniacs. Combustible from the soul. If he wanted to go out with this girl, he was going to have to put his foot to the pedal.

"*Akchik*," Haik used the familiar term, even though he had just started flirting with her. "Every Armenian likes fire. If six hooded monks sit around a fire, how can you spot the Armenian?"

"The one that growls," she asked with a smile.

"I said he was a monk."

"I don't know," she said, reaching for the hot sauce.

"He's the first to poke at it. The pyro."

Naturally, she laughed. For the first time, she looked directly, deeply into his eyes. Hers were the tawny color of honey flecked with bits of dark brown. Like the stuff his *Tatik* Ruby collected from the hive that grew on the old apple tree back in Armenia.

He was trapped in the amber of her eyes.

And just like that, Haik fell for a girl so out of his reach, he was playing Little League to her Majors. But this is the city of possibilities. If the stars aligned, a handsome Brazilian valet could bed a Hollywood actress. Theoretically, Haik *could* get the favor of such a high-class girl.

The problem with theory is that it's still a guess. Class doesn't always disappear when you deplane at LAX. Some of its citizens insist on living in a self-imposed ghetto. Following its rules. Giving it power.

"So you want to grab a coffee sometime?" Haik asked, hoping the assumption worked in his favor.

"I don't think so." She got up, but Haik insisted on carrying her breakfast tray to the conveyor belt. She was charmed by his smile and those impossibly long eyelashes. He batted them because she was staring.

"They're very long," she whispered.

"You should see the rest of me," he whispered back.

"That's a great line," I said, laughing. I took the brownie back.

"Yeah, well. I have my moments," he said.

"What did she say next?"

"Nothing. Some asshole chief resident interrupted us," Haik said.

The lovely Christine was from one of those well-to-do families who had never even *lived* in Armenia, the beautiful, soon-to-be mob-ridden homeland. Her parents were both doctors trained at the best schools. They had a summer house in Cannes. Even knew Charles Aznavour, who once brought Edith Piaf over for dinner. Running around with a boy like Haik was going to start up that auntie gossip machine, the kind that cranked for decades and even then was impossible to turn off until you choked one of them to death.

"What's the big deal with going out with me?" Haik asked her a month later after several more breakfasts, although he knew the answer.

"Nothing's the big deal," she replied. "My dad's a little crazy after my mom died, you know. He wants the best for me. For him, that's people he grew up with."

Let me tell you, she was being polite. She didn't want to say the unsaid. That his type wasn't good enough for her.

But sex was a whole other thing. Sometimes, people just do it without thinking of the consequences. This applied to me, too. It's been a good decade since I've had this sex. The last time I held a woman's naked body, it was a younger admirer, someone I tried to forget I'd made love to. Armineh's daughter, Alice. She must have been almost fifty, and it had been only a year after my wife died. She was ripe and full of sexuality, like a double cream French brie. She always wore makeup and high leather pumps even if she was at the bakery.

Alice said she needed some *advice*. I knew that was code because other women had asked me for this type of counseling. But I missed my wife so much I let myself be seduced in a Hilton hotel room that overlooked the freeway. I asked her to close the burgundy drapes and turn off the light. I tried not to think of her idiot husband who was running for the community college board. Or her father, whom I would see the next day at the park. I would let Levon win at backgammon. But I had to make it look difficult, like he really won.

Alice undressed me, making little striptease noises, flinging my shirt over the lamp and my pants on the mini bar. I kicked my reason under the bed and slipped under the covers with the sheet up to my neck like a virgin. I watched her undress herself. She freed her creamy body out of an armature that looked like brown scuba wear and crawled on top, making soft growling noises. She shook her long, dark locks out of its coif, like Armineh used to do after she baked the midnight loaves in that basement bakery in Yerevan.

Later, after she'd had her way with me and I'd had my way with her, I tried to politely escape, reaching for my shirt, toasty from the lamp bulb.

"I've always had a crush on you, Uncle Rupen." She turned on her stomach, her cascading hair glinting red in the lamplight.

"Darling, maybe you shouldn't call me 'Uncle' anymore." I buttoned up my shirt.

We saw each other once more, the second time at the Holiday Inn. There was no striptease, just a quick hard session. Afterward, I told her we mustn't see each other again. That was the last time I had felt sensual pleasure from another body.

I ordered another brownie dessert special from the waitress.

"So have you done it with her yet?" I pushed the empty dessert plate to the side and leaned forward.

"Like I would tell you!" Haik fluctuated between being incensed and disgusted, his body moving from side to side, dodging my words.

"Why not? You think I'm going to spill the soup?"

"No. I haven't slept with her. She thinks I'm too young for her. I'm only a couple years younger." Haik sighed a bitter coffee breath.

"Yes, that's probably it," I said although we both knew.

Haik slurped his coffee.

"You know what you need? A grand gesture," I said.

"What?"

"When I asked my wife to marry me, I took the whole Yerevan Folk Symphony with me up five flights of stairs. She was teaching the neighborhood children how to dance. I entered the studio alone and started playing the *Laz Bar* on my duduk. She was surprised at first, then started to laugh. She remembered. Then, I stopped playing and approached her where she stood, her arms in mid dance, the kids scattered about like tea rose petals in the wind. My friends at the symphony spilled into the room, playing the *Laz Bar* where I'd left off. I reached for her hand and we danced together. Then, I dropped to a knee." I finished the brownie and licked my spoon clean. "That is how you get a woman."

He considered this while he slurped the crunchy dregs of coffee where the sugar still hadn't melted. "I need to use your penthouse," he said.

A vacuum sucked all the moisture from my mouth. "That is not a grand gesture."

"Maybe she'll sleep with me," Haik said. "That's a start."

"So you don't mind lying in a sinner's bed?" I asked.

"Well, last I heard, you're not admitting to your sins."

"But you think I'm evil, so doesn't it bother you?"

"I'll change the sheets."

"Please, not the apartment. How about the studio?"

"No. I want to take her some place impressive."

"How do you know my place is nice?"

"Are you kidding me?" Haik got up and refilled his own coffee.

"Okay. Fine. How do I get everyone out of the house?" I asked when he returned.

"Figure it out. Middle of the day on a Tuesday or something."

And just then it happened. A pain so strong in my gut, I couldn't stand up to demonstrate my indignation at his cheekiness.

"What's going on? Is it your stomach or your conscience?" Haik leaned over to my side of the table.

"Very funny. It'll go away." But it didn't. It got worse until I could only breathe in short, Morse-coded breaths. S-O-S.

"You shouldn't have eaten all that cake. Do you feel like throwing up?"

"A little bit. I have so much pain these days."

"Like gastrointestinal stuff?"

"Something like that."

He paused, considering his options. "Come on. I have something in the car that might help." He ushered me to the BMW, holding me by the shoulders. "I give it to my *tatik* when she can't sleep at night."

"You're very good at this." I felt the strength of his youth propel me across the empty parking lot. And who was this bee-keeping, ruby-wearing grandmother of his?

"I'm a highly skilled orderly. Glendale General's best." He nested me in the passenger seat, the neon of the traffic cones blinking in my peripheral vision.

He reached into the glove compartment and took out a small plastic bag with what looked like the dried bits of driveway grass you can only get at with a small brush and pan. He rolled it carefully in the same kind of cigarette paper the accountant used, sealing the ends with his smoky spit. He lit it between his lips and took a puff. A sweet, slightly skunky smell drifted toward me. Upon his approval of the smoldering clippings, he said, "Here, your turn."

"Are you trying to get me into bigger trouble?"

"Look. It will help with the pain."

"If it were good for me, it wouldn't be illegal, now would it?"

"You're telling me you didn't know anyone who smoked something different in the old country?"

He had a point. My father was an occasional opium user.

"It's illegal here," I insisted.

"So is what you've done," he said.

"I haven't done anything against the law." I doubled over with the pain.

"Don't get technical. Take a puff. You'll feel better very soon."

He straightened me up and brought the joint to my lips.

I inhaled just a little, and then a little more.

"There you go," soothed my pusher. "Hold it in your lungs and then release it slowly."

I sank further into the soft leather seat and let the rich smoke soothe me. Through the windshield, the Big Boy in his checkered pants winked at me. I thought I saw him mouth, "Uncharted territory, Rupen, old boy."

I took another puff.

CHAPTER TWENTY-TWO

I hid from Haik after that night.

With hindsight and my re-sharpened pencil, I see how futile it was. I didn't fully appreciate his desperation. He was like one of those courting Bower birds, bringing his female a colorful bit of whatever he could find—a string of homemade walnut *soujouk*, a collection of perfume samplers pocketed from a department store counter, a ring fashioned from sea glass and bronze paper clips. But nothing he offered seemed to catch this girl's fancy. He didn't stand much of a chance against the other suitors with their golden boxes of Godiva chocolates and U2 concert tickets. (Viktor tells me their lead singer, the man with the thick glasses, has heard me play the duduk.)

I was only marginally interested in his predicament because my recent bout of pain had put me into a dark mood that led me to play songs I wouldn't normally touch.

In the time of the great ruler Artashes, around 180 BC, funeral songs were highly formulaic, like pop music. First, you asked the deceased to wake up from this deep slumber and go about his daily routine, then you scolded the dead person for not listening to you. Next, the song described the departed's final steps. Followed by praise for his or her good deeds and a rousing farewell.

"Rupen, is that *Leaving on a Jet Plane* on the duduk?" The accountant asked from the other side of my locked door.

"Maybe," I said, opening the door and nearly shutting it. Haik stood next to him.

"One of your students," the accountant said. "I let him in."

"Yes, you did," I said.

He nodded and left. Haik stepped in and closed the door.

"No," I said before he could say anything.

"I'll tell your old lady friend," he said, sniffing around my refuge.

"Try it, you little worm. You'll never be allowed back in Bakery Opera."

"Well then, your daughter." He ran his fingers along the edge of my grand table.

"I won't let you get near her. Don't touch my things."

"Ara, then."

"No. Don't!"

"Oh, he's the one that matters?" Haik raised an eyebrow. "What a good patriarch. Caring what the heir thinks."

"It's not like that. All my grandchildren are equal in my eyes."

"Sure, you old sexist."

I conceded to the apartment. But that was only half of the equation. He had to convince his lady bird that he was worthy. How do you do that when you're a poor, unschooled artist?

"I told her I read the *Kama Sutra* and only researched the positions that gave women the pleasures," Haik said.

That seemed to outweigh the boxes of chocolates and expensive concert tickets. At least on a provisional basis.

"What are you going to do when you get to the zebra position?"

"There's no zebra position," Haik said. "She'll like me by the time I'm done with my repertoire. She'll beg me to be her boyfriend."

* * *

On the day of their maiden coupling at my apartment, there was not one but two major earthquakes. One in Landers, the other up in Big Bear Mountain. And there was smoke in Griffith Park. The Santa Ana winds had kicked up in a dry, wanton frenzy. This non-existent thing people call earthquake weather. Haik and Christine watched it from the south side of the balcony as it swirled in a thin spiral on the ridge above the cemetery. A cobra let out of its basket.

"It's probably just the ranger setting a control fire," Haik said to his Christine, quietly emptying his pockets of loose change, cigarettes and lighter. He was trying to quit smoking. She thought it was low class (not to mention unhealthful). He kissed a hot trail down her neck.

"Is this your place?" she asked even though she knew the answer.

"Maybe someday." He gently rubbed her shoulders.

"Your friend has a beautiful home. Very tasteful."

"Would you like me better if this was all mine?" Haik asked as he led her inside the apartment.

She didn't say anything and he didn't press her.

They took off their shoes on the rosewood floors that I had specially brought in from Indonesia. He turned on my Venetian chandelier although it was afternoon. The twinkling lights flirted with Haik.

"Who's this woman? She looks familiar." Christine picked up a photo in a Tiffany frame of my wife, the goddess with porcelain skin, barely wrinkled although she must have been in her late forties at the time. She sat in a rattan café chair with the Eiffel Tower behind her, her pink lips slightly parted and her eyes lit.

"That's my friend's wife. She used to be a dancer back in Armenia."

"She's beautiful," Christine said, putting the picture back down.

"I can think of someone more beautiful," Haik said, caressing her neck.

"What are we doing?" Christine whispered against the warmth of his arm. "This can't go anywhere." Haik had his answer but he wasn't about to believe it.

"Sure, my *jahn* of *jahns*." He said anything she wanted to hear. "We're just playing."

She let him lead her down the hall to my bedroom. He slipped off her yellow silk dress, pulling her hair out of the twist she unconsciously coiled on top of her head. "I like your hair down."

"Oh, you're one of those Armenian guys, huh? Like their women in tight Gucci, four-inch heels, long hair and nails."

"I just like you." Haik's voice was raspy and not from cigarettes.

While they teased and flirted, whether out of politeness or because Haik disliked me, he looked for a towel to put down over the comforter.

"What's this?" Christine asked, opening up the book with the gold medallion embossed with an olive tree, worn down from many caresses. "There's some writing on it. The letters look Eastern."

Wish well, be well. It had been my mother's and her mother-in-law's before her.

"What kind of friends are you keeping?" Christine joked. "Not any sultans, I hope."

"Probably got that at a yard sale," Haik replied, putting the medallion back in the book. He pulled her close to him until their skin touched.

"I'll marry you some day," Haik whispered into her golden curls.

"You're so dramatic." She pushed him with her elbow.

"I mean it." He kissed the elbow that had bruised him.

"Don't think too much." She tapped him on his nose with her forefinger.

"Oh, you're one of those girls who like their men in tight Versace and empty heads." He pulled her onto the bed. "Let me show you what I've learned."

On the hillside, the slow spiral met a confluence of wind and brittle brush, igniting into something fierce and unstoppable. Motorists on the 134 Freeway stopped and gaped at its voracious force. Skunks, rabbits and coyotes fled its magnitude. There was no room in its heart for anything other than itself, the burning fire.

CHAPTER TWENTY-THREE

Haik startled me one afternoon when he stopped by the studio to return my house key. By now, he and Christine were spending every other Tuesday at the penthouse. I rushed to cover the joint burning in a silver saucer on the windowsill as he jiggled the door.

"It's just me," he yelled out.

I let him in. "You look like you had a good time." I went back to the window. "How's the *Kama Sutra* treating you?"

"Wonderful." He closed his eyes, his eyelashes tendrils on his cheeks. "It smells like sugar in the spot where her breasts meet."

"Mmm," I said, taking a puff. I placed the joint back carefully on the saucer.

"There's a constellation of beauty spots on her stomach. It's the path to ecstasy." He reached over behind me and brought the joint and makeshift ashtray to his lips as if he were taking four o'clock tea.

He sat on the carpet and told me the details of their lovemaking, more than I expected or even asked for. I understand now that if he told me, that would mean it really happened. I was his witness. But it's not polite to share everything. I'll just say I liked sleeping in my bed on the days when they'd lain there in the afternoon. I collected the strands of her golden hair held hostage on the bedpost and kept it with my sheet music on the side table to remind me of my goddess.

* * *

I married my wife, Artemis, on a moonless night on Lake Sevan. We saw a shooting star sail under Orion and I told her, as impulsively as Haik, that I wanted to marry her right then and there.

"What's stopping you?" She turned on her heels and weaved among the ancient *khachkar* stones behind the monastery. The cross stones, green with moss, looked like lace in the glow. Back then, I was young and fit and I chased her, catching her at the top of the path leading down to the inky lake.

"*O night, be long—long as an endless year! Descend, thick darkness, black and full of fear! Tonight my heart's desire has been fulfilled—My love is here at last—a guest concealed!*" I recited the first few lines of the Kuchak poem.

She replied. "*Dawn, stand behind seven mountains—out of sight/Lest thou my loved one banish with thy light; I would for ever thus in darkness rest/So I might ever clasp him to my breast.*"

I consider that our true wedding night.

* * *

"You know how the back of a woman looks like a cello?" Haik asked after a second puff.

"Yes. And the front of a man looks like an oboe."

"That's funny." He snorted spit.

"Ouch." I felt a sharp stab.

Haik passed me the joint when he saw me cringe.

"Pain?"

"Yes." But I didn't tell him where. The doctor had warned me that if I got aroused, it would pinch a little in the "penile region" as if it were a remote location in the Himalayas. I'd told the doctor my active love life stopped at a bowl of coffee ice cream. Three scoops, and now Bob's Big Boy brownies were on the list. But he was worried about my potential sex life. Keep all excitement to a minimum, he'd said.

"Try to visualize something else," Haik said.

It felt like a roadside bomb exploded in my *joodgik*, bits of nails and shrapnel flying in my innards, but I took his advice. I thought of the accountant downstairs with his shirt off. That did the trick.

"What's new at work?" I changed the subject from young firm

bodies for the sake of my poor manhood.

"Outbreak of MRSA." Haik put the joint back on the windowsill.

"What's that?" I asked. "Is it a test like the SAT or GRE?"

"No." He giggled. "It's when you pick up a severe infection as an inpatient."

"You get sicker going to the hospital?"

"I know! It's funny."

We both laughed. Everything was so funny.

"I've been working on a big project," he confessed after a few minutes.

"*Eench*? Selling Mexican antibiotics to the MRSA patients?" I prompted him with my big toe.

"No. I'm building something."

"*Vonts*?" I knew what kind of "building" he was talking about.

"Nothing." Excitement crept into his voice until it burst. "I'm doing something with the boxes we get toilet paper in. My grand gesture," he said getting up from the floor.

"Really?" I had my doubts about the romantic value of cardboard.

"The hospital goes through three thousand rolls a week and I deliver it to all the units." He moved my duduks aside and perched on the work table.

"That's a lot of shitting,"

"Huh? Yeah, a lot of people go through the hospital every day. Once I empty the boxes, I take them downstairs. We're supposed to break them down and give it to housekeeping for recycling. But I don't. I sneak them into the basement. We haven't had a building inspector in months."

"Is whatever you're doing worth it? You could get into big trouble if someone sees you."

"Isn't every big gesture worth the trouble?"

"Still."

"I'm building it for her."

I nodded. It's no use arguing with a person in lust.

Birds swooped outside the window, stopping to fight over the dried bread I regularly tossed on the ledge.

"Have you ever seen parrots?" Haik asked.

"My friend Armineh has an African grey with a red tail." I answered as if his question was completely natural.

"No. I mean a group of them."

"You think this is Hawaii?"

"My grandma said she saw a flock of parrots."

"Your *tatik* is losing her noodles. She thinks she knows me."

"I told you she never lies. There must be parrots flying around L.A." Haik's phone sang the Armenian national anthem.

"Hi, brat," he greeted one of his sisters. "She wants to talk to me? *Barev, Tatik,*" he said to the woman who had kept my identity a secret for so long. "You want sunflower seeds? Yes. I have your special medicine. Of course, *Tatik,* I won't tell Mama." The phone wedged between his head and shoulder, he waved goodbye as he left my studio. As if we were friends.

Maybe I should have stopped him from the folly of love. I'm not trying to absolve myself after the fact. And I'll admit I craved the details of twisting limbs and sticky juices, firm flesh and soft skin. Just because obsolescence was built right into my body parts didn't mean I wasn't still intrigued by carnal experience, even if it was my enemy's.

And of course, there was the marijuana, which I'd come to like more and more each day.

In exchange for my complicity, he brought me a small bag of dried herbs twice a month. I wondered if I'd drifted permanently to the other side. What would the priest at St. Gregory's think of my personal frankincense? Whatever guilt I felt, I channeled into ordering some juniper incense to mask the odor. But instead of covering up the smell it mingled with it, creating a rabid superscent.

I made sure to smoke Haik's offering only in my studio, and even then, on the accountant's side of the building. If anyone came sniffing, I hoped they'd blame the poor bastard with the calculator. His parakeets swung in their cage under me as I leaned out the window to exhale the forbidden smoke. I hoped his birds felt as good as I did.

"Rupen, the building smells like an ashram," the accountant

said one day shortly after my new regimen. "Are you teaching the sitar now?" He pantomimed a swami type with his turban and instrument.

"You just don't understand artists," I said, holding my baggie under my coat. "Incense helps creativity."

I couldn't wait to get upstairs, drag my chair to the window, light up and let my mind go. Sitting there with my feet propped on the sill, joint between my lips, my life blurred into a Monet-esque canvas, blues, purples and grays, greens and yellows ignoring their regular paths. Lulling me into silence.

CHAPTER TWENTY-FOUR

One night, I dreamt of a bright green parrot tapping at my balcony window. It was twice the size of a normal bird and had a streak of crimson through its tail. And although it had a beak, it had teeth. Like a dinosaur. It pecked at the glass with its strange mouth. I tried to shoo it away but it wouldn't stop. It put its round, yellow eye to the glass. Did parrots have eyelashes? This one did. The eye got bigger and bigger until I woke up with a fright.

I lay still in the dark but the noise didn't go away. It was Haik, crouched on my end of the balcony, smiling.

"What are you doing here?" I mouthed the words from the safety of my bed.

"Come out," he mouthed back.

There was no door leading from my room to the balcony, so I had to walk around to the living room. I went to the bathroom first. Then, I packed a few almonds in a plastic bag.

"This is too much," I said when I got outside. "You've gone far enough."

"Come on. It'll be fun. Bring this downstairs." He handed me my own pot of late harvest tomatoes. Little orbs of emerald had just started to turn to ruby. I watched them every day, waiting for the perfect moment to make a tomato and oregano salad.

"Here, take this, too." He handed me the little pot of oregano.

I put on my Zegna slacks and a black cotton shirt that were draped on the back of a chair and crept downstairs with the two pots.

"How did you climb up to the balcony?" I asked, getting into the BMW.

"Fire escape." He started the car. He drove us through the sleeping city. Haik smoked a cigarette with the window down, the

123

cool air and smoke floating back to me.

"We don't have a fire escape," I said after a few minutes.

"Fine. Someone left the door open so I took the elevator to your floor and took the service ladder up to the roof and jumped."

"What are you going to do with my plants?"

"Something that will benefit others."

"At Home Depot?" I asked. He'd pulled up to the gardening area located at the tail end of the store on San Fernando Boulevard.

"This is a temporary stop."

Haik climbed over the fence and handed me beet and pumpkin seedlings, romaine lettuce, tarragon, cabbage, and even a sad little apricot tree that should have been planted in someone's loving garden months ago. Then the alarm went off and we had to run. Haik tripped over the fence and scraped the side of his face.

"Why didn't we wear masks?" I asked. "We're going to get caught!"

"Not if you stop talking and get in the car!"

We sped off down a residential street but we could hear police sirens in the distance.

"Let me see your face." I took out my hanky, but he kept driving until we got to Brand Boulevard.

"Motherfuckers took out the peppers I planted last time," Haik said, parking next to the Cuban bakery where we'd first met.

"Who?"

"The stupid city people. I planted peppers down the median enough for a big barbecue."

"What kind?"

"Armenian barbecue."

"No. What kind of peppers?"

"Anaheim."

"Those are good barbecued. Why did you plant them?"

"So everyone can have peppers."

"Everyone can buy their own peppers."

"That's not the point."

"You want some almonds?" I pulled out the bag from my pocket.

"Maybe later." He got out of the car and opened the trunk.

It was still dented from backing into the utility truck during our traffic cone harvest. He stood for a minute wondering where to plant his future crops.

"We have only a few minutes before the cops come back from Home Depot."

"Let's mix the tarragon in with the grass. It'll blend right in," I said.

"Okay. I'll plant the cabbage next to this purple plant that looks like a cabbage."

In less than twenty minutes, we were done with most of our dissident garden.

"Where should we plant the apricot?" I asked.

"In front of the Alex Theater," he said. "Maybe one day, you can make a new duduk."

"Maybe." It came out of my mouth even though it wasn't true.

"You should be able to pick your precious tomatoes in a few days," Haik said.

Me and everyone else.

CHAPTER TWENTY-FIVE

I was at the doctor's office, its walls yellowed and the air-conditioning shuddering and bleating every ten minutes, reading the same *National Geographic* I'd read on three past visits. A story on vibration-sensing animals. The earliest written record of rats and weasels leaving their burrows before a large earthquake is from 373 BC Greece. The latest is when this rat had to leave his penthouse for his useless checkup.

Like animals, we have the ability to sense danger before it happens but we often choose to ignore the warning. I closed my eyes. What did I feel? A jet of air from the cooling system. The smooth paper of the magazine, bent along the edges. The rigidity of the hard plastic chair. A touch of urine against my thigh. And a rush of body heat. Him.

"I thought I saw you walk in earlier," Haik said, shifting several bags, his orange knapsack firmly on his back. He was still wearing scrubs, his ID badge flipped so you couldn't see his name. His face was scratched and crusty from the Home Depot escape. He waited for something.

"Sit if you're staying," I said after a few moments. It was too late to move to safer ground.

He put down a Kmart plastic bag filled with books: *Algebra & Trigonometry, Eleventh Edition; Government and Economics; English Literature with World Masterpieces.*

"Studying, eh?" I asked after rifling through the sack.

"There's a job opening in the lab. I need to finish my GED and take one college class to apply."

"Good. It'll keep you from blackmailing people."

He didn't smile, but I knew from the wiggle of his eyebrows he appreciated the effort.

"How's your grand gesture?" I put down *Government and Economics* with the thud it deserved.

He shrugged as if he'd never mentioned it.

We sat for a couple minutes while he fiddled with his array of bags.

"Glad I ran into you. I have something for you." He handed me a brown paper bag with fancy rope handles.

"For me? Donuts? A traffic cone? The letter K, perhaps?" I reached through the delicate blue tissue and touched cloth. It was a pair of jeans. "What are these for? Will we be defacing the Gap?"

"They're for you. Much easier to wear than your designer slacks . . . for when we go out at night." To the untrained ear, it sounded like we had reservations for dinner. "You don't have to dry clean them."

"You got me a gift? I'll look like a missing Rolling Stone. The fat one."

"Do they have a duduk player?"

"No. That's Peter Gabriel's territory." I was still stung he'd asked Vache Hovsepyan to play the score for *The Last Temptation of Christ*.

"What are you here for?" Haik asked, settling back in his chair.

"Just a regular checkup." I showed him my teeth in what I hoped was a smile, just to throw him off.

"No one goes to see Dr. Scaly Skin for a regular checkup."

"Well, I'm getting old. The plumbing doesn't work the way it should." I folded the jeans down the middle like slacks. "Thanks. But you shouldn't have spent your money on it."

"Don't worry about it," he said. "Congratulations, by the way."

"For what?" I knew he was referring to the article in the *L.A. Times*.

"The story. 'L.A.'s Secret Musician.'"

"It's nothing." I shrugged offhandedly. Off the record, I thought the three-page spread was the summation of my life's work. The acknowledgement of all I'd accomplished.

"Why do you say that?" He laughed a little, scratching his head. "How do you get to be *somebody* and say it's nothing?" He got up from his seat and loomed over me.

He really meant, how could a fraud like me make it big? I imagined he might hit me. I felt my ears flatten like a stray crossing the path of a drunk. Instead, he raised his voice.

"I just want to know!"

Only one other person was in the waiting room, a tall black woman with a long blond wig and shiny golden nails.

"Don't worry, ma'am, he's completely harmless when he takes his Valium," I said in her direction. I saw her here every week and I knew she wore a hearing aid that she turned off to save the battery.

The boy started, flinging his backpack off his shoulders, but I put my hand on him.

"What's the matter with you?" I pointed back to the chair. "Is it that girl?"

"Leave her out of this." He didn't sit.

"Fine." I bit at the callus on my ring finger until it was red.

"They don't even know, do they? Your family? What would they think of you?" he asked.

I shook my head although I thought of that very question every day.

"And you got so rich." He left out the rest of what he was thinking—*living a lie.*

"Not that rich," I said. But the truth hurt much less than I thought it would. Maybe because he didn't know the depth of my sin.

The nurse opened the sliding glass window. "Is everything okay?"

The deaf woman said nothing.

"Yes. Sorry, nurse. It's just a silly little game we're playing."

She said something under her breath that looked like "Crazy Armenians."

Haik sat down hard, shaking the row of plastic seats, knocking his books and the jeans to the floor.

"I'll tell you what you want to know." I picked up the jeans and folded them again. I wasn't sure what he really wanted to know but I had to start. It was time.

I told Haik of what happened when I was just a child. That was 1915. My home, in the little village where his grandmother and I both probably grew up outside of Sis which, as I mentioned earlier, is now called Kozan in Turkey—but then was part of a crumbling Ottoman Empire and way before that, belonged to the Armenian Kingdom of Cilicia, and even further back in time, was home to the chariot-driving Hittites—all of it had been burnt down to charcoal.

The soldiers under our new leaders, the Young Turks, were ordered to dispose of Armenians and confiscate their land. Things were rough. A huge influx of Muslims from Eastern Europe had moved into Anatolia. Bellies and minds were rumbling. The Young Turks turned around and promised the Armenians' riches to their Turkic supporters.

This scheme wasn't new for my hometown. The year after I was born, thousands of soldiers had moved across the Adana countryside with the precision of starving locusts. They riled up the local Turks into a fury that would only be sated by rape and murder, fire and destruction.

Our small village had been spared during the Adana massacre six years earlier, which, when its evil belly had been fully satisfied, had sucked more than 30,000 Armenian lives. But the beast was hungry again. Starving.

Up in the hills that day, I was herding the family goats. I sat on a piece of limestone so smooth I imagined it a dinosaur egg. What if it hatched while I sat there playing the duduk I'd stolen from my father's chair that morning? Would I be swallowed up by an ancient monster? It was a girl whose name I've forgotten who showed me this wonder.

Below in the distance, while I counted our animals up high, some soldiers I'd passed on my way to the mountain pasture set fire to Armenian homes to punish them when they resisted eviction. But the fires didn't discriminate. They spread, whipped up by the winds that traveled from the ocean and slammed into the mountains behind us.

It was only when I lay on my back with a wild rosemary–aromatized baby goat on my chest that I saw a thin white loop across the clear sky. I turned on my stomach and peered over the dinosaur-egg stone to see smoke spew into the sky near St.

Sophia's monastery bell tower. It was Sis's most honored land-mark.

I told myself it was the traveling carnival. With a boy's enthu-siasm, I penned the goats and hurried home so I wouldn't miss the evening fireworks. The year before, they'd had a tightrope walker, a boy about my age, in a turban too big for his head. Steady in the air, only his lips trembling. I wondered if he'd grown into his cos-tume as I scrambled as fast as I could down the narrow paths, the dry brambles drawing blood from my bare legs. Halfway down, the wind carried the wailing and the smells of burning meat. It still took an hour to get to the village. And the closer I got, the more I knew there was no circus. No fire eaters. No tightrope.

By then the village square was empty of living beings. Dead bodies everywhere I looked. Naked and draped from the branches of the big olive tree as if set out to dry. I threw up on my feet. It was hours before I could go near our house, which was on the outskirts of the village. The fire had consumed everything and everyone in its path, including many Turks.

"Yeah, right!" Haik snorted. "The Turks set the damn fires!"

"Yes, that's true. But it killed *everyone*. Everyone I knew," I said.

"I'm glad," Haik said.

"I'm not who you think I am." Something hot and wet welled up behind my eyes.

"You're exactly who I think you are. Go on with your fantasy."

I sat quietly, slumped over my belly.

"I said go on," Haik said, his voice full of hot pepper and vinegar.

"I fainted and must have fallen asleep. The next morning," I continued, "the weather was beautiful. Perfect for hunting the little wild fruit that look like tiny blackberries." That's what I thought when I woke up and looked at the sky, lying in the soft ravine in the field behind the house. Then I remembered. I got up and ran toward the house.

I found my father's blackened body at the charred back gate. I knew it was him because of his hat. Oddly, the deep green wool had barely been scorched.

I opened my mouth to say I'm sorry but bile rushed out instead of words. The wind swirled hot embers around my legs.

"What did you have to be sorry for?" Haik asked.

I couldn't bear to tell Haik why our village was destroyed. Instead, I told him I went inside where my mother's body covered my two little brothers under the kitchen table. I think my brothers were smothered to death because they looked perfect. I touched the gold medallion my mother wore around her neck, a wedding gift from my father's family. It was warm as a freshly baked cookie. The surrounding olive trees, some that were hundreds of years old, had caught fire, turning our home into an oven hot enough to steam her flesh. It also burned to a crisp my grandparents and my two aunts who huddled by the well.

"Do you know what that smells like?" I asked him. I was ashamed to tell him the aroma of cooked flesh made me hungry. I hadn't eaten in more than a day. Humans are definitely a red meat.

Haik shifted in his seat but kept quiet. I told him I couldn't speak after I saw my family. Not even when the troops who were sent to clean up the mess found me. It felt like a jagged rock had lodged in the base of my throat and it would dig into my flesh if I opened my mouth. I swallowed and I swallowed and it wouldn't go away.

"Shock," Haik said, nodding his head. "I've seen that in the ER before."

I shrugged and continued.

The soldiers looked at my vomit-crusted feet and the duduk in my hand and shoved me onto a path going east.

Soon, I was swept up with the Armenian leftovers—old people, women and children, herded to the Syrian Desert—still holding my father's duduk. The cylinder of wood reminding me that I would never be like him. I was seven.

I walked behind a beautiful girl and her family. Her name was Altoon. I'd never seen such fair skin or such blue eyes, tendrils of her pale hair escaping from her scarf. The soldiers soon carried her away to become a girl who would never grow up to be a woman.

They marched us further into the desert. They made sure there was nothing to eat. Nothing to keep us cool or warm except the debris of other people's lives. I watched a once-rich woman trade her heavy gold belt, the kind with dangling little coins, for a glass of water. The soldiers asked her if she had anything else. She removed a silver thimble from a leather pouch around her neck. It was the last of her possessions. They gave her a few raisins for it.

Once we'd gotten far enough into the sands of another country, the soldiers melted away back to their masters.

I wandered alone for months, attempting to play a song for anything people might give me. The lump in my throat slowly dissolved to sand but I rarely talked to anyone. I walked when I had the strength and waited to die when I didn't. There are hills in the Middle Eastern desert made up entirely of our bones. Those days oozed together into a pool of time. I couldn't even remember what happened during that period even when I thought about it months later.

"Why didn't you tell someone who you were?" Haik asked. "They would have sent you back."

"Boy, you can never go back," I said. "And what for? Everyone was dead."

He made an impatient noise. "Then what happened?"

Only one day stood out very clearly during that time, I told him. It was in ar Raqqah—that's in Syria. I sat outside the biggest building in the city at that time. I heard it's now a museum. My body was just another link in the cadaverous chain leaning against the wall. I stared at the putrid sores on my bare feet and waited to die.

"Mr. Rupen. Mr. Rupen." The nurse, in her flowery pink scrubs and bifocals, stood right in front of us. "I've been calling your name for minutes. Do we need to check your hearing, too?" She clucked and led me to the examining room. A poster against domestic abuse loomed on the far wall.

Haik squeezed in as the door closed. "I'll stay with my *grand-father*," he said as if it were a swear word. The nurse turned to me for permission and I consented.

"Your blood pressure is much too high, Mr. Rupen," the nurse said. "Meditation and deep breathing help." She demonstrated deep breathing with her eyes closed and her hands folded. "Try that for a few minutes. And try to limit your salt."

Or blackmailers.

"The doctor wants another quick exam." The nurse looked at her notes. "Please undress and put this gown on. Take off everything."

She left us alone in the broom closet with an examination table, torture devices of every shape and form and a window. It was the same room where the doctor had informed me I was dying.

Haik sat on the butt-pinching, cracked plastic chair against the wall, staring past the streaked window to the sky changing from blue to pink. He waited for me to explain why I was still alive.

I struggled onto the table and tried to untie my shoes. I couldn't reach my feet. Haik sighed loudly and fumbled with the knots Lucy had tied that morning. His fingers were long and beautiful. They were the hands of an artist. An artist-thug.

"*Merci*," I said. There was a pink scar on the top of his head. It looked like a map of Greece with its complement of little islands.

"Have you forgotten I'm Glendale General's award-winning orderly? I do this shit all day," he said. "Your shoes are very nice." With brutal envy, he caressed a leather tongue with his index finger before he placed the shoes neatly under his chair.

"They're Bruno Magli, straight from Italy. You can't get that style here."

I took off my socks. My khaki pants. I passed him my checked shirt. He handed me the pale blue gown, soft and limp from so many washings. I slipped it on and took off my boxers. I spread them over my lap exactly where they'd normally be worn.

"How did you get that scar on your head? One of your projects?" I asked, mostly to fill the space embarrassment creates when you take your clothes off.

"You could say it was my first *oeuvre*." He actually used the French word. "When I was eight," he continued, "I took the pot of hot oil that my mom used to fry *kuftas* to burn a swear word into the grass. There was a spoon in the pot that tipped onto my head."

"A marked man for life."

"That's what it feels like."

"So what did you want to write on the grass?"

"*Toon vor es.*"

"Hey! I was just asking."

"No. That's what I wrote on the grass: You are an ass."

"Oh, that's ambitious to write in hot oil. And after you burnt your head. You should have just stuck with 'ass.' It would have gotten the point across."

"Yeah. My dad beat me good. Burnt head and all. But *Tatik* thought it was funny. She laughed about it for years."

It was quiet for a few minutes. We could hear the wail of the malfunctioning air conditioner outside and the nurse yelling to the black lady with the gold nails to turn on her hearing aid.

"You clearly didn't die in the desert," Haik said. "What happened next?"

I must have shivered because he handed me a white cotton blanket with dark blue embroidery that looked like a Greek pattern. On closer examination it said *Property of Glendale General* in block letters.

To cover my fear, I recited poetry. *"I know the desert is beautiful for I have lain in her arms and she has kissed me."* Those were lines from *The Poet in the Desert*. Lucy's class was assigned to read it. She thought it sounded lovely. Romantic. I can't even go to Palm Springs without feeling faint. And I've never been to Las Vegas for the same reason. The desert is an infinite prison of shimmering gold and pink, choking your throat and clutching your ankle with every step you take. The murderess.

I told Haik about the boy named Levon who found me holding up the wall that fateful day.

"You're the duduk player, aren't you?" Levon asked me in Turkish. I must have nodded because he said "I heard you out there." He gestured into the nothing.

"He spoke to you in Turkish?" Haik asked.

"Of course," I said. "Speaking Armenian in public could get your tongue cut out."

Haik swallowed. He moved his tongue back and forth as if to make sure it was still there.

Those words saved my life.

I think of Levon as my creator. I don't mock God when I say that but he baptized me and gave my lost soul a new name. And one day, so far in the future I couldn't even dream of it, those words would lead me to become Maestro Rupen, the best duduk player in the world. (This is not my proclamation. The journalist wrote that in her story.)

I keep wondering even after all these years why on that day my life changed. Did I step on the right side of an unseen line? What did I do differently to deserve being saved when everyone else I knew was dead?

Levon tore the sleeves of his shirt to bind my feet. When I asked him why he was helping me, he said he liked the way I played. He assumed we were on the same path. Why else would I wander the desert? So I made his journey my journey and joined him to find what remained of his family in Lebanon. That's where most Armenians were heading. Except we wouldn't see the sparkling Mediterranean for another year.

Levon was from an Orthodox Christian family. They went to church twice a week. Sometimes more. The monks at St. Sophia taught him to recite all 150 psalms during the course of the day, just in case he went into the priesthood. He continued this tradition as we picked our way past indistinguishable piles of bones human and animal, objects of great value and items of the mundane.

"*Yea, though I walk through the shadow of the valley of death, I will fear no evil. For thou art with me,*" he would repeat in the strong, high-pitched voice of an altar boy.

"Do you go to church, Haik?" I asked.

"Nope. That's for people who feel guilty." Haik shifted in the cracked chair.

Good Soviet.

Although I didn't have a formal religious education, I understood the balm this book had to offer. The Book of Psalms was meant to be uttered in the vast void of the desert. Our personal inferno. Psalms were meant to be recited by the lonely and suffering. By us. If a book could be an instrument, it would be the duduk.

I liked Psalm 88, a lament, which I memorized while Levon recited the verses in Armenian. He spoke in the insistent open-voweled sounds that used to make me think every Armenian conversation was a fight. "*Why, O Lord, do you reject me and hide your face from me? I have suffered your terrors and am in despair."*

Reciting the Psalms didn't do as much for Levon as it did for me. Even as we repeated Psalm 123, verse 3. *"Have mercy upon us, O Lord, have mercy upon us: for we are exceedingly filled with contempt."*

It was as if God had inadvertently reminded Levon to *be* filled with contempt. "I will slay the first Turk I see," Levon shouted when he remembered his dead family, which was often. "I will kick him in the face when he's dead." Levon's darkness simmered below his heart. Psalm 123 be damned.

"My fear that Levon would snap passed just as his anger did," I explained to Haik, who had moved in so close I could smell his sour, smoky breath. "Levon wasn't in any shape to commit murder." Without his sleeves, which had long fallen off my feet, you could see his arm bones.

Haik sat back and fingered the box of cigarettes in his shirt pocket.

"Mr. Najarian." The beady-eyed doctor poked his head around the corner. "Sorry to keep you waiting. I just got out of surgery."

"That's okay. I had some company." I pointed to Haik.

He hesitated, then asked Haik to leave the room. Could the doctor feel danger, like those animals? He must have read that article on vibrations, too. That magazine had been there long enough.

Haik got up. "I'll pick you up tomorrow, *Papik* Rupen," he said, handing me a folded piece of paper with a smirk on his lips. "We just don't spend enough time together."

It was a shopping list scribbled on pharmaceutical letterhead. Lipitor. In red block letters it instructed:

Bring the following—
100 white standard envelopes
100 stamps
1 ream of copy paper
2 pens
2 clipboards
1 large pack Dentyne mint gum

I folded the paper and pretended to listen to the doctor. After he told me I was still dying, I'd put him on mute. An hour later, I picked up my prescription for Diethylstilbestrol. The bag was very light for containing the last source of reprieve. I took a shortcut through the parking structure but felt tired even though I'd only walked a few yards. My haunches shook as I sat on the staircase under the employee parking sign and pulled out the medicine. A yellow pamphlet attached to the box informed me Diethylstilbestrol was a high dose of estrogen that was a current medical alternative for advanced prostate cancer.

Estrogen? I couldn't even use my penis as a paperweight, but maybe I could grow bigger breasts?

CHAPTER TWENTY-SIX

Medicines had the same effect on a dying man as prayer circles, witch doctors and Susie's beam ray machine: To make me feel like I was in control of my destiny. I might as well have called for Aralez, the most ancient of Armenian pharmaceuticals. One of the oldest gods, his powers included the ability to resurrect the dead by licking their wounds clean. As you might have already guessed, he was a dog. (Probably something like a greyhound.) When I see a dog picking its way through a battlefield in the Middle East, the pagan in me feels strangely relieved while the Christian in me feels horror. In dog we trust.

That day, I put the pharmacy papers back in the bag and took a deep breath, just like the nurse had shown me.

Expensive cars were parked on that floor. These employees, probably cancer specialists, were clearly well paid. Too well paid, with my insurance money. An egg yolk–yellow Lotus was brazenly parked across two spots. If I weren't Aralez-tired, I'd have walked across and keyed the car myself. There were several Mercedes of varying pedigree. And a gray BMW with a horizontal dent across the trunk that looked very familiar. I assumed he must have been called back to work for an extra shift.

I don't know why I decided to stay seated on the step—the everlasting humor of the universe, perhaps—but not three minutes later, Haik walked to his car accompanied by a blond girl in a white coat, her hair twisted into a knot. He slipped his hand under the coat and cupped her breast, tenderly approving its shape and heft.

"I can't really take a break right now." Her breathless voice carried across the open floor. They kissed outside the car for a few minutes. She bit his upper lip, pulling it gently away from his mouth. Haik's hand traveling low to caress her rounded derrière.

"No, sweetie," she said even as they both slipped into the backseat.

It was like I knew her, by Haik's descriptions at least. I sat there quiet as a cockroach while the windows fogged up first in the middle and then up the sides. I waited for the car to shake, but it didn't. That's a BMW for you.

When they concluded their tryst, she stepped out of the car and smiled as Haik blew her a kiss before he drove away. I struggled up and did my best to tiptoe to the elevator at the top of the staircase. I practiced the nurse's zen breathing as I heard the girl's footsteps cross the floor and patter up the stairs.

A bell rang somewhere close to her.

"Hello," she said.

I thought she was talking to me, and was about to answer.

"I'm still at work," she spoke into her mobile phone. "No. I ran into someone." She giggled. "No. Nothing serious. Just having some fun. Mmhmm. He's very good."

"Did I startle you, dear?" I asked in English when she saw me and let out a small scream.

She dropped her adding machine of a phone. Her lips were red and swollen, a lacy strap showing on one shoulder. An aroma of yeast and pollen lingered in the air.

"I'm sorry. I wasn't expecting anyone here at this time," she said as she straightened her disarray, embarrassment in her topaz eyes. Her ID read Christine Helian. Christine of the sun. So this was the girl who left her hair behind on my bed. My virtual lover.

"I should be the one to apologize." I tipped my beret, took the elevator to the basement and waited for her to leave. I don't think she recognized me as Maestro Rupen.

CHAPTER TWENTY-SEVEN

I've read that a surface wave is the most destructive of earth-quakes. There's a type of surface wave called a Love wave. It moves along the top of the earth like a rattlesnake zigzagging to-ward a field mouse. Its vibrations create jarring shocks as it travels its destined path, making it very damaging.

I'd just put my socks on and slipped the soft leather of Bruno Magli back onto my feet when Haik showed up at the studio. I had a Love wave in my back pocket. I just didn't know it yet.

"Did you get everything on the list?" he asked instead of greet-ing me respectfully.

"I'm on my way to the park," I said.

I'd only seen my friends once that week. They wondered, and not quietly, why I no longer spent my afternoons with them.

"Sorry. Duty calls. Did you get everything I asked for?" he asked again.

"Yes. It's all here." I showed him the sea of white paper cover-ing my work table.

"Good. I need you to address the envelopes to the following address: Turkish Consulate, 6300 Wilshire Blvd., Los Angeles, CA 90035."

"I understand your need to torture me, but do you want me to get caught?" I worried about what he had in mind. Tainted Tyle-nol? MRSA germs?

"You won't get caught. Get moving, Maestro. You have a hun-dred envelopes to address." He reached into his backpack and brought out a pair of latex gloves and a knife.

"Are you going to stab me?" I moved away from the knife's range.

"Not today." He gathered the ream of bonded linen paper to

140

the window and started folding each sheet into thirds.

"Why don't you give me a pair of those gloves, then?"

"You don't need them." He didn't even look up at me.

I went back to the envelopes, considering if I should write in cursive or capitals. I decided on block letters with no serif, a style I remembered from a long time ago. I must have been on the fifth envelope when he spoke.

"So what happened that made you wander the desert for a year?"

I wondered if I should tell him even more than I already had.

"I'm not in the mood to chat," I said, but I slipped my shoes back off.

"Of course you are. You don't have anyone else to talk to," he said.

* * *

One day, I continued, while Levon and I gathered bits of firewood to trade for food, we got very lost. So lost that we walked in circles for a whole day until two men in head wraps and shawls that covered their faces found us. They talked amongst themselves, once in a while, poking and pinching us. Not that there was much to poke or pinch. Finally, one of them grabbed each of us by the arm and marched us over an outcrop of rocks, eastward. It wasn't long before we realized they'd kidnapped us. It sounds like something out of a Charlton Heston movie, but many children like us were stolen and sold into slavery.

The men brought us to the head of a nearby Bedouin household. His name was Abu Yassar and I remember that he had three moles on the left side of his chin. One that sprouted hair. I stared until Levon stepped on my foot.

Abu Yassar looked at our rags and sores with the same mixture of pity and greed one bestows on livestock. He paid our kidnappers with a skin filled with goats' milk and a basket of fresh dates—that was our entire worth—and became our master.

His women fed us a bowl of milk each and some flatbread, scorched over a wood fire. We scooped the flecks of fat that floated on top of the bowls with our fingers and sucked its richness, comforting as our mothers' breasts. I hadn't tasted milk since I'd left the village.

Abu Yassar had four wives, eleven children and a handful of grandchildren. We rarely saw the older women but they made an impression when they walked by in their voluminous, black *thobes* embroidered in red (if they were married) or blue (if not). Their foreheads, chins and arms were tattooed with little crisscrosses to show they were taken. Part of his clan and his property, as we now were. Sometimes, they tousled our curls. Other times, they slapped our ears.

We took care of the goats and camels, making sure they were fed and safe from the jackals (both human and animal) that wandered the flat stony face of the Al-Hamad. I was a natural with the goats because I discovered something about them during my career as a herder. Goats are music lovers. Rhythm is part of the natural world and animals, including humans, understand the concept. Goats are one of the oldest domesticated animals and they've listened to millennia of human music. Melody is now in their DNA.

"Are you smoking too much weed?" Haik interrupted my story.

"You think we're the only animals that compose music?"

"Why? Did you catch a coyote rapping last time you drove through Griffith Park?" Haik asked.

"Laugh all you want," I told Haik. And he did. "But humpback whales compose music."

"Yeah, but that's probably just functional, like trying to get a mate."

"You could say that about humans, too. Who is to say that whale songs aren't purely creative? We just don't know."

Today, they would've called me a biomusicologist. Back then they called me something similar to the pied piper, keeping hoofed creatures happy till they were slaughtered. While the goats weren't great singers, they were an appreciative audience—even prancing and rolling to their favorite melodies—so I played the duduk for Abu Yassar's goats.

But herding was the least of my tasks. Since I was malnourished and very small for my age, they forced me to race camels for their celebrations. If you're afraid of heights, camelback is its own special kind of bumpy aerial torture. If I won, Abu Yassar gave me a shirtful of dried apricots that I shared with Levon. To this day, I turn the channel when I see camels on TV. Apricots, I have no fight with.

In return for our labor, Abu Yassar kept us marginally fed and clothed.

"You know, my *tatik* lived with the Bedouins for a few years. They saved her," Haik said.

"That's my point, boy. Not everyone is bad."

Haik snorted but halfheartedly.

"How did your grandmother survive?" I asked. "I thought everyone was dead."

"Not her. She was napping high up in a mulberry tree. She heard the noise and stayed there till the fire got out of hand. Then she climbed down into a well and hid. But the soldiers caught her a few weeks later and sent her to the desert. She was very sick when the Bedouins found her. They nursed her back to health and she lived with them for five years. Then, when she was fifteen, they found her my grandfather to marry. He was staying with another clan near their oasis," Haik said.

I nodded but didn't say anything. It was true. Bedouins helped many Armenians stay alive during the terror. But my relationship with them was colored.

It was there that I had my first taste of coffee. The Bedouins drank coffee that boiled for at least forty-eight hours over a low charcoal flame, until it was reduced to its purest expression. Part of my floating duties was also to watch the family coffeepot at night.

I didn't tell Haik that having to watch the coffeepot while they slept wasn't the bad part. Abu Yassar's eldest son, the opium-addicted Abu Ahmad, was the worst. How he liked little boys! He was probably in his thirties, with children of his own. At night, he would come to the goat pen where we slept and carry one of us off. Levon, being bigger, would yell and beat him. Abu Ahmad hit him so hard he knocked out a bicuspid. Once, he even cut Levon with a knife. It took weeks for it to heal and then, it left a ropey scar.

The first time he took me, he pulled my rags off and saw my circumcised penis.

"Well, what have we here? What are you, boy?" He lifted my eyebrows with his fingers and peered into my terrified eyes.

"I don't know," I replied. *"Yea though I walk in the shadow of the valley of death, I will fear no evil,"* I recited Psalm 23 out loud in Armenian. It seemed to excite him all the more. He licked his lips.

After he was done, I walked back to the pen trying to stifle my whimpering. I told myself I deserved it for what I'd done to my village.

"You should forget about this," Levon whispered from his side of the pen.

I nodded in the darkness. We never talked about it, even after we ran away six months later during a sandstorm. If you talk about it, it means it's real. But Levon's hatred moved beyond the Turks to include the Bedouins.

Eighteen months after I left my home, Levon and I made it to Antelias, just outside of Beirut. More than six hundred miles. On foot. It was the makeshift seat of the Armenian Apostolic Church, the Catholicos of Cilicia.

Sahag II was a man in his late sixties, worn and wearied by all he'd seen happen to his people. Just like us, he wandered the Middle East, looking for a new home until he reached the shores of this Lebanese town. There, all you could hear was the Mediterranean crashing into the sun-baked stones, erasing the Bedouins, the desert, the fire and all that had occurred before.

We were among hundreds of orphans. Many, like me, were the sole survivors of their family. The crazed nuns from various relief organizations, in their flurry of white habits and gnarled feet gripping brown sandals, set up dormitories and makeshift classrooms. For most of us, Antelias was our first formal education. I started school when I was nine. It was a blessing since it gave me a chance to learn how to properly read and write Armenian, not just the slang and half-words I used with my village friends. If you were older than fifteen, the nuns made matches on the spot to marry off this torn generation.

"Did you notice any Turks there?" Haik interrupted.

"God, you are obsessed." I sighed into my block letters.

"Well, we have to be vigilant. Keep our blood lines clean."

"Why?"

"It's our heritage. Our identity!"

"Whether you like to hear it or not, Armenians have enough Mongol blood to start an invasion," I said.

"You always make shit up." He sent a stack of paper flying about the studio.

"So convenient to believe what you want," I said. "Less than a thousand years ago, Genghis Khan's grandson, a little shit like you, conquered Armenia along with Afghanistan, Iran, Iraq, Turkey and Syria."

Haik snorted but didn't say anything so I went on.

"In the 1400s, it was fashionable for Armenians to wear Mongolian clothing. Marriages were arranged between the wealthy of each group. Alliances were made. Fine. Don't believe me. Hand me more envelopes and pick up the mess."

Haik grumbled as he gathered the paper. I asked him to light a joint. I inhaled several times. Now that was zen. He motioned for me to continue the story.

"Things changed when I was twelve," I told him. "I became a man of the cloth. Aha! You thought Levon would be the monk."

"I wouldn't doubt you'd find a way to worm your way in," Haik said. "You're a weasel."

I prefer rat.

"Why do you care? I thought you were an atheist?"

"Sure. But you're not." He sneered and went back to folding more paper into thirds.

"It's kind of you to look out for my soul. Do you want me to go on with my story or not?"

"Go on." He reached for the joint and took a puff.

"I didn't become a novice in Lebanon, though. I went all the way to Italy."

"You're just making shit up again," Haik interrupted me.

He put his gloves on and started scraping pigeon droppings off the windowsill with the knife. He slid the droppings in between the pristine folds of the finest linen paper.

"You wouldn't say that if you hadn't skipped Armenian school on Saturdays."

He conceded with a nod that he had skipped many a class and handed me the folded sheet, full of bird shit, to stuff in the envelope.

"Why do you need the Dentyne on your list? To seal the envelope, right?"

"No. I ran out of gum yesterday." He took out two pieces, unwrapped them with the heel of his palm and his teeth. "What happened in Italy?" he asked with his mouth open, green gum stuck to his back teeth.

"I went to St. Lazarus," I said, referring to the Armenian monastery in the Venetian lagoon. "It was so beautiful there. The incandescence at sunset . . ."

"So you came back to life," Haik said. "Saved again."

I knew he was referring to the story of Lazarus in the Bible, but I gave him a lifted eyebrow.

"I know stuff," he said.

"I doubt you know what it used to be in the twelfth century."

"A prison?" Haik asked.

"No. A leper colony."

"I wouldn't have guessed that."

"Do you know how an Armenian monastery ended up in Venice?"

"Is this a quiz, teacher?"

"No. This you'll appreciate. In the early 1700s, Venice's ruling council gave it to a group of Armenian monks who were escaping Turkish persecution."

"Man. I *should* have guessed that. How did you get to Venice?"

"I hitchhiked."

"You're not as funny as you think." He stuck his chewed up gum on the inside corner of the sill and took a hit.

"Fine," I told him. "On a ship carrying cedar planks and mail."

The Benedictine Mekhitar Order of St. Lazarus guarded its

literary traditions closely. They often searched for poor, bright Armenian boys among the diaspora to educate and train to protect the ancient works—some 4,000 manuscripts and 150,000 volumes. They even had their own printing presses, which were finally shut down just a year ago, in 1991. I was good at languages, so they took me.

The monkish life suited me just fine. I wanted to be alone to stare at the lagoon's turquoise water and bloom into Rupen Najarian, Armenian from Sis. I studied Latin, French and Italian with fifty other boys. (My village hadn't even had a school.) We woke up before sunrise and had two hours of chores before lessons. Then more after classes. And then some more in between prayers. My job was to wash dishes after our meals. The cooks were patients from the mental institution on the neighboring island. They made delicious pasta with sardines on Fridays.

"That doesn't sound tasty," Haik said.

"Trust me. The prick of red wine vinegar and chopped onions— brilliant! It's like the highest C you can play on a grand piano."

I'd never seen art—paintings—until I roamed the upper gallery. Tintoretto. Veronese. Aivazovsky. A poor boy's personal museum. I didn't even have the vocabulary—that those canvases were called paintings. But their purpose was clear. Just like we know what rain or sunshine is for.

"Which one was your favorite?" Haik asked.

"*Chaos* by Aivazovsky. It's a storm on the open ocean, strong and erratic like the spin cycle of a vengeful washing machine. And there near the heavens, the fury squeezes out God, bright and clean, bringing calm over all that is dark. It's breathtaking."

"Well? Do you have one?" It was only polite to ask him what his favorite work of art was.

Haik thought about it. I knew him well enough to know that he'd pick some spot of graffiti off the 101 Freeway.

"It's a sculpture made by this Romanian dude, Constantin Brancusi—*The Kiss*." Haik picked up the wad of gum he'd left on the sill and started chewing it again.

"I've seen a version he did in Paris at the Montparnasse Cemetery," I said, taken aback.

"You're lucky. I've only seen it in photos at the library."

"What do you like about it?"

I almost thought he wasn't going to answer.

"He takes out just enough of the stone so you see the man and the woman kissing. It's naked. It's about the truth."

Warming up to his subject, he then went on to tell me that Roman sculpture was the pinnacle of the art form and anyone who disagreed was an ass.

"How do you know so much about Roman art?" I asked, now truly astounded.

"We spent two months there before our papers cleared to enter the States," he said. "It was a shitty two-bedroom apartment that we had to share with another family. My parents were so stressed out, half the time they didn't even notice when I took off."

"So you have a criminal record in Rome?"

"Nah. Not enough time to get in trouble. I just walked around a lot and snuck into museums when it rained."

"Think of the trouble you could have created if you had an extra month," I said.

We worked on our individual projects for a while before he asked me what happened next in Venice. I knew he would.

I was one of the only students allowed to assist in the printing shop, I told him. My favorite was an eighth-century press from China with movable wooden blocks. Whole pages had to be carved onto a piece of wood and pressed onto paper. This was state-of-the-art technology till Gutenberg came along with movable type. Mostly, we used a press made by a Venetian local, a transplanted Frenchman named Nicholas Jenson. He came up with the first standardized type sometime in the 1400s. He was inspired by the clean letters carved into Roman marble, which was different than Gutenberg's Gothic type that looked more like calligraphy. *The Times* newspaper in England can thank Jenson for their Times New Roman font. It was based on one of his original typefaces.

Boys came and went, but I stayed. I was good at printing and washing dishes and whatever else they wanted me to do. I was great at blending in. If I wasn't working, I practiced the duduk. The monks encouraged me to play. They believed this instrument was of Armenian pedigree, just like I told the journalist, and that it should be preserved.

They asked me how I learned to play and I told them the truth. That my father taught me. He learned from a very old Armenian herder when he was a boy.

It was this concentration of time at the monastery, more than a decade to think about the duduk, that made me who I am today. And maybe a little suffering. "You asked me how I became what I am. The answer is simple. Become a monk."

Haik didn't seem convinced that my fame came from little else than hard work and concentration.

"You think you can take shortcuts to greatness?" Not that I was calling myself great (the journalist did that, though) but I was no cheap cut of meat.

Haik was quiet. Was he trying to choke the little voice? The one that said anything worth being takes a lifetime of work? I wondered if I should tell him it's easy to ignore the truth because you don't feel worthy enough to make the effort. He probably didn't even hear the little voice to want to choke it. I believed his type always looked for the easy life and blamed everyone else when they didn't succeed.

But my life in the Venetian cocoon was soon over.

"It's time for you to leave, my son." Father Grikorian's voice broke through my sleep one morning. He sat on the edge of my bed, gazing out the pinhole window of my cell. The day dawned slowly, gracing the ocean with light. Fishermen below squabbled over their secret spots.

"Why, Father?" Had he discovered my un-Christian ejaculations? I masturbated regularly in the soft grass behind the roses, which the monks grew to make their famous rose petal jam. But so did everyone else. Or did he see me kiss the smooth stone lips of Venus? The latter was a dare. But I liked it and had to rush out to the rose garden.

"Your place is not with us." He looked around the ten-foot room. The white-washed wall with the crucifix. The small desk. The single bed. The armoire that held my change of clothing.

Had he found out something else? I was so weak with fear, I felt my bladder loosen.

"It's your duty to go home," he said, smoothing my hair.

"Where are you sending me?" I pinched my bladder shut. "This is my home."

He shook his head. "To the land of your forefathers," he whispered in my ear.

No, I thought. I'm going to the land of my children.

It was April 24, 1936. My twenty-eighth birthday. We listened to the sound of the sea lapping hungrily on the monastery walls. Did the waves tell Father Grikorian it was a ruse? That most of the men who returned to our newborn country would be sent to war or to perish in the mines of Siberia?

In December of that year, Armenia became one of the fifteen Soviet Socialist Republics. But there was a catch. Stalin demanded that enough Armenians be present in the new republic. Otherwise, *Hayastan* would be dissolved. Till that moment, Armenia had been a place found only fleetingly on modern maps, but it lived in the collective brain as the grand kingdom it once was. A magical place to retreat to when everything fell apart. Armenians walked, sailed, drove and flew from India and Ethiopia and from every country in the Middle East. From France and England and even from the comfort of the United States, they came to transpose Armenia from the brain onto real land. Even if it was a stony shadow of its former glory, the *Hayastansi* would breathe into the cold earth and give it life.

A few days after Father Grikorian's visit, I finished setting the printing press for his translation of the *Chronicle of Matthew of Edessa*. The monks stuffed an extra set of clothes, unfashionably sturdy, and a warm wool coat that belonged to the prior Father into a leather satchel. I hid my father's duduk between its folds before I left the safety of the monastery's stone walls.

The inmates in the kitchen hugged me, tears in their eyes. They had seen me grow from a scabby boy into a man. And now, I had their recipe for *Bigoli con le Sarde*.

I stepped back onto that mail ship, going in the direction of Lebanon. There were Armenians onboard heading for the new, lighter Armenia.

The vessel left Venice, picking up speed, the saltwater spitting on my face. I turned away from the islands and that's when I saw her. My goddess. She was on the bottom deck, wearing a bright blue full skirt, dancing the *Laz Bar*, a fisherman's dance from the Black Sea, the crashing waves her music. She held her hands out to unseen partners, twirling in a solo circle, her body a writhing fish, her head held high but her feet winged like Nike until she collapsed to the ground.

"How did you know she was the right one?" Haik asked.

"You were probably very horny."

"She heard music in the ocean." But I conceded that I was also very horny.

"So what happened then?"

"I helped her up. Her hand was so soft I wanted to hold it forever. But her uncle pulled her back inside." When he noticed my erection.

I smiled at the memory.

"What happened to Levon?" Haik asked.

"Levon stayed behind in Lebanon." His surviving family, one sister, a couple of cousins and an uncle, eventually found each other in Beirut. After finishing high school, he and his uncle opened a bakery. "We lost touch for twenty years or so."

"That's wack." Haik perched on the table, his bird-shit hands suspended above his knees.

"What is this 'wack'?"

"I mean, it's crazy."

"You can't imagine the state we were in. Many people couldn't find their own children. Forget about friends."

"So how did you meet up again?"

"The next time we saw each other, I was no longer a priest in waiting. He was married with three little girls. And we were in another country." Our own.

"You ran into each other by accident?"

"Nothing's ever an accident."

"What, you're saying 'God' intervened?"

"Let's say the humor of the universe."

In 1936, I told Haik, Yerevan, Armenia's new capital, was

desperation trapped in a wagon wheel. That's what people called architect Alexander Tamanian's circular master plan for the city. Up until the tumult of the 1900s, Yerevan was a sleepy outpost. More Eastern than Western. But in a matter of years, a city of a couple of thousand people who sat on floors to eat their meals spiraled upward to sit on chairs. It gave up its wide-legged pantaloons and jangling belts of gold coins for three-piece suits and replicas of Parisian dresses. It opened up, trying to accommodate the thousands who entered its limits. In the process of creating Tamanian's new layout, a Persian fortress, mosques, Turkish baths, houses made of mud, colorful bazaars and caravansaries were all demolished. Good riddance. Who needed reminders of the oppressors? They tore down a few ancient churches, too. Progress.

Those early days, I spent time admiring Tamanian's Republic Square but not on purpose. It was still under construction, but the pattern of a traditional carpet was emerging as they lay the volcanic tufa rock. I sat on the new stone, playing the duduk for my daily bread, having spent the little money the monks had given me. My hat was often empty, although people lingered to hear me play.

"Have you eaten, duduk player from Sis?" an unfamiliar voice asked. But the face. Take away twenty years and the gravelly voice he'd grown into, add twenty pounds and a few burn marks on his knuckles, and it was Levon. He wore the drab olive of the Soviet Army and carried two baskets of freshly peeled ash bark.

It was the second time Levon saved me.

"Here, hold this." He thrust a basket in my arms. "It will work up an appetite." As if I weren't already hungry.

"What's this for? To make a fire?"

"You'll see." He kissed my cheek and thumped me on the shoulder. "Good to see you're still alive."

We descended with our baskets into the cellar of a new building on Boulevard Mashtots, the city's fresh thoroughfare.

"Meet my best friend," Levon introduced me to his wife. Armineh. She looked like Amelia Earhart in her chocolate brown men's wool trousers belted high at the waist and sheer white scarf around her neck. Her chestnut hair was pulled away from her delicate face into a ponytail, so you could drown in her melted chocolate eyes. Two little girls clung to her sides and the third slept in a laundry basket next to the cold oven. A long wooden table was covered lightly with flour. Dough sat under threadbare cloths, willing themselves to rise in such austere surroundings.

"Welcome, Rupen Najarian." She bowed slightly as if I were someone. She placed a clean towel on the counter and laid out a small square of lavash, olives and a few dried plums. What a feast for a man who hadn't eaten in twenty-four hours.

While I ate, Levon built a fire and lightly toasted the tree bark in a cast iron skillet. Then he pounded it in a large mortar with a pestle. Such unusual customs in Armenia, I remember thinking. He carefully mixed the ground up tree bark into the flour bin.

"There won't be enough to eat if we don't make more bread," he said in response to my gaping mouth.

To thank them for the meal, I played *Dle Yaman*, "I Miss My Beloved," one of our ancient songs that describes a woman longing for her shepherd husband late from tending his flock in the mountains. Armineh kneaded one of the balls of dough, tears falling into the mixture as she punched it halfheartedly.

"Now look. The dough is too wet. I'll do it myself," Levon said. He took the bowl away and Armineh turned to leave.

"You can't go out in men's pants," Levon insisted. "What will people think?"

"They'll think what they want." Her scarf trailed behind her, full of unsaid words.

I lived with them in the bakery until I passed my audition for the State Orchestra. Every so often, Armineh asked me to play *Dle Yaman* when Levon wasn't there. But she never cried again.

CHAPTER TWENTY-EIGHT

In 1942, Levon fought in the Russian Army. I escaped the front because of my rising status. I did my service in the army band, playing a flute. I still lived at the bakery with Armineh and the girls—there were four now. The neighbors raised their eyebrows at our household but didn't say anything. They knew to keep their mouths shut if they wanted any bread or *gata*, the slightly sweet Easter bread which, when baptized in coffee, will extract an amen even from sinners.

We saved eggs and butter for weeks, storing them in the coldest part of the cellar. This was easy since it was still snowing outside. Near the oven, Alice, Armineh's eldest daughter, and I monitored two small pots of lentils. When they finally sprouted into velvety grass close to the fortieth day of Lent welcoming the coming of spring, Alice hugged me. Armineh petted the grass each time she went to the oven. We'd slipped into a comfortable rhythm of baking and music.

With Levon gone, Armineh preferred to bake at night rather than early in the morning. The children bedded and me working the parties of Soviet generals who didn't observe religious holidays, she kneaded armfuls of dough for sweet round loaves of the Easter *gata* with only her thoughts for company.

One night, I quietly opened the door so I wouldn't disturb her. Sitting on the top stair of the basement, I unlaced my shoes while she buttered her slender fingers, starting with the pinkie on her left hand and ending with the pinkie of her right hand, so they wouldn't stick to the dough. Curly, acorn-colored tendrils fell on her white neck. She moved to a baker's rhythm, rolling her shoulders back and forth. Shifting her weight forward then settling into her hips, then back and forth, her large dark eyes in a trance.

Every so often, she would sigh with pleasure.

The nebulous mass of flour, yeast, milk, sugar and butter miraculously divided into smaller orbs on the universe of wood and metal.

Armineh plucked one portion at a time and rolled it out to a thickness of less than a fourth of an inch. She brushed the face of the open dough with melted butter, then folded it to a square. She licked her lips.

"I know you're watching," she said.

"Sorry." My cheeks felt hot. I got up from the stairs and put my shoes under the staircase. "I'll help."

"No. Your hands are dirty." She continued to divide the filling—the *koritz*, a blend of butter, flour and sugar—into equal portions. Placing one portion in the center of this square, she hid a metal button, to represent a coin, which we had so few of, in the *koritz* and brought over opposite corners of the square to cover the filling.

It was in the hiding of the button that she seemed to come alive. As if the golden disk she buried was her own treasure to find later. She examined each button gathered from threadbare coats and dresses, with a keen interest before tucking it in carefully. Then her face lost its glow.

She rolled out the filled dough to the size of a small pie, brushing the top with beaten eggs, and drew the tines of an aluminum fork over the top in a lattice design. This she let rise with the thirty loaves she'd made earlier. Then she wrapped her arms in strips of fabric against the wooden inferno. With a deep breath, she whisked a few of them into the oven. We watched over them as they left on their final journey out of our floury realm to be cooked and browned for a half hour, turning into a flaky, chewy, coffee cake–like bread.

I passed her the remaining loaves, one by one, my breath rustling the hair that had escaped her bun. I inhaled her vanilla scent.

"You need a wife, Rupen," Armineh said.

* * *

The next Easter, Levon came back from the front, wheeling a young man not much older than Haik. He was missing his legs. Hovannes.

"He shouldn't have saved me," the young Hovannes said, punching dough fiercely, his black hair flopping over his eyes. "I don't want to live like this."

Armineh silently swapped the dough in front of his fists every ten minutes before rolling them into the long measures of *lavash* and tendering them to Levon, who slapped them into the clay *tonir* dug into the ground. My dancing goddess, Artemis, had become my fiancée. She watched the spectacle in tears.

"We're not usually like this," Armineh assured my wife-to-be. "We're much less cheerful."

"So how were you two introduced?" Levon asked, since it was still improper to find your own spouse.

"My uncle," she lied. Her uncle didn't want her to marry a dirty-minded musician. He still tried to hide her when I went to call on her. What really happened was that she'd told me on the boat she hoped to become a ballet dancer. I searched all the dance classes in Yerevan until I found her rehearsing *The Whims of the Butterfly* in an unheated studio. The rest is history.

"Rupen makes a wonderful impression," Levon said. "He's a very good person." He handed Armineh the cooked breads. She stacked them in a long basket lined with a thin towel. Their buzz of activity continued within the bakery microcosm—Armineh placing a ball of raised dough in front of the inconsolable Hovannes. Hovannes punching its lights out. Armineh rolling out the dough and handing it to Levon. Levon baking the bread and passing it back to her.

"I'll help," my Artemis offered. She relieved Armineh from collecting the cooked breads.

"Ach!" She dropped the first piece of hot bread on the ground.

"Careful!" Levon said. "You don't want to feed the evil spirits. It's bad luck."

"It's the spirits above ground we should worry about," Armineh said, taking the next piece of bread.

"I'm sorry. I'm not good at this," Artemis said.

"That's okay, sweetheart," I said, blowing on her burnt fingers. "Bread always comes with a story," Armineh said.

"Really?" Artemis asked.

Armineh nodded. "Once upon a time," she said. "Vahagn, the god of war, fell head over heels for the goddess of love. And what's not to love? She was beautiful and perpetually young, undamaged. She fell in love, too, and they decided to marry. The father of all gods, Aramazd, placed a long piece of *lavash* on the goddess's shoulder on her wedding day. But on her way to the groom's house, the bread fell on the ground. She didn't notice in her excitement, but Aramazd did. He denied the two lovers their wedding, saying 'The one who drops bread on the floor can never be a wife or mother.'"

"Mind her words, Artemis," Levon said. "She talks from experience."

* * *

With each visit to Stalin's fronts, Levon came back a slightly different person. Levon, but through a complicated prism of love and hate. He still introduced me to everyone as his best friend, even the airline clerk who took their tickets as they left for California in 1975.

"He saved my life. For that I owe him everything," I told Haik, who had just finished filling the last envelope with bird shit. Levon considered me his best friend, maybe because we had shared the desert and its offerings. "But he was a tough dude." I used Haik's nomenclature. "We all have faults but the desert had deepened the fissures of his flaws. Sand turns to glass, and glass is sharp enough to do that."

"Maybe it makes you feel superior to judge him. He could have easily found out you were a f-a-k-e." Haik spelled each letter out.

"Did I not just say we all have our faults? Why do you want to make me angry?" I stopped addressing the envelopes.

"I don't want to make you angry. Your type is predisposed to violence. Put a helpless woman in front of you and your rape instinct comes. It's just your nature," Haik said.

"What the hell kind of nonsense are you talking about?"

"You should read Noel Buxton's *Asia Minor's Tendency Towards Violence*. It'll open your eyes."

I wanted to open his eyes and take his eyeballs out.

"He traveled around Anatolia right before the genocide." Haik folded the last of the papers. "He wrote down what he observed."

Like Komitas, I thought. The Armenian priest who travelled Anatolia during the same time, collecting Armenian songs like that lullaby Lucy likes to play. He saved so much from destruction. What did the stupid Englishman do?

"You know what your deal is?" I asked. "Everybody else is at fault for your problems. Take me out of it, you'd find someone else to blame. You're a mental cripple."

"Fuck you!" He spat out. "As if you have any right to judge me."

"See. Look how you talk to someone old enough to be your grandfather. No. Fuck you." As if he'd been a bartender at the Hilton, I'd told this boy way more than I should have and he used it against me. "Are we done? I want to go home for dinner."

"Fine. We'll mail these envelopes tomorrow. Hold onto them until then," he said as he unwrapped two more pieces of chewing gum. He zipped up his backpack and sauntered out the door.

After he left, I crossed out all the addresses. And wrote this in its place in my own cursive: Consulate General of Armenia, 50 N. La Cienega Blvd., # 210, Beverly Hills, CA 90211.

CHAPTER TWENTY-NINE

From time to time, an Armenian prick so rich will hire me, Rupen Najarian, the world's most famous duduk player, to perform at his granddaughter's baptism or his son's wedding (and he is almost always a prick). Viktor, my agent, will pimp me out. And I'll do it because this fellow will hand over—in cash, i.e., tax free—at least $10,000 for no more than three hours of musical masturbation. It's easy money for me, and definitely for Viktor.

This is exactly what happened on a Saturday, not long enough after the pigeon shit episode to forget the little bastard. There I was in my carpet vest and Zegna pants practicing village songs on the duduk with a tired *zurna* player, a drunk *dhol* drummer and Ara in the part of reluctant *dam* player. He hated performing with me, especially now that I spent so much time with Haik, "the Armo," as he liked to call anyone or anything that smacked of a certain grade of Soviet Armenia. He used it to describe clothing of dubious taste as in "that shiny black shirt is so Armo." Or hairstyles, certain foods, even songs. So much so that his mother finally reminded him that he had proposed the family return to Armenia.

"You don't get it, Ma," Ara said. "It's a state of mind."

"What kind of state of mind?" Keran made those air quotation marks over the word 'kind.'"

"A cheap-ass one," he retorted.

My musicians and I were booked that entire Saturday for an epic wedding party. It started at the groom's home at ten in the morning and ended at the newest banquet hall in town, The Black Sea, at two the next morning.

We picked up my American student, Brian, who wanted to practice playing the duduk in front of a live, mostly friendly audience. Ara drove us into the hills above Brand Boulevard, past the tasteful Spanish Revival houses and the modest mid-century homes to the new outcrop of mansions, charming as bank safes. I closed my eyes to rest. The event hadn't even started and I was already winded.

Outside the largest house at the end of the road, a row of limousines lined the circular driveway paved with concrete made to look like cobblestones. Armineh's son-in-law, Aram, saluted from the fleet. It was a hot August day but the men of the groom's family leaned against a grove of Greek-inspired statuary outfitted in expensive wool suits, smoking Cohibas.

"Welcome, Maestro," the father said as we emptied out of Ara's car like circus clowns. "We are grateful you could come today." He offered me a cigar. "This was rolled on a woman's thigh," he said with a wink.

"Oh, how exotic. I'll smoke it later in your family's honor," I said, pulling out my duduk. He tucked a few cigars in my vest pocket as the *dhol* player pounded out a rhythm, wincing with each beat. He was nursing a stage-three hangover. And it felt like I was, too. Without the benefit of liquor.

The groom's family and friends, some forty people, spilled out of the house, flashy as parrots and smelling like a Macy's perfume counter. We were instructed to get into one of the limousines for the drive over to the bride's house.

Aram waved us over from the limo corps. He offered us rosewater cookies from a purple pastry box next to him.

"How much time do we have till the bride's house?" I asked, resting my head on the seat, clammy from the effort of being the public Rupen Najarian.

"We're almost there," he said. "Would you believe the girl lives only two blocks away?"

"Drive a little slower," the *zurna* player said. "Let me finish my cookie."

"Ara, my young handsome friend, did you see all those pretty girls?" The *dhol* player asked my grandson. "That family is well endowed in the chest area."

"Including the men!" the *zurna* player added.

"Women love musicians," Brian said. "You can get all the

pussy you want."

The other musicians agreed, but I kept quiet. No one needs an endorsement from his grandfather.

"Dude, I play the duduk." Not the electric guitar," Ara said as we climbed out of the limo.

"An electric guitar has nothing on the duduk," I said.

"Yeah, even my *dhol* is sexier than a stupid electric guitar," the *dhol* player said as he started drumming again. "It reminds women of the pounding they might get later," he whispered with a wink.

An emissary from the bride's family came out to greet the groom's party with a silver platter piled high with freshly baked *gata*.

We entered the bride's living room, an homage to the world's marble quarries, playing a wedding song from Shatakh, where the groom's father's family came from before the genocide. The bridesmaids had spent the previous evening decorating the room with fresh orange-colored roses and silk bows embellished with real grapes.

"Shit, who pays for all this?" Brian whispered.

"The wedding? The groom's side," I said.

"You're shitting me?"

"I shit you not."

"The girl gets enough jewelry to hock off later," the *dhol* player said.

"So is this where the wedding's going to take place?" Brian asked.

"No, this is decorated just for the pleasure of the family," I said. "They're going to the church after this and then tonight to a banquet hall."

The family women, fresh from the hairdresser's, danced around us, snacking from the gift baskets of baklava and chocolates the groom's family had bestowed the night before when they delivered the bride's veil. The groom's side entered bearing bottles of cognac, flower arrangements, and even more chocolates and baklava.

The ladies danced us into the den, which had been converted into the bride's dressing room. The girl sat on a purple velvet upholstered bench amidst the white fluff of her dress. She lifted her skirt to show her bare feet. Her toenails were manicured with tiny rhinestones.

We played several more folk tunes. Her brother was supposed to enter any minute to help her into her shoes, but he was delayed. The younger cousins had hidden her footwear and wouldn't release them until the groom paid a ransom.

"What was that all about?" Brian asked as we took a little break.

"Well, they're not going to let their girl go that easily. There was a time when girls were scarce. That's why the groom has to pay for everything," I said.

The groom forked over a selection of twenty-dollar bills to the little cousins and we started to play a romantic melody as the bride's brother came in with a pair of ivory silk pumps. He placed a folded hundred-dollar bill in her right shoe for good luck and helped her into the Louboutins. The bridesmaids giggled as they read their names, which they had signed on the red sole of her shoe. I told Brian the girl whose name remained on the sole after a night of dancing would be the next to get married.

"A room full of girls, and *we're* the only men." Brian elbowed Ara. "It's like shooting fish in a barrel."

Ara straightened his shoulders. But he didn't get his chance. We went back into the grand room to play for the guests.

Inside the bride's room, she took her veil and circled it around the heads of her bridesmaids, wishing them love and marriage. Then she handed it to her mother, who kissed her and placed it on her head.

The young bride came out, a shimmering vision, as the family applauded and danced around her. Her father sang her a teary song. I imagined what Lucy's wedding would be like and remembered I wouldn't be around for it.

"So now what happens?" Brian asked as we were driven the two blocks back to Ara's car.

"We're on standby till tonight's party," Ara said.

"Thank the gods," The *dhol* drummer said, "I need a nap."

I nodded.

"No. I mean with them. The couple. What happens next?" Brian asked

"They go to the church and the priest marries them," I said.

"Then they spend hours taking photos in Brand Park," the *zurna* player said. "The photographer takes longer than the priest." He spoke from experience. His daughter had recently gotten married.

"What are your church services like?" Brian asked.

"Well, the priest blesses the rings. Oh, and he puts it on your middle finger." the *dhol* player added, showing us the bird.

"No one's done that for ages," I said, pushing his hand back down.

"No way. The middle finger?" Brian asked.

"Once, long ago, we believed that a vein carrying blood went directly from that finger to the heart," I said. "The Romans called it *veni amori* in Latin, the vein of love."

"I like it when the priest tells the bride to be obedient to her husband," Ara said.

"Be careful what you wish for," I said. "Obedience might bore you."

"We have that bit here, too," Brian said. "Tell me more. What else do I need to know?"

"The crowns," the *dhol* drummer said. "After the vows, the priest crowns the bride and groom."

"Yeah. It looks like they went to Burger King," Ara said.

"I haven't seen that here," Brian said. "What's with the crown thing?"

"They say it's from the Bible," the *dhol* drummer said.

"Sure. Except where did the Bible get it from?" the *zurna* player asked.

"It's Greek," I said. I remembered from my days at the monastery. "It's a recognition of an achievement, like in antiquity when an athlete won, he got a wreath placed on his head."

"I thought it was from the *Gospel of St. John*, the marriage at Cana," the drummer said. "The priest always read that passage when you wear the crowns."

"Everything we do is from before the Bible," I said. "When we all had more in common."

"Then they drink booze," Ara added.

"That we still have in common," Brian said.

"They're still at the church," I said. "It's like Catholic Mass."

"They drink from one cup as a promise to share the good and the bad," the *zurna* player said.

"Then everybody prays and the party starts. Black Sea banquet hall, here we come!" The drummer sang out.

"See. We're not all that weird," Ara said.

"Well, there is the morning *after* the wedding," I said.

"What happens then?" Brian asked.

"Back in the days when the new couple spent their wedding night at the groom's house, his family would send a bowl of red apples if the bride was pure until her wedding night," the *zurna* player said.

"How do they know that?" Brian asked in awe. "Do they watch?" he said with a gleam in his eye.

"No!" the *zurna* player exclaimed. "They look at the bridal sheets the next day."

"That's gross," Ara said. "Do we have to keep talking about this in front of my grandfather?"

"Well, he brought it up," the drummer said.

"No one really does that anymore," I said.

"Yeah, right." The drummer snickered.

CHAPTER THIRTY

The Black Sea's opening, in just three months from start to finish, was a feat in Glendale, where the planning department saddled private projects with the city's own responsibilities—sidewalks, crosswalks, street lighting—they were yours if you wanted to start a business here.

But somehow not for The Black Sea.

The park pigeons rumbled that Karlen had harnessed the planning department's individual weaknesses and past sins like an alternate energy source. In fact, his banquet hall was approved, designed, decorated and staffed, all thanks to human failings and the desire to keep them secret.

I liked him despite his heavy ways. Although Karlen was a mobster, he was a music lover. I suppose the two aren't mutually exclusive. Karlen especially enjoyed the folk arrangements of our musical hero, Komitas. He spent his vacations researching and cataloging Komitas' works according to geography.

I wasn't at The Black Sea that evening because some rich man had paid me enough money to put Ara through another year of college or heaven forbid, I owed Karlen a favor. No. I was there because the universe would have it no other way.

From my vantage point, I could see the benefit of many imperfect characters. The room might as well have been the main salon of the QE2. Czech crystal chandeliers, an interest payment collected from a trembling architect. Silk wallpaper, black and gold carpet and an inlaid wooden dance floor from a family whose generations Karlen had helped smuggle to the U.S. The erect upholstered chairs wrapped in lengths of sheer cream fabric from a factory he protected in Downtown L.A. The circular room smelled pleasantly of cinnamon, jasmine and the fear of others.

I was secretly honored to be the first to play here, but my employer still had to uphold my list of requirements. I expected my own table, where I could invite whomever I wished to join me, and I only played after I sampled the *mezze*. Although beautiful and air-conditioned to within a breath of a blizzard, The Black Sea had to prove itself, culinarily speaking, against the town standards, Arbat on San Fernando Avenue and Yepremian on Central Avenue. It had a good chance because Karlen had poached a chef from Spago. A Lebanese man with a string of Las Vegas debts, or so Armineh had implied. The man knew his way around mousse just as easily as hummus.

"There you are," Armineh said to me but kept surveying the room. She was a frequent wedding guest since her five daughters had married into five different Armenian families. Somehow, Armineh was related to everyone but me. But there was a good reason for that. She wore a floor-length shantung silk gown with a deep purple sheen and an olive cashmere wrap. Delicious as a slender Japanese eggplant.

"I wondered when you'd stop flirting and sit with me," I said.

"I haven't stopped," she said. "Should you be working so much?"

"I'm not working *that* much. I took a paid nap this afternoon. Besides, I'm bored."

She nodded sympathetically as her eyes continued to roam the corners of the room.

"My! I'll be talking about this place all week." She squeezed in next to me. "Karlen has wonderful taste."

"Why don't you ask him out on a date?" I poured her a double brandy as she stretched past the *zurna* player to pinch Ara's cheek.

She lightly slapped the *zurna* player, who in turn had offered her his bread-stuffed cheek.

"Stop. I'm old enough to be his mother." She lowered her eyes. "I like men my own age. Now shut up and eat."

Brian just stared at the heaving table, shocked at its epic nature.

An Armenian banquet is a symphony where you have every instrument known to man present and you're playing a rococo arrangement, like one of those pieces from Rameau or Couperin where every phrase ends in heart shapes and kisses. You pull out all the stops, to belabor another musical analogy. "So can we eat this stuff?" Brian asked.

"Of course," I said. The correct Armenian celebration table is pre-set not only with plates, silverware and a flower arrangement, but with appetizers, or *mezze*, and booze. Even if a priest is coming to say grace, he's not there to bless the starters. "But pace yourself," I warned him. A torturous piece of advice for me to follow, too. The beginning, the cold *mezzes*, is my favorite part of the meal. On the banquet table, the entire Armenian diaspora is represented. Foods from Russia, Lebanon, Syria, Turkey, France, you name it.

"The pickles are marvelous," Armineh said, following a noted benchmark. If the pickles were good, then The Black Sea was a contender for best banquet hall. "Our good luck that the chef had a gambling problem, eh?"

The gold-rimmed chargers heaved with fifteen items—house-cured meats, including a rabbit in gelée, Russian salads of chicken and potato redolent with mayonnaise and dill, hummus seasoned with toasted cumin and a murky green olive oil, eggplant two ways: roasted and pureed, raw beef *chi kufta*, caviar and smoked sturgeon, three different fresh salads, Bulgarian feta, French Brie and Armenian sheep's milk.

And the bread. Charred pita and *lavash* from the *tonir*, still puffy with warm air.

Armineh, the musicians and I sampled the goods while we watched the first act, the "Mermaids," a dance troupe Karlen had hired exclusively for The Black Sea. The six girls, with flat stomachs, long limbs and firm breasts covered lightly in exotic peacock blue costumes, sashayed across the stage with giant feather fans in a fifteen-minute routine. Then the lights dimmed. This was our cue to exit behind the stage and through the courtyard and enter back into the foyer, where the bride and groom waited.

When Karlen gave the nod, the lights came up and we struck up a lively wedding dance, escorting the new couple into the hall. The guests jumped to their feet, clapping to the rhythm. The groom's mother placed a length of *lavash* on each of their shoulders to symbolize prosperity. And of course, the bride made sure not to drop the bread. Then the groom's mother placed a dinner plate from the bride's house on the floor. The bride tried to break it with her shoe, but it was Corelle. A waiter brought a cracked plate from the kitchen and the young lady smashed it with her Louboutins, meaning she had now broken with the past and had entered her mother-in-law's house with a clean slate. And The Black Sea was out one plate.

The bride and groom danced around for the guests to admire them as a married couple, then joined the extended wedding party at a table with so much frippery it looked like a can-can dancer's dressing room.

We went back to our table. Sweat poured down the back of my neck. I wanted to sneak away to the bathroom while a fashionable fluff band sang Armenian pop tunes during the meal. They were definitely Armo.

I was about to get up when I felt someone blow air on the back of my neck. I tightened my insides.

"Try this vodka," Karlen whispered from behind my chair as he poured the clear spirits into my shot glass.

"It's Grey Goose," I said, sitting back down. "I've had that before."

"Sure. But it's *my* Grey Goose," he said. "I have a guy downstairs distilling it from the bruised fruit that Masis Market can't sell. It tastes the same, doesn't it?"

"I suppose," I said. The French are good at a lot of things, but in my opinion, vodka is not one of them. "So you're getting into the counterfeit liquor business?"

"I think of it as recycling," he said. "It's a shame to throw away empty bottles when you can reuse them, no?" The lights drifted back on.

"Looks like you're next, Maestro," Karlen said as the band exited in a blur of rhinestones. He patted my shoulder and strode on stage and introduced me in the voice of a circus ringleader. "Tonight, your host has arranged a very special event, indeed. Introducing the exceptional, the one-and-only Maestro Rupen

Najarian!"

Armineh clapped with two pickled green beans.

And in this heady midst of favorite foods and shots of strong drink, the anticipation of possibility was warm and comforting as a lover's breath.

Some musicians like to perform their best pieces at the end of their concert. I like to play them at the beginning. It's the promise of promise. Possibilitude. Now I know that is not a real word. But humor me.

With my lungs filled with air, my bladder held tight, I played *Tonight the Moon Is Full*. The main lights dimmed and pin spotlights swirled like stars while fresh jasmine flowers floated from the ceiling. Karlen, that romantic.

As white petals snowed on the guests, a few came to rest on Armineh's hair like jewels. She gathered them up, inhaling deeply before blowing them in my direction. Her eyes sparkled under The Black Sea's lighting extravaganza. She looked away and I thought she blushed. I felt my chest tighten and I wondered if it was a heart attack. My feet wobbled but not because the earth had moved.

It wasn't plate tectonics or pastries that had finally done me in. It was . . . *love*? No. I remember thinking I was too old and nearly dead. I couldn't look directly into Armineh's aubergine brilliance again that night.

I tried to calm myself as we played *Maralo*, one of my favorite circle dances. I looked over the expanse of dark heads, bobbing up and down to the rhythm, a haze of swirling cigarette smoke and jasmine about them. The bride and groom danced among a gaggle of their friends.

That's when I saw the halo, ringlets of gold weaving through a black sea. She wore a pale green, sequined dress, a mermaid of yore, with filigree earrings that cascaded onto her glowing shoulders. A groomsman, sharp in his charcoal Versace suit with suede trim, gazed down her plunging neckline through the corner of one eye, as did the waiter who had ascended the basement staircase with a tray of Grey Goose. An older man stood at the shore of the dance floor, watching the golden girl and the rich young man with satisfaction.

Realization slapped me so hard I missed a note. It was the beautiful Christine. *Haik's Christine.* And the older man? He was her father. I knew him because he was on the board of the Alex Theatre. We both watched the couple twirl in their orb of light, holding pinkies, crossing feet and swinging from side to side, laughing breathlessly as the music spun faster and faster, eddying out of control.

This was not the epicenter. No. That's just a random point on the surface. This was the hypocenter. The true point deep underground where an earthquake begins.

I don't smoke. Tobacco, that is, but that night was different. I longed for the textured feel of the leaf, the grassy debris that saliva traps on the tongue. The snip of the tip. The millisecond after it catches on fire. And that first inhale. And the glorious exhale. Watching Christine dance unleashed the same satisfaction as if I'd had sex with two whores and a midget on a trapeze. Nothing could compare to the tingling that swept my body.

"*Papik,*" Ara, who took up the melody when I stopped playing, whispered during the *dhol* drum solo. "Are you okay?"

"Like a tray of warm baklava," I assured my grandson. "Let's take a break." I gave the signal and the *dhol* drummer faded out. I grabbed Ara's arm to steady myself. He escorted me outside next to the giant ceramic pots of dwarf lemon trees. The *dhol* drummer lit up his unfiltered cigarette.

"What are the lemons for, scurvy?" the *zurna* player joked. He hated the nautical theme, having been conscripted in the Russian Navy during the Cold War.

"Hey, those girls were at the house," Ara said as he and Brian drifted off into the crowd of nicotine addicts. "Hi, beautiful ladies, make room for the band," he called out.

Brian nodded in approval.

I waited.

Christine's father, Serge Helian, crossed the patio in long, decisive steps. People unconsciously cleared a path for him as he walked toward me. He wasn't tall, but he was well built. He had light hair like his daughter and the red face of a wine drinker. Côtes du Rhône.

"Maestro, I enjoyed your selection this evening. So touching."
He grabbed my shoulder with both hands. "And congratulations
on that great article in the paper. You're one of our shining lights."
I gave him a Cuban cigar.

"*Merci*, Serge. This cigar has been rolled on a woman's thigh,"
I said.

"Oh? Let's see how tasty it is," he said, lighting it.

"Are you here alone?" I asked.

"No. With the two women in my life. Not my wife and my
mistress, but my daughter and my sister." He chuckled at his own
joke. "You must have met them both before at the Alex. They're
such fans of your music. We all are."

"That's very kind."

"I'm not supposed to be smoking. My daughter is very strict."
He chuckled again. "She takes very good care of me."

"Every man needs a daughter," I said.

With impeccable timing, Christine walked through the doorway in search of her father.

"Here," he said. "It's best if you were the one holding this."
He handed me the Cohiba and I took a puff. It tasted like vanilla,
wood and I suppose a woman's thigh.

"There you are, Papa," she said. "You're not out here up to no
good, are you?" She kissed him on the cheek.

"Do you see anything in my hands?" he asked, holding out
his palms.

She turned to greet me. "Oh!" Recognition flooded her eyes.

"You remember Maestro Rupen," her father said.

"Hello, young lady," I said.

"*Bari gisher*, Maestro Rupen." She looked down at her golden
slippers and convinced herself I didn't remember her from the
stairs.

"Are you having a good time, dear?" I asked Christine.

"Yes. What a beautiful party!" She was grateful for the
new topic.

"And you seem to be getting along with the groom's best
friend." Her father winked at her.

"Papa! Please."

"Well, it wouldn't be the worst thing to be paired up with him, my dear. His family is very well established. They were diamond dealers in Beirut," he explained for my benefit.

"I'm not ready. I'm still in school," she said.

"Your mother and I were married when I was still an intern. You have to get the good ones while they're still around. You're almost twenty-five. That's five years older than we were. Think of the jewelry your mother-in-law would give you."

Something like doubt mixed with fear clouded Christine's tiger's eyes. She nodded. I put out the cigar and excused myself to play the final set.

"You look like you got a mouse," Armineh said as I sat down, brushing against her warm shoulder.

"Something even better, my darling." I got the cat. "Oh, Karlen," I summoned him over with a wave of my shot glass. He refilled it from the Grey Goose bottle and poured himself one in an espresso cup.

"So, Maestro, are you still in need of my special expertise?" he whispered.

"Not anymore, my bald friend."

"Better that way." He toasted me with his cup. "Now when are you going to play something from Komitas?"

CHAPTER THIRTY-ONE

I ironed my new jeans while listening to Alan Hovhaness' *Requiem and Resurrection*. The key to his music is his enduring melodic sense. Melody is nothing more than a bunch of notes strung together on a musical clothesline. The thing we hum when we like a song. Hovhaness once said he believed in melody, and to create melody one needed to go within oneself. His work is happy and luminous, accepting of the world and sure that tomorrow will be even better than today. But what if what lurks inside is not as beautiful as music? What if it's as jarring as a rupture, that harsh boundary between solid, unmovable earth and the dim recess of the underworld?

I tucked that thought back into the darkness. Hovhaness celebrated all that was good and so would I.

"It's scorching outside. Earthquake weather," Lucy said. "I couldn't concentrate in school today." She fanned herself with *Seventeen*.

"Can you still read that magazine when you turn eighteen?" I asked. I tried to iron the space between the belt buckle tabs.

"Oooh. I love this measure," she turned up the stereo. Then turned it back down after the good part had ended. "Jeans, Grandpa? You're not supposed to iron them like slacks, you know."

"Nonsense. Pants are supposed to be pressed, my dear. That is the mark of a proper man," I said. "Do you think they look good?" I held them out in front of me.

"Very fashionable," she replied, trying to erase the crease with her hands.

"Young lady, I worked hard on that!" I swiped the pants back. "Why are they stretchy?" I pulled at the fabric.

"There's Lycra in it," she said. "It's a new thing."

"That's for women's underwear!" I threw them at her.

"Oh, *Papik*. Be cool." She threw them back.

"Where did you get those?" Ara walked into the living room, throwing his books on the ironing board, sweat lining his temples and his face a dark cloud.

"It's a gift." I couldn't lie. I didn't know where to buy sand-blasted jeans.

"From Haik?" Ara asked.

"Yes. Haik." I was embarrassed. "He couldn't afford to pay for his last lesson."

"You spend a lot of time with that Armo. I see him coming out of the studio every other day." Ara licked his lips. "What do you see in him?"

"He just needs extra practice," I said. I should have stopped there but something made me want to defend Haik. "There's no need to call him names." Maybe I said this too firmly. Something changed for Ara, as if I'd pushed him to the brink of some unseen edge and he was hovering, trying to gain his balance. Then he fell.

"Just say it, *Papik*. He's better than me. Otherwise you wouldn't bother with him."

"Ara," was all I could say.

"Maybe he can be your *dam* player." He made it sound like "damn player."

"Are you an idiot?" Lucy asked her brother. "What's the matter with you? Stop yelling at *Papik*. You're the stupid successor."

She didn't know she was the best duduk player in her generation because I never told her.

"You idiot, haven't you noticed that our loving grandpa is MIA half the time? And now he's wearing Guess jeans? Oh yeah. How could you be bothered to notice what's going on with your family. Sucking some *odar's* face at school is your top priority." He made lewd gestures with his tongue. "Don't think I don't know what you're up to."

"He's not a *foreigner*. He's American!"

"He's not one of us."

"Two-face! You can have a life but I can't? Don't think no one knows you're humping that black girl who works at RadioShack but you're scoping out virgin-of-the-month, Nouneh Benzatyan, to get engaged to. That's really enlightened, asshole."

"Don't compare yourself to a man."

"You creep! At least I love Joaquin."

"Everybody we know died so you could fuck that Mexican? Bravo. Pa would be so proud."

"Shut up!" Lucy yelled. She lunged for her brother. He stepped aside and let her fall, hitting her head on the bookshelf.

"Jesus Christ! Enough, you devils!" I threw the iron on the kitchen counter, cracking the Parthenon marble I'd ordered from Greece. I'd never raised my voice to my grandchildren before and I'd never thrown anything larger than a wad of paper.

Lucy started to cry. Ara stormed out, slamming the door behind him. A chunk of the counter fell on the ground. The noise jolted me out of my internal fires.

"Oh, God. I'm so sorry, Lucy *jahn*," I said as I picked up the iron. "Is your head okay?" I helped her to the couch and got some ice to wrap in a towel. She sobbed till she had hiccups. She held the side of her head with both hands.

"Everybody we know isn't dead." She sniffled. "I didn't do anything wrong, did I?"

"There, there," I said.

"So is this guy, Haik, better than Ara?"

"No. He can't play at all. It's a long story." She nodded but didn't ask anything more. "Ara hates playing the duduk. So why's he acting like this?" I asked after a while. I hoped she knew something about her brother.

"I don't know. He wants to be like you, I guess."

"No. Nobody should be like me." I sighed.

Lucy lay down and I sat next to her, holding the icepack on her head.

"I hate him," she said, her voice stuffy.

"He didn't mean it."

"Yeah. He did."

"No. You two just release a lot of energy, like when the earth shakes."

"You talk a lot about earthquakes."

"I do?"

"All the time."

"Your *papik* was born because of an earthquake," I said after awhile.

"You mean during an earthquake?"

"No." I shook my head. "The ground moved, sending your great-*tatik* into labor."

"Wow. That is so cool."

"So, what's going on? Are you really seeing a boy?" I shifted a little so her head was on my lap.

"Would you be mad?" she said into the paunch of my stomach.

"You're not even eighteen. You have a lifetime to be with men." I cringed when the last part left my mouth.

"I know. But I love him, *Papik*." She sat up and put her head on my shoulder.

I kept quiet. It's no use arguing with someone in love.

"Are you upset he's not Armenian?"

"No. I'm not upset." I held her hand up to my face and kissed her palm. "We're all what we should be."

"Ma doesn't know."

"I'll let you tell her. But if you want my advice, tell her sooner than later."

Below us, the grandfather clock chimed in the policeman's apartment.

"I've been thinking of playing the duduk with you more, Grandpa," she said after the clock's last dong. "Would that be okay?"

"I would love that, Lucy *jahn*." I held a lock of her long hair, curling it around my forefinger. "You are a wonderful musician." I didn't know why I had waited so long to say it. We sat and watched the sun wane, leaking its heat so slowly it never realized it lost its power to the night.

CHAPTER THIRTY-TWO

I wore my jeans to Armineh's bakery. Technically, Bakery Opera was now her five daughters' business operation. Armineh to the fifth power, as I branded the girls.

It was a new concept for Glendale Armenians. They called it a "Paris-style" bakery although nobody was sure what that meant. Did they sell baklava on the Champs- Élysées? Just as well. It was my favorite place in the city, and not just because my friends owned it and I could have anything I wished—on the house, of course. They made the regular Armenian and Persian breads but also baked French baguettes, Lebanese-style baklava, Russian cookies, lavish cakes including their famous espresso opera cake, two kinds of Napoleons, chocolate bombs, rum babas, éclairs, pancake-sized chocolate chip cookies and miniature jam cookies by the pound in their trademark purple boxes for Sunday family visits. Even flan, *tres leches* cake and something called a *quesadilla*—the sweet kind, not the one with melted cheese—that the Salvadoran customers first looked upon with suspicion but came to consider acceptable.

"We don't need other customers," Armineh had argued with her daughters over the Latin American pastries. "We have plenty of business now." But the daughters knew that every *quinceañera* needed a traditional sweet. With the new menu additions, the Opera gave the Cuban bakery stiff competition even with my occasional lapses.

Levon opened the first Opera when he immigrated to Los Angeles. With a small loan from the Armenian Benevolent Society, the original, a hole-in-the-wall next to a pawnshop and a free clinic, was in Hollywood where the first wave of Armenians settled. He didn't name the bakery after the famous cake, though. He didn't know the difference between almond sponge and a Scotch-Brite scrubbing sponge. Levon was a lifelong Puccini fan. That's why he called it Bakery Opera.

What Levon didn't know about pastry, he knew about bread. He was the first to build a clay *tonir* in Los Angeles and he used it to make the perfect *lavash*. The toothsome and fire-pocked sheets of bread brought Armenians from all over Southern California to his door. A few years before he died, he followed the exodus to Glendale, bringing his bakery with him into less modest surroundings.

Last year, the daughters decided they needed to change with the times. They hired an interior decorator who painted scenes from *Carmen* on the walls. The decorator, a gay Persian, wearing dress shirts the colors of icing and cufflinks that looked like birthday candles, had this peculiar habit of walking in figure eights. The regulars stopped in front of the windows to watch him mince across the linoleum with bolts of fabric. We didn't believe gay Armenian men existed. Naturally, we thought there were plenty of Persian homosexuals.

He sewed golden brocade curtains and upholstered two opera chairs in plush red velvet. No one was allowed to sit on them for fear of crushing the fabric. He designed a false stage in the window, replete with two dressmaker dummies outfitted as a bullfighter and a gypsy both holding wedding cakes mummified in layers of fondant.

The girls even ordered a musical clock from Salzburg that disgorged Mozart on the hour. It was the talk of the neighborhood for months, to their satisfaction. They played operas to further the ambiance. There was a moment of musical chaos at the top of the hour when the clock chimed in with *The Marriage of Figaro*.

I adored the confusion.

"Haven't seen you at the park lately. Getting too good for us?" Armineh had snuck up behind me as I sampled broken morsels of almond cookies that they offered on a bronze platter on top of the counter. "What in God's name are you wearing, Rupen?"

"My checked shirt and the green beret Lucy got me." I wanted to touch her cheek. I knew it would be soft as old laundered sheets.

"No. Your pants." She pinched my thigh lightly.

"These?" I said breezily. "These are called jeans, Armineh. It is our custom here to wear them." I gestured like an English explorer with an uncomprehending native.

"I know what they are. What are you doing in them?" She enunciated the words.

"It's my new look. What do you think?"

"Makes you look young."

I was momentarily pleased.

"Not a day over eighty." Armineh never gave me a compliment unless it had to do with the duduk. "Actually, they make your legs look too skinny," she said.

"Nonsense. I weigh as much as the bullfighter and Carmen put together. But it might be the Lycra. They make the pants tight." I turned slightly to model my rear end.

She shuddered in mock horror, itching to make a joke. "How are you feeling today?"

"Goodness, Armineh! Just say you don't like the jeans." I kissed her on the head.

I sat down by the window with a cup of mint tea and a few rosewater cookies. A river of traffic flowed by on Verdugo Boulevard. Occasionally, a car would swerve to the side and its occupant would cajole a passerby into running in for a loaf of bread. Finding parking in front of the bakery was as good as winning the lottery.

The pungent vapor steamed up a perfect circle on the window. Armineh's daughters boiled fresh spearmint leaves with a heap of sugar to make the drink. I'd taken up mint tea after remembering an old wives' tale that men shouldn't drink too much of it because it dampened their testosterone. In fact, our bewhiskered ladies were instructed to drink this infusion twice a day. It works, so my theory was if I drank mint tea instead of water it would reduce the raging manliness that was about to kill me. I took another hot, sugary sip.

"We have work to do, Maestro." Haik's raspy disembodied voice whispered in my ear. He placed a box of very large rubber bands in front of me.

The first act of *Tamerlano* started on the stereo. It was the scene where the defeated Ottoman Sultan is brought in chains to the court of Tamerlane, the emperor of the Tartars.

"You should quit smoking," I counseled him. "You sound like a carrot being grated." The music picked up.

"*Vonts*? Whatever. Just keep the lecture to yourself." He dismissed me. "You really like these rosewater cookies, don't you?" he said, helping himself to one from my plate as he sat down.

"I suppose so. Why?"

"You eat them every time you come in here."

"I haven't been to the bakery for a while. How do you know?"

"I've seen you in here before."

"What do you mean 'before'?"

"I don't know. Before we talked at the park." Haik looked embarrassed. "You used to come in every Tuesday and eat all the samples. Sometimes, I watched you from over there." He pointed to the little market area where you could shop for prepackaged goodies.

"Why did you watch? You didn't know me."

He shook his head. "Everybody knows who you are. I was just curious, I guess. Then my grandmother told me who you were. Who you *really* are." His tone changed. "Be ready at eleven tonight." He got up from the table.

"I'm not in the mood to go out tonight. I think I'll take it easy." I leaned back and placed my hands behind my head, the picture of relaxation.

He raised his thick eyebrows. "Pardon?" He feigned deafness, cocking one ear. "I don't think I heard you, my oppressor."

"Oh, I'm the oppressor? You treat me like your slave," I hissed, straightening back up.

"Change is good. Not a bad thing to see what the other side is like."

"Change *is* good," I agreed. "So tonight I thought I'd listen to some music first. I was thinking of Ella Fitzgerald, since we're in the mood for shaking things up. Then barbecue some *lule* kebabs.

I have a recipe that would kill you. The secret ingredient is toasted allspice. Then, a little later, I'll go have a brandy with Serge Helian. You know him? I ran into him and his very lovely daughter at a party last week. He invited me to visit his gorgeous home so he can show me his stamp collection. Can you believe he has stamps from every single country? Even principalities. Have you ever seen a stamp from Andorra?" I slurped my tea loudly.

Haik's face was a meter of emotion. First impatience, then boredom followed by confusion and finally fear.

"Please . . ." He trailed off. He didn't know if he should sit or stand.

"Please what?" I have to admit this was an enjoyable situation. Like having a pet perform tricks.

"Please don't say anything," he said.

Roll over, Haik.

"To whom?"

"Christine's father."

Now shake a paw.

"Oh, you know him, too?" I rubbed his nose in it.

"No. She never . . . I mean, we've never met."

"Why? It's not like you're black or something."

Now beg.

"I'm the black of Armenia." He looked down at his slender hands. Hands that had instructed me to pile donuts, cut letters without my glasses, steal traffic cones, sacrifice my tomato plant, address envelopes, mail bird shit.

"Does your young friend want something?" Armineh asked, taking my empty cup, her hand lingered on my shoulder.

"Certainly," I said. "He's just having trouble making up his mind what it is he wants."

"That happens a lot in here," she said over her shoulder as she walked back to the register.

"What do you want?" he asked after a couple minutes of defeated silence. "Ask me anything."

"Anything?" I leaned in, "That's a very generous offer. Why do you care so much? She's just a girl. There are plenty more beans in the pot."

"None of your fucking business." He felt his left pocket for his cigarettes. His hands trembled. There was a thin line of sweat above his upper lip. "Well. What do you want?" He repeated the question, softening his tone.

"Wait. I get it." It dawned on me right then and there in the heady aroma of vanilla and sugar, of mint and roses. That uncontrollable unleashing of the soul, like when you hear Mahler's Ninth for the first time. The intensity of a tsunami hitting shore. The release that only comes with ejaculation. "You love her, don't you?"

Haik said nothing.

"Ha! You love her!" I exclaimed maybe a little too loudly. Armineh eyed me from the counter. "You poor, terrible idiot!"

Haik got up, knocking over a display of candied almonds as he wove himself through the afternoon crowd surging in for bread and cookies.

"So what's it worth to you, my young punk?" I called after him. I laughed, slapping the table like the homeless man in front of the main library. I laughed and laughed till I coughed and pissed a little.

It was almost four in the afternoon. I thought I'd go to the park. Triumphant.

"Armineh, my darling flower," I called out. She'd timed a visit to the kitchen during my spectacle. "Shall we walk over?"

"Feeling lucky, are you?" she asked, gathering her shawl.

"I have a premonition I'll beat you at backgammon today."

I got up and stretched my arms wide to the ceiling. Jeans do feel more comfortable!

CHAPTER THIRTY-THREE

Now that I had the upper hand, I willed everything to go back to the way it was pre-Haik. Of course, I knew you could never go back. But still, I wished for it just the same.

I immediately put a stop to his Tuesday trysts in my home, although I'll admit I enjoyed Haik's X-rated accounts. Twenty strands of Christine's hair resided in my notebook. But it's not like I aimed to make a wig. No more late nights of small crimes. And then there was the question of the 25K. I wanted that back. Haik would not get away with insulting me and taking my money. It was a recession year, after all.

In the months I'd come to know Haik, he'd never told me where he lived. I knew he used to walk home from the hospital and it would take him about fifteen minutes. That might put him in Maple Park, or the slums of Glendale as Ara called it. Maple Park was so Armo even the dogs barked with a Russian accent. It was rapidly becoming an all-Armenian enclave, wedging eight to ten recent immigrants into an apartment. There would be a lot of boys named Haik there.

The hospital was probably the best place to start my stalking. He often worked in the ER where he'd first seen Christine on her rotation. That was where I'd wait for him. I had a little chest pain anyway.

I asked the admitting nurse if she knew of an orderly named Haik. "Haik Bedrossian or Haik Topalian?" she asked, not bothering to look up from the newspaper she hid between patients' charts.

"The tall, thin one with short hair," I said.

"They're both tall and thin," she replied, turning the page.

The nurse put me in one of the cubicles with the curtains

drawn. Its white walls and shiny floor hypnotized me to sleep. I napped on the bed for a couple of hours, waiting to see the doctor.

"Knock. Knock. I'm Dr. Helian," a breathy voice woke me up. I rubbed my eyes. It was *her*. "*Barev*, Christine *jahn*," I gulped. She held my chart in her hand, the look of a wild rabbit in her eyes.

"Oh, Maestro. I am sorry to see you here." She bit her lip and opened up my chart. I knew what she meant. I felt the same way.

"Your heart hurts?" She asked in Armenian, not looking up from the chart. She twirled a lock of her golden hair on a pen. She still didn't know that Haik and I were personally acquainted.

"Yes." I was the wild rabbit now. Fearful. As if the earth had moved under my safe burrow, sending sharp stones on my head.

"I'm sorry, dear. Is there another doctor I can see?"

"Don't worry, Maestro. I've taken care of many men before," she said, not looking up from the chart.

"It's just that . . ."

She kept reading. Then her eyes widened. "I see."

She knew. She knew I was dying.

"Please don't tell your father," I said.

She shook her head. "Doctors can't discuss their patients with others."

"Of course. *Merci, achik jahn*." But I knew for certain there was no such rule stopping patients from discussing their doctors. "So, are you in love with that young man from the wedding? Or is there someone else?"

She blushed. "Let's concentrate on how you feel."

Christine sent me for a cardiogram which took another hour of waiting. The shift changed and it was time for her to go but she stayed.

"Well, your P-wave looks a little off," she said, returning with the results.

"I like P-waves," I said. "It's the first signal to reach the seismograph. You know, like a warning jolt before the big shaking."

"It's not quite the same in cardiology," she said. "I want you to know there's nothing to worry about right now. I've prescribed a potassium supplement that you can pick up. Just take it easy."

I heard the first bar of the Armenian National Anthem. *Let*

Armenia be glorious forever. I bolted from the bed.

"Maestro, please," she said, putting a hand on my shoulder. "That's just one of the orderly's phones ringing. Everything's okay. See."

She pulled back the curtain, exposing me to Haik in his ugly green scrubs, phone to his ear. Haik looked from me to Christine. Christine looked at Haik, then me. I looked at my prescription for potassium.

"What are you doing here?" Haik asked, dropping the phone on the shiny floor with a clack. "What did you say to her?" He rushed toward me and grabbed me by the shoulders.

"Haik!" Christine exclaimed. "What is the matter with you? Take your hands off of Maestro Rupen!"

The nurses at the work station looked up. Christine put her hand up like she had the situation under control.

"He's a liar," Haik hissed.

"Maestro Rupen, I apologize." Christine's face turned pink.

"How dare you talk to my patient like that!" She said through clenched teeth, pushing past Haik. "Come with me before you embarrass me any further."

"Look what you did," he said to me as he picked up the broken phone.

"You did that all by yourself," I said with a little smile. I took my time putting on my clothes. Savoring the moment.

On my way to the pharmacy, I saw Haik push a side door open like he was picking a fight with it. I tracked him as he stomped outside. He bummed a cigarette off of a ponytailed Latino dishwasher whose tattoo sneaked up from above his turtleneck. They sat on the ledge by the parked ambulances and faced the sun, drenching themselves in the last rays of UV and Vitamin D. The nicotine seemed to calm him down.

They argued about the previous Sunday's soccer game, Kitchen vs. Orderlies: 3:1 in Kitchen's favor.

"You can't make a goal if you kick like a fat girl," the dishwasher explained.

"How about if I kick like a skinny girl?"

"*Cabrón.*"

"*Pendejo*," Haik responded in a Russian-accented Spanish.
"Can I ask you something?" the dishwasher asked.
"What?" Haik drew on his cigarette.
"Why you guys so angry at the Turks?"
Haik's muscles tensed up. "They took everything from us. Killed us. Then they tried to get rid of any proof that we were ever there. *Comprende?*"
"Yeah, Homes. My grams was Navajo. But I still gotta live here."
"I can't forgive him."
"Who you talkin' about? God?"
"Nobody."
"Is it true them Turks never run in the L.A. Marathon 'cause they'll get their asses shot up?"
"You have to ask them." He thanked the man for the cigarette with his accented *gracias* and swiped his ID badge at the side entrance that led to the basement. Home of his grand gesture. The door locked behind him.

* * *

I waited by the BMW the next morning at six when Haik clocked out. He turned off the car alarm by Braille as he felt around in his pocket, mesmerized by the fiery sunrise. When he saw me, it was too late to lock the doors. I'd already opened the passenger's side.
"Did you think I wasn't going to find you?" I asked in the meanest voice I could summon.
"Why did you have to come here? he asked. "She's very angry with me."
"I had a little chest pain," I said. "I didn't tell her anything."
"What do you want from me?" he asked with the resignation built from years of doing others' bidding."
"How about you make me breakfast?"
"Here?"
"Why? Do you cook *here* often?" I gestured to Space 252 and its surroundings.

"You want to come over to my house?" He was incredulous.
"Why, thank you. I don't mind if I do, especially since break-fast is one of my favorite three meals." I got into the passenger side of the car and buckled myself in. "Everyone will be sleeping. No." He paced outside my door. "I'll be very quiet." He huffed and grunted but he walked around and got in, slamming the door. I watched how he handled the car as we exited the garage. There's a way to decelerate by downshifting, even though it was automatic transmission.

He drove us to the bungalow on Maple Street, the car squealing his displeasure at every corner. I'd have to get the tires realigned when I reclaimed my property.

A sentry of sunflowers long past their bloom lined the perimeter of the yard. We parked behind the Ford Fairmont on the cracked driveway, bumpy from the outstretched roots of the neighbor's sycamore tree.

Haik's grandmother, in a long black wool skirt and matching sweater, stood outside in the thin morning light, searching the win-dowsill.

"I left an apricot cake here to cool. Someone took it!" she told Haik. She hadn't noticed me yet. She turned around and caught a honeybee with her bare hands. I knew only one girl who could do that. But it couldn't be her. She was dead.

"It's okay, *Tatik*. I'll look for it later."

"Oh, you brought *him* home!" she said at the top of her voice when she saw me. She let the bee go. "Maybe *he* took the cake!" She pointed a finger in my direction and laughed like she'd told the best joke ever. "He's a trouble maker!"

"*Tatik*, shhh. Okay?"

Haik's grandmother ignored him. "Such a cute little boy. And have you seen him play the duduk? One day, he may be as good as his father," she said, taking my stubbly chin between her fingers.

"Come on. Let's go inside." Haik shepherded his grandmother to the doorway.

She nodded, wiping her eyes. "But check if he has the cake," she whispered as Haik opened the screen door and pointed her to the bedroom.

"I promise," Haik said. "Now why don't you take a nap?" Ruby shuffled away in her bedroom slippers. Haik finally looked at me and said, "Come inside. It's not like your home or anything."

I nodded in agreement.

He turned his back in embarrassment and went into the kitchen, its beige linoleum floor cracked stiff in places. Haik put the samovar on the stove. "Tea okay, Maestro?" He didn't wait for my response before turning it on.

A large brown couch and an enormous dining table took up the entire living room. Every surface was covered with crochet and hand knotted rugs—no doubt Ruby's latter-day handiwork. A blue ceramic *achk* hung on a silver thread from the door to ward against the envy of others. No risk here, I thought.

I could see the backyard from the living room. Through the sliding glass door, a tall block of stone soared in the dry, uncut grass, a modern dolmen of sorts. I went outside to take a closer look. It was grey basalt. The artist had carved intricate crosses that looked as fine as lace but on different facets of the pillar, leaving some of the surface in its natural form and polishing others. My fingers had a mind of their own, drawn to the uneven surfaces. I followed the meandering patterns; modern yet ancient. Someone must have worked on it already for a long time. It was a minor piece of architecture.

It reminded me of the ancient stones you find in fields and the shores of lakes and rivers all over Armenia. Ornate as carpets. A monument to eternity.

"Rupen, you bad little boy," Ruby whispered behind me.

"Aren't you supposed to be in bed?" I asked, snatching my fingers back.

"Shhh. I saw you steal the duduk. But I won't tell anyone if you come to the pond with me. I'll show you how to catch a wasp without it stinging you. There's a trick to it. Come on!" She took my hand and led me around the yard. "Hurry before my mother finds us."

"Why, Ruby? What did you tell him?" I asked but she didn't understand.

She pulled me to the side of the house, looking for the pond from our youth. "Now, isn't this better than being cooped up inside the barn with all that smelly yarn?" Ruby giggled.

* * *

Ruby came from a family of famed carpet weavers. That meant the balance of estrogen was higher than testosterone in the family. Women were simply better at the job. In Ruby's family, the men had died off, been killed in assorted pogroms, run away or failed to produce any males. The clan of widowed aunts, unmarriageable second cousins and young girls made the most beautiful rugs in our valley. They were known for their ram's horn designs and they signed each carpet with a small ewe at the right bottom corner, in yarn dyed red with cochineal. Ruby's great-grandmother had heard from her great-grandmother that the family's wares were found in homes as far away as Florence.

They lived on the other side of the hill behind our house, on the border of the Armenian part of the village. My father had known them a long time. They had traded with my family for a century for our sheep's wool, which Ruby's grandmother claimed was the best quality in a hundred miles.

Ruby wasn't interested in carpets. She didn't care about the family history or that there was a record of Armenian textiles dating back to the first century. Ruby was great at catching the winged and torturing boys who were younger than her. She knew how to skim rocks. Which pond had the laziest fish. Where the first berries of spring grew. She was the first to show me the dinosaur egg stone. I must have been five years old. Ruby. Ruby. Ruby.

* * *

In the kitchen, Haik scrambled eggs over a skillet of potatoes and peppers awash in butter. He had the look of a man who had spat in the food. He set out a plate of cured *basturma* and other cold cuts, Bulgarian feta, olives, *lavash* and homemade apricot jam. He poured our tea into clear glasses with silver handles. Haik carried everything on a tarnished bronze tray to the dining table. I didn't help.

"Here's your food." He thumped the tray on the table.

"Did you know *basturma* is the forefather of pastrami?" I asked, making myself a sandwich of jam and *basturma* on *lavash*. Cured meat with preserves is my favorite breakfast side dish. This *basturma* was dark, marbled with fat and covered with a layer of spicy *chaman* paste.

"What's pastrami?" He sat down but didn't take a plate.

"It's like *basturma*, but less tasty."

Haik grabbed a slice with his fingers and lowered it into his mouth.

"You know, it's Turkish in origin." I'd waited till he started chewing to needle him. "Turkish soldiers put salted beef in their saddle bags and pressed it with their thighs on their long rides.

"Long pillages," Haik corrected me. He slurped his tea and smacked his lips.

"Is that a *khachkar* you're working on in the back?" I asked.

"Yeah. I guess you can call it that," he said after a long pause, admitting he was the artist. "But it's not religious or anything."

"The very first cross stones weren't religious. The markings were actually an equal grid and later converted to a cross after the king accepted Christianity," I said. I'd studied them at the monastery. *Khachkars* were placed on roads to assist travelers; they served as talismans. They were also carved to commemorate exceptional events like battles and miracles.

"It's interesting," I said after a moment.

He lowered his eyes to his plate and permitted himself a small smile.

I didn't tell him it was the most amazing sculpture I'd ever seen. No. Right then, I couldn't permit myself to encourage my blackmailer. All I gave him was the stale crumb of "interesting."

That's how his mother, tucked in the last remnants of sleep and a mothy tan robe, found us.

"Oh my goodness! You brought a guest home? I would have cleaned up a little last night if I'd known. . . " her voice trailed off as she tried to place me.

190

Haik stood up, unsure what to do, so he glared at me. His mother's eyes widened. "Rupen Najarian? *In my house?*" She clasped and unclasped her hands. "Gracious! Why didn't you tell me, Haik? Oh, Maestro, your 1969 concert in Moscow! We still watch it on video. And when we won those two tickets for your birthday concert, I knew my mother would enjoy it so much. She's always been such a fan."

"Ma, calm down," Haik said. "I made eggs." He sat back down, his fingers pressed to his mouth for a minute, afraid of what I would say to his mother. Then he turned to me and said. "Maestro, please meet my mother, Hasmik Bedrosyan."

I stood up and shook her hand. She looked like Ruby, but less spirited.

"Rupen Najarian is eating eggs in my house," she said in disbelief, impervious to her son's discomfort. "I beg you, please sit down."

"Thank you. Your son is a very good cook. The tarragon is a great touch." I kissed my fingers like a French chef.

She tittered. "He learned that from me."

"I. We. My husband and I were so worried," she said, her eyes darting to Haik's bowed head."

"Oh?" I asked.

"Well, the car. The late hours. We thought he was getting into trouble. I'm so glad he is with you. You know, a good influence."

Haik growled under his breath.

"I'll do my best, Madame. Would you mind terribly if I borrow your son for a minute?"

She held out her arms as if to say, help yourself to anything I have. I pulled him onto the front porch.

"Boy, I expect you in the lobby of my apartment tomorrow at 6:30 P.M., and wear something nice. I have something for you to do." With that, I said goodbye, a flurry of questions, exclamations and seething in my wake. Ruby waved to me from the bushes in the side yard.

"I didn't take the cake," I told her.

"It's okay if you did. Apricot was always your favorite."

* * *

191

Haik waited for me downstairs at our designated time. He stood by the cacti, testing the needles of a saguaro with the tip of his finger.

"Great! You're here!" I boomed, startling him to prick his finger.

He sucked the blood from the puncture but didn't say anything. He was wearing black pants and a white shirt. He could have moonlighted as a waiter at The Black Sea.

"I hope you're hungry. I made reservations for dinner. We're going to Newport Beach."

"That's an hour and a half away!" he said, stopping by the large glass doors.

"I'm not asking you to drive me to Mecca. Get going." I nudged him toward the car. I slid in as soon as he clicked the doors open just in case he decided to rush off without me.

"This car sure is smooth," I said once we got on the freeway. "Did you rotate the tires?"

He nodded. I quizzed him on the car the entire journey. When was the oil changed? A month ago. How were the windshield wipers? In good shape, but the replacements were $30. He looked at me sideways, but I didn't let on the car would be mine soon.

I didn't notice when we got off the Jamboree exit until Haik asked if he should turn left or right. Left.

"There it is. I've been *dying*"—a little joke entirely at my expense—"to try this place." I pointed to a restaurant in a mini mall next to the gas station. A neon blue sign read *The Bosphorus.*

"You brought me to a Turkish restaurant?" Haik asked in disbelief. He parked in front, the car still running.

"I thought you might enjoy the food. The *L.A. Times* said the chef is great."

"I'm not going to eat anything," he warned, still strapped to his seat.

"Really? Maybe a quick call to Serge Helian would get your appetite going."

"Okay. Fine. But I won't enjoy it." He turned off the engine, got out and slammed the door.

"I will," I said feeling superior.

Inside, the restaurant was decorated like a seaside tavern. Wooden benches and chairs on a tile floor. A mural of fishing boats at sea on one wall faced an advertisement for Efes Pilsener on the opposite wall.

"I thought they weren't supposed to drink." Haik clenched his fists as he sat down on a wooden chair. He didn't acknowledge our host, who was also the owner.

This was my first encounter with a restaurant full of Turkish people. I noticed my fists were clenched, too. There were no Turkish restaurants in the tri-city area, and for good reason. Someone would burn it to the ground. No matter. We were in Orange County. Very few here understood or cared about the Molotov cocktail of our relationship.

An old man in a vest fiddled on the *kemenche*. A sullen youngster played percussion on the *darbuka*.

The owner weaved himself around the musicians with a tray of hot tea flavored with cinnamon. He poured it out in a thin stream into two glasses and handed us the menus.

I ordered for both of us, since Haik refused to participate. For *mezze*, we had the spicy tomato dip and small warm pastries stuffed with sharp cheese and dried thyme. Then, they brought us minced beef Adana kebabs on a plate of rice pilaf, the spicy fat drippings soaking into the rice. I also ordered Iskender kebab, a layer of thinly sliced grilled lamb basted in tomato sauce, served over chopped up pieces of flat bread and drizzled with melted butter and yogurt. All of which you had to eat before it turned into a congealed mess.

"This tastes just like regular food," Haik said. He meant it tasted like Armenian food.

"What did you think it would taste like? Sushi?"

"I don't know."

"Delicious, yes?"

"Whatever." Haik had cleaned his plate.

"We're not done yet," I said after the meal. "Now that you've enjoyed someone's hard labor, you have to say thank you." I motioned for the host to call the chef.

"I'm not saying anything," Haik hissed.

"Serge Helian. I've got his number." I patted my shirt pocket for effect.

A few minutes later, the chef, a wiry man with a thick black mustache, came to our table. I applauded and motioned for Haik to say something. "You must be very pleased with your cooking," Haik said through a tight jaw. The chef took that as a compliment.

"Come back again," the owner called out as we walked out the door.

"I doubt he'd say that if he knew we were from Glendale," Haik muttered. "Probably chase us with a butcher knife. Turks love a good throat cutting."

We drove back in silence, the air occasionally punctuated by a garlic-infused burp. He dropped me off at the front entrance just as Ara turned into the garage.

My grandson and I had an uneasy truce since the argument. Ara hadn't apologized and neither had I. He pretended not to see Haik so we could keep détente.

CHAPTER THIRTY-FOUR

I summoned Haik to the bakery soon after our dinner at The Bosphorus. Armineh wasn't there but I'd cornered the best table in the house, right next to Carmen and the bullfighter. It had a perfect view of the entrance, where I watched him pull the BMW into a prime parking spot in front. A lucky omen. He got out, his shoulders sloping, and entered the bakery. He looked at me warily as he sat down.

"I got your note at the hospital. So why did you want to see me?" he asked. "You want to drag me around town?"

"No. You don't have to drive me anywhere from now on."

"That's a relief." He relaxed a little, almost his old self. "I need to work more hours."

"Well, I've been thinking," I said, picking the lint off of Carmen's red skirt. "I can drive myself."

"Huh? Did you get a car?"

"Yes. You were right to have chosen a BMW. They are good cars. I'm glad I have one."

"Really? Where is it?" He sat up straight, interested.

I looked outside the window and he followed my stare. Then, I turned my gaze on him and stuck my palm out. "Keys, please," I said.

"What the hell?" He shot up, upsetting what was left of my mint tea. "You can't do that!"

"Control yourself, boy. You make a mess every time you come in here." I sopped up the tea with my handkerchief. I was glad Armineh had already left for the day. "You're like a billy goat."

"I love that car. I worked . . ." He trailed off.

"What? You worked hard for it? Is that what you wanted to say?"

He sat back down, smoldering in his self-made briquettes.

"I suppose it depends if you want a chance with Christine," I said. "Although you made a pretty good mess the other day."

And on cue, Serge Helian walked in dressed in turquoise golf pants and a plaid hat. To the inexperienced eye it might have looked like kismet. But Armineh told me he came for Napoleons every Wednesday after his game. He didn't see us, but we saw him. And that was enough.

"Make sure you only put super unleaded from Chevron in it." Haik threw the keys on the table, those dark eyes boiling over.

"I will. I've heard a BMW impresses women." I called after him as he fled my taunts.

Haik didn't look at the car when he walked back toward the hospital but he touched it lightly, sending it a love note with his fingers.

I snuck out before Serge Helian could see me. Two freshly blonded ladies lunged for my table.

It had been years since I'd driven. How hard could it be to remember? I sat behind the soft leather covered wheel. I was too nervous to turn on the engine, so I checked the glove compartment for the manual. There was a big bag of weed on top of the booklet. I lit up a joint right then and there on the street. If Haik had taught me anything, it was that no one suspects old people of being criminals.

Serge Helian strode out with his box of Napoleons. I ducked, exhaling smoke on the foot pedals.

Fifteen minutes later, I was calmer, maybe even a little don't-worry-be-happy. But just a little. I looked at myself in the rearview mirror. I wanted to look good when Armineh saw me pull up at the park. I christened the car Aralez after the dog god that could cure a person with a lick of his tongue.

I drove up and down Brand Boulevard—I believe the correct term is "cruising"—at twenty miles an hour till I got the feel of the engine. If I pressed it a little too hard, it shot out from under me. The other drivers gave me dirty looks as they passed by. I pretended to look for a parking space.

Armineh was the first to spot me when I screeched into a space on the corner closest to Trader Joe's. I bumped the delivery truck behind and the Honda in front. The girl who drove the Honda wouldn't mind. The driver's side was keyed up anyway. It was almost 5 P.M. and the park was full. Armineh's eyebrows arched so high they disappeared into her hairline. I hoped that meant she was impressed. She said something to Robert and Hovannes and they immediately crossed the street. By immediately, I mean it took them a few minutes to put away their snacks, find their sweaters and wheel Hovannes over.

"When did you take up driving?" Armineh asked. "Are you too tired to walk?"

"Why would he be tired?" Hovannes asked.

"Unlike you, he doesn't have a magical electric chair to get around town." They bared their swollen gums at each other.

"I've just been lazy," I said, patting the car on its hood. "You know how us celebrities are." I huffed on my fingernails and polished them on my sweater.

"It looks like the car your student whatshisname drives, doesn't it?" Hovannes asked. His mongoose eyes always noticed everything. He hadn't forgiven me for my outburst from months ago.

"I can't get a thing past you," I flattered him. "I bought the car from the boy."

"Really. Why? I thought you only liked brand new things," Robert said.

"His family has some money trouble. I wanted to help out," I said just as I'd rehearsed in the car.

"That's very generous of you." Robert said, patting me on the arm.

"How great you can afford to help them," Hovannes added somewhat coldly.

"Well, what are we waiting for?" Armineh asked. "Let's go for a ride!"

They piled in without asking.

"Why does the car smell like skunk?" Hovannes asked.

"Not skunk. It smells like—nah—maybe it's skunk," Robert said.

"Um, yes, it got sprayed last night," I said rolling down the windows. "Damn animals."

We drove up Scholl Canyon to the golf range, hoping to catch the sunset.

"Drive faster than this silly forty miles an hour," Armineh commanded.

Happy to do her bidding, I took a deep breath and pressed my foot down, charging up the hill at eighty miles an hour. They whooped like teenagers.

"This is one powerful car. It must have been expensive. How did Haik get it?" Robert asked, knuckles white.

"He probably stole it," Hovanness said with a snort.

"Please. Do you think I would be involved with a criminal?" I asked. "It was a gift from a hospital patient when he died. There's a will and everything."

We sat on the wall at the top of the canyon, the sunset displaying tropical shades of red and orange. We shared the same view the Tongva Indians had enjoyed while they hunted deer up in the canyons—not knowing that José Maria Verdugo, a strapping Spanish corporal, would own this vista as he surveyed his new land grant, any more than Verdugo knew that Charles Lindbergh would admire it 132 years later as he took off on the first transcontinental flight to New York. The same view that four friends with so many secrets enjoyed at that quiet moment.

"It looks like downtown is on fire," Robert said.

"Downtown was on fire," Armineh said.

"Well, you know what I mean," he said. "It's just beautiful. So alive."

I put my arm around Armineh and put my other arm around Robert so they wouldn't suspect. But I only squeezed her side.

As the sky darkened, a crescent moon appeared.

"It's the beginning of the new month," Hovanness said.

"My father used to tell us it was good luck to show the waxing moon your money," Robert said, reaching into his wallet for a dollar bill. "It means you'll make more during the month."

I don't believe any of that nonsense," Hovanness said.

"I do," Armineh said, snatching Robert's dollar bill and tucking it into her blouse. "See, I made a buck already."

They fought with each other to see who would drive back. Armineh won. She adjusted the seat and mirror, and proceeded to refresh her lipstick.

"Is that for the benefit of the police when they stop you?" Hovannes asked.

She brushed him off and drove remarkably well until she ran into a bank of trashcans on the last hairpin turn on Chevy Chase Drive. Robert drove us the rest of the way. I left the car on the street until I could explain it to the family.

I recited the same story at home.

"That's nice of you, Pa, but you didn't have to buy the car," my daughter said as she stirred a pot of *borscht*. "You don't like to drive."

"Not true. You always insist on driving me."

Ara looked up from his homework, but didn't say a word. He knew I was lying about something and it had to do with Haik.

"I like it," I continued. "I feel free."

"My father, the eighty-four-year-old stud." Keran laughed as she handed me a bowl of soup. "You'll get all the ladies."

I only needed one.

I took the car everywhere. Even if my destination was just a couple streets away, I drove my roaring beast. I pulled up to the bank in it.

"You should have gotten your loan through us," the manager chided me.

"I paid cash," I told her.

I parked in the red zone in front of the grocery store to buy coffee.

"I knew that car had to be yours. Not the boy you came in with last time," the pretty clerk said.

"Oh, he was just borrowing it." I twirled my bag of freshly ground coffee.

I maneuvered it into St. Gregory's parking lot. The priest blessed it. (I didn't tell him I had named the car after a pagan god.)

I played Hovhaness' *Requiem and Resurrection* loudly as I drove down the street.

* * *

Within days I'd replaced Armineh's limo-driving son-in-law, Aram, as her personal chauffeur. She only felt a momentary guilt that disappeared when she realized I wouldn't be around forever. And I didn't argue. Every moment I could spend with her gave me new meaning.

"Rupen, do you think we can drive to the beach?" she'd whisper during Sunday services.

It was hard for me to veto a trip to the ocean. The cacophony of waves rushing to shore was the sound of a little boy's salvation. But our jaunts were all-day trips because I refused to take the freeway. We drove through Los Feliz, admiring the beautiful homes that surrounded Griffith Park. My favorite was a Moorish-style walled house painted white with blue trim. Bougainvillea the colors of a psychedelic Pucci scarf lined the narrow stairway leading to the roof. Then down through the close quarters of Koreatown and the stately expanse of Hancock Park. From there, I took Venice Boulevard in all its gritty splendor down to the ocean.

Sometimes we'd stay in Venice, listening to the crazy turbaned man playing the guitar on his roller skates, or we'd drive along Pacific Coast Highway to Malibu. Wherever we ended up we always took off our shoes and walked into the ocean in our Sunday best, the icy water shocking the very core of our souls.

"Think of it as a free spa treatment for your feet," Armineh responded to my brrring. I thought of it more like shock therapy.

We sat just yards away from the surf on a white towel I found in the trunk of the car.

"Why does this towel say *Property of Glendale General?*" Armineh asked. "Is it from your doctor's visit?"

"I'm there twice a month these days."

"Oh my. What's that like?"

"What? Seeing the doctor? I could sleep through it. I don't know why I keep going."

"No." She paused, trying to figure out how to phrase her question. "I mean knowing. Knowing you have a certain amount of time as opposed to being surprised."

"It's good and bad. I'd rather be hit on the head from behind. Let me ask you something," I continued. "Why do you always smell like cloves?" I mainly wanted to change the subject.

"That is a very indiscreet question." She slapped me on the arm.

"No, really. Is it all the baking?"

"Do you like the way it smells?" She turned pink. It took a lot to make her blush.

"Yes. It reminds me of a dark wooden chest filled with treasure. Maybe pearls and cinnabar."

"I keep a couple cloves in my brassiere. Look." She fished out a bud. "My mother used to do it and years later when she was gone, I wanted to be just like her."

"It smells very nice." I took the bud from her hand and slipped it into my mouth. She put her head on my shoulder, the blush traveling down her neck. I wrapped her in my arms.

We stayed till late afternoon. Then we drove the two hours back before the sun set. I didn't like to drive at night.

"Pick me up tomorrow," Armineh would say when I dropped her home. "If you feel up to it," she'd hasten to add.

I'd never felt as carefree as I did in those days driving my Aralez down the palm-tree covered streets. The finely calibrated air-conditioning humming while the seat warmer toasted my buttocks. Perfection. I even forgot I was dying until I wet myself or worse, couldn't take a piss.

CHAPTER THIRTY-FIVE

Joy, however, eluded Haik. I came to find out he felt unmoored without his status symbol. Overnight, he'd gone from a man who'd commanded respect among his peers to his pre-chariot days—the geek who walked home with the high school kids. His parents were secretly relieved. They still believed Haik had borrowed the car from me, and using someone's expensive possession for more than an emergency was just bad manners.

Haik felt especially emasculated around Christine, stripped naked of his metal persona. Not what he needed after his unexplainable outburst in the ER. When Christine asked him what happened to the BMW, he told her it was in the shop. Did she care about appearances? Who didn't? Even those who claim they didn't, did. That in itself was keeping up an appearance. She knew that most of the fancy cars in Glendale were borrowed, leased or stolen. Nevertheless, she might have felt the car would give Haik some credibility in her father's eyes—a contender for her affections, like the rich groomsman or the other ER residents with their shiny trinkets. Not that she'd ever introduce Haik to her father.

Haik told me Christine drove a sparkling white Acura. Serge's gift when she finished medical school. Her license plate read *Voski*—"golden" in Armenian. He promised to upgrade her to the Mercedes-Benz of her choice if she got engaged to an eligible bachelor within the year.

Christine offered to drop Haik home after work but he refused, saying he was going to the library to study. He'd rather have his worst enemy see where he lived than her. No. Not after their long afternoons in a deluxe apartment in the sky.

Haik doubled his shifts, thinking he could save up for another car. He made team T-shirts and sold them to the hospital soccer league. Anything. *Something* that would be worthy of Christine. His anger bloomed exponentially to my freedom. It was clearly Haik's turn to get back at me, or get back just enough so the car would be his again. From the outside, it looked like that was all he cared about. The car. Revenge. It wasn't just that. Haik needed me. But at that moment, I wasn't paying attention. Haik's emotional status was his own concern. I was busy feeling the air-conditioning freeze my cheeks, bopping and humming *I Love L.A.* to the radio as Armineh looked at me askance from the passenger side.

CHAPTER THIRTY-SIX

The following Tuesday, I picked up Armineh in front of Macy's on the way to the park.

"Getting this car was the best thing you ever did," Armineh said, stuffing her bags in the backseat. She handed me a half-eaten snow cone. Pineapple flavored.

"You mean the best thing for *you*," I teased her, but my chest puffed up.

"Naturally," she agreed with a shrug. "What's this? Did you bake brownies?" She brought up a rectangular Tupperware that had slid out from under the seat and between her feet.

"That? It's old." I panicked and threw the snow cone out the window. I was tired of smoking pot and I'd read in the back of *L.A. Weekly* that I could get the same benefits by ingesting THC in a handy chocolate recipe. I used the last of Haik's supply to make a batch of brownies. I was going to drop it off at the studio later.

"Nonsense. If it's a little dry, we'll dip it in our coffee." She placed the dish firmly on her lap. "Where's my ice?" She looked around for her treat.

"Gone," I said.

Coffee had already been served when we got to the park.

"You two are always together. Are you dating?" Hovannes brayed as we approached the bench.

"We don't believe in dating," Armineh said. "I'm waiting for you to arrange our marriage." The table erupted in cackles and coughs.

"Rupen made some brownies." Armineh offered the Tupperware of marijuana-laced goodies around.

"Uh, I don't know. I think they gave me a stomach ache," I said, reaching for the dish.

"Don't be silly," Armineh said, moving the brownies out of my range. "You probably ate too many of them."

"Good timing. I was craving something sweet." Hovannes grabbed a couple with his gnarled fingers. Robert reached for one. Hovannes insisted he take two. Robert read a copy of *Asbarez* with concentration, tracing the letters first with his index finger, then mouthing the words. We often forgot Armenian was Robert's second language. And it didn't help that like most Armenians who didn't live in the Russian Empire, he had trouble understanding what some of the words meant in the standard Eastern Armenian adapted during Soviet times.

"Robert, it's not the Dead Sea Scrolls," Susie of the beam ray machine said. "Give me the paper. I'll read it to you and then explain it."

"Not bad," Armineh said, chewing a corner of the chocolate confection. "It's not dry at all. There's a strange taste, though. Did you put fennel seed?"

"I might have done that by accident. I thought it was clove." I winked at her. She popped a morsel in my mouth.

The wind shifted, blowing curled up sycamore leaves across the park. They skidded down the road, pebbles on a concrete lake. Armineh tightened her scarf.

"Have you people ever seen parrots flying around Glendale?" The brownies had loosened the stiffness in my shoulders and my tongue.

"It's glaucoma," Hovannes said. "I've heard it makes everything look greenish."

"No. No, I've heard about them," Robert said. "Did you see some?"

I shook my head. "I thought it was a joke."

"Parrots aren't from here. They shouldn't be here," Hovannes said.

"True. But they're here now." Robert ate another brownie.

"How did they get here?" Armineh asked. "I love my Minnette. She's smarter than my kids."

"They immigrated like us," Robert said.

"Like *us*," Hovannes said, pointing to everyone but Robert.

"*You* were born here."

"So?" Robert asked, his voice still strong but his eyes glazing as the marijuana took effect.

"Never mind him," Armineh said, "Tell us about the birds."

"No one's sure, but some people say there was a big fire at a nursery in Pasadena and some parrots escaped from their aviary," Robert said.

"They still don't belong here," Hovannes grunted. "I wonder if they're tasty like pigeons."

"Did I tell you Minnette laid an egg for me? She thinks I'm her mate," Armineh said with a giggle.

"I think they're monogamous," Robert said.

"Maybe you and your bird should get married." Hovannes made flapping gestures at Armineh.

"Listen to this," Robert said, his words slightly slurred. He'd taken the newspaper back from Susie, who was leaning heavily on his shoulder. "There's an ad in the back of the paper from a group called the National Armenian League. Have you heard of them? I haven't. It says beware, there's a Turk parading amongst us as a hero."

My heart skipped a beat. Then three. I looked at the sky, the shedding treetops rotated in a counterclockwise pattern. Everything I'd worked for swirled into a celestial vortex. Dry leaves rained on our heads.

The humor of the universe, I remember thinking. Why Haik? He'd never understand that it was all a big misunderstanding. I could have explained everything to anyone else and they would have absolved me. They would have looked right through me and asked "who cares"? But these people next to me did.

"What nonsense those ads are!" Armineh snorted, looking up from the empty coffee cups she tried to read but kept picking up and putting down. She grabbed the paper. "Ooooh, there's an ad for a used beam ray machine. It's good for glaucoma. We should get it."

"Oh, that's mine. I put it up for sale," Susie said.

Armineh continued searching for the offending ad. She read it carefully.

"Well, I believe it," Hovannes declared. "I've always said the

Turks will keep trying to destroy us, even from within." He tapped at his heart for effect.

"You've never said that," Armineh said.

"Just because I didn't tell *you* doesn't mean I didn't say it."

Armineh got up from the table, walked around our concrete Stonehenge.

"Better to have remained pagans," she said. "Should have continued worshipping fire."

"What's the point? The water worshippers would have killed us," Hovannes said. "No. *We* should have killed more of them."

"Maybe the Turk *is* one of us." Robert waved his hands above his head like a bogeyman.

"Well, what if it was me?" I asked, looking at my fingernails. I squeezed the infected callus on my index finger until a little pus came out. "What would you do?"

"I'd kill you with my bare hands," Hovannes said, straightening up in his wheelchair and pantomiming choking a person.

"Hovik, put your hands down. It looks like you're shaking a coconut to see if there's water in it," Armineh said.

"I'd be very confused," Robert said. "How can you be the most famous Armenian if you're not?"

I thought of Mount Ararat.

Armineh remained silent. I nudged her with my elbow. "Well, we all have our secrets, right, my flower?"

She sighed. She was thinking of her little boy. He'd be around sixty-seven now. And she was also thinking of me dying. I waited for her to be generous.

Instead she said, "Pretending to be one of us would be unforgivable."

We ate another brownie each.

"Unforgivable because I'd be a Turk or unforgivable because I hadn't told you?" I pressed on. I heard nothing but the wind dragging the leaves across the street. Did they keep quiet because they were high, or because they didn't know the answer?

I got up and left without the rest of my brownies. I needed a break.

"Come back," Armineh said. "I want to play backgammon."

I didn't feel like going home, so I walked to Trader Joe's. They were sampling spanakopita, the frozen kind you can bake in twenty minutes. The three samples I had were tasty enough, so I thought I'd take a packet home for the kids.

It was in the frozen food aisle that I remembered a song. The cold wind from the freezer dislodged the words from my memory.

It's white everywhere
Winter has a different taste
The sky is a bit darker.
Water is frozen in the small creeks.
Come on, let's make a big snowman.
If you are not afraid of a fall;
Let's slide on ice.

It was a nursery rhyme my father used to sing to me. His songs came from a snowy village high in the Taurus Mountains, the kind of place where the entire village decamped with their flock for the summer months. I hummed it over and over again. I forgot the spanakopita. Somehow this song would set me free. But first, I had to find Haik.

CHAPTER THIRTY-SEVEN

He found me instead. Haik was waiting in the lobby of the apartment when I walked in later that evening. I'd gone back to the park and Armineh had just beaten me at backgammon, five to two. It appeared my winning streak was over. How she rubbed it in my face.

"I have dethroned Rupen the Great." She clasped her hands above her head like a prize-winning boxer, the skin of her triceps flapping back and forth.

"Maestro," Haik whispered behind me. I could feel his breath on my neck. It seemed he had taken up smoking for good. He stood between the saguaro and the aloe vera in the atrium, rolling two river stones between his fingers, a copy of *Asbarez* under his arm. I knew which issue he held. "Perhaps you're tired of driving yourself around in such a gas guzzler?" The purple circles under his eyes assured me he hadn't slept much, and his hair had grown long enough to cover the Greek Isles. The boy was a redhead.

"It's over, Haik," I said. "I'm so tired. I don't want to do this anymore. And the car belongs to me."

"How I see it, you don't have a choice," he said, tossing the stones back under the cacti. "Did you see this week's newspaper?"

"I don't need to see the moon or the stars." I brushed aside the paper he tried to hand me. "I told you, I'm done."

"What, you're done being a Turk?" he asked.

"I can't change that!" I'm ashamed to say I started to cry. "What if I am a Turk? I didn't mean to hurt anyone. Go ahead, tell anyone you want."

But he didn't have to. When I turned around to flee, right in front of me were Lucy and Ara, schoolbooks in hand, mouths wide open.

Some people describe the moment when a secret spills as eternity, that instant unfolding so slowly and painfully as if steaming open a forbidden letter and inserting a butter knife in between the glued ends. This wasn't like that. It happened like an instantaneous sharp jolt. An earthquake centered underfoot. I still can't recall everything that occurred from the second I turned around to the moment I left the building for good.

Here's what I do remember: a look of disappointment on Haik's face. I thought he'd be happy, but I suppose he no longer had a secret to tether me. Ara, who rushed at me and shook my shoulders until my molars knocked against each other.

He might have asked a question, like "what is this retarded Armo talking about?"

Haik might have replied, "Armo and proud of it. At least I'm not a Turk like you, motherfucker."

Lucy threw up in the cactus, but not before she broke off a piece of a saguaro and used it to batter Haik. Ara pushed him to the ground and pulled Haik's shoes off, hitting him with his own Reeboks.

I couldn't control their fury no matter how much I shouted. They kicked him as he lay on the ground, covering his head with his arms. I remember thinking for a second how pleased I was that Ara and Lucy had finally stopped fighting with each other. Maybe this was a turning point for them.

Then I looked around for some way to stop them. I saw the tempting red box with the simple command "pull." And I did. The bells rang and sprinklers turned on a moment later, an unintentional bounty for the cacti. The kids stopped, stunned by the shower.

Haik limped out, feet bare, two minutes before the fire trucks arrived. I cleaned up the blood on the floor with my cashmere sweater.

"*Papik*, it isn't true what you said? Is it?" Lucy asked, her hair plastered to her head.

I couldn't say anything, so I nodded.

Ara said "no" over and over again.

I didn't know what to do. I remembered Captain Cooper

who lived below us. I fantasized about snatching his revolver and shooting myself, drinking bleach, hanging myself with my belt, drowning here in the lobby. Then I realized I was a dead man anyway.

"You need to know something else," I said.

"Shut up!" Ara said. "Don't you dare say anything. Just shut up!"

"How dare you talk to your grandfather that way!" My daughter, dressed in a soon-to-be-ruined Chanel suit, stood by the entrance. "What's going on here?" She looked from Ara, to Lucy, to me holding the sopping pink sweater, her eyes wide with fear. "Pa?"

"*Papik* is a fucking Turk," Ara replied. "He's lied to us all our lives."

I was done lying just then. "I'm dying. I have cancer," I said, thinking this might be better news than their newfound ethnicity.

Lucy threw up again. Her vomit flowed in a thin opaque stream toward the cacti, incorporating slowly into our private lobby storm.

I walked out, my clothes clinging to my ribs. I heard fire engines turning on Wilson Avenue, their sirens providing the soundtrack to my exit.

CHAPTER THIRTY-EIGHT

At eighty-four, I finally moved out. Independence found me in aisle ten, staring at a wall of linens: 300-thread count? Poly-cotton? California King?

Finally I had to face reality, but I couldn't make up my mind. Should I get red or green? And did thread count really matter? I'd never bought sheets. Ever. *Did I really tell them I was a Turk?* I didn't. They overheard. Technically, I only told them the bit about dying. I put red-and-white striped sheets in my cart. Then an inflatable bed, some towels, pajamas, slippers, underwear, kitchen things. I wandered the supercenter until the security guard shooed me out.

I'd spent most of the evening driving to all the places where Maestro Rupen, the famous Armenian, had thrived. The park was deserted except for a fluttering Masis Market plastic bag. Carmen and the bullfighter eyed me suspiciously from the Bakery Opera window. St. Gregory's wooden doors were chained, Noah's face in the shadows. The marquee above the Alex Theatre shone bright white, empty of any lettering.

The phone rang in my studio as I walked up the stairs. It rang again and again. Nothing moved in the building except for the fluttering of parakeet wings.

The strange closet for the Murphy bed—I never thought I'd need it. I pumped up the bed and diapered its enormous vinyl skin in cheery circus stripes. I'd forgotten to buy pillows, so I rolled up the towels into bolsters. I took my shoes off and tested the bed. I could see out the window from my vantage. Radio towers communicated their cryptic messages from the top of the mountains. I changed into my new pajamas and slipped under the stiff sheets but there was no sleep. The lights on the mountaintop kept blinking a devilish red.

I struggled off the slippery mattress and sat at my desk, tracing the dark brown vein that started in the middle of the table and split in two as it meandered off the corner. The man at the lumber-yard who planed the rough wood called it a flaw. But what a thing of beauty this flaw was.

I took out a stack of leftover paper from Haik's mailing project. I drew a musical staff and wrote three notes on the first page. It was the last three notes of that nursery rhyme my father used to sing. I looked at the circles and lines and didn't know where to go next, but a certainty flashed through my twisted muscles and jumped into my bloodstream, hitching a ride in the white blood cells that rushed around to save me from cancer and narrowed out through my arms and into the fingers that gripped the pencil so tightly. Trembling.

I took out my notebook, a secondhand Moleskine I'd bought at a Paris flea market. A leather-bound book in which I never wrote music, but I hoped people would think otherwise. Instead, here we are.

I've written down everything from when I met the boy to all the things he made me remember. Just in case someone, you, want to know my side. You might hate me, but at least you would hate me knowing who I was.

In the beginning, I waited.

I switched from the pile of white paper to the notebook every so often, anticipating that any second the starter's gun would be shot. But sometimes you have to shoot the gun yourself.

The mountains changed from looming dark form to purple outlines and then into dull greenish peaks without the benefit of time-lapse photography. Three little notes. I could think of nothing else.

"Pa! Pa!" My daughter pounded on the door.

"I didn't see Maestro Rupen come in this morning," the accountant called out.

I must have fallen asleep at the desk after sunrise. The notes still danced in front of my blurry eyes. I didn't want to open the door.

"I know you're in there. Your car is parked outside," she whispered, trying to hide her conversation from the accountant's ears.

"*Bari luis,* Keran." Neck stiff, I opened the door in my pajamas. I should have bought a robe.

"Pa, why didn't you come home last night? I was so worried."
She came in but didn't kiss me. Her dark curls were tied in a ponytail. I hadn't seen this hairstyle since she was a teenager. She wore
my old trench coat over her college sweats.

"I needed some space," I responded.

"Space? That's for Americans!"

My girl had a point. We stick close even if we hate each other.

"I brought you some coffee and pastries." She placed the bakery box on the big table, blotting out the flaw, and handed me a
flask.

"The kids told me what happened. They were very upset."

"And you?" I asked.

Keran started to cry. She wiped her eyes on one of my new
kitchen towels.

"Nobody else knows," I said quickly. I was afraid to touch her.
To comfort her. What if she slapped my hand away and called me
a dirty Turk monster?

"Why didn't you tell us?"

"I didn't even tell your mother."

Keran looked confused. "No. Not that." She trembled. "About
the cancer."

"I don't know." It was only half the truth.

"So why didn't you tell us about the other thing? Why didn't
you tell Mama you were a . . . um?" She couldn't bring herself to
say Turk.

"It's a long story. Don't you have to go to work?"

"I called in sick." Keran sat in the old leather chair and pulled
her knees to her chin. Her socks were mismatched. "So?" The
testy teenager reared her head.

"Well, when was I going to tell your mother? When I saw her
on the boat from Venice? When I followed her to the conservatory
in Yerevan? When I gave her the sweetest red apple I could find on
St. Sarkis Day? Or when she sent it back studded with cloves in
the shape of a heart?"

"What a romantic," Keran said, pulling the armchair closer.

"That's what we did back then when we wanted to marry someone."

"Okay. So what happened?" She let out a long breath. "Tell me everything."

"It was 1915," I started, glancing at the notes scribbled in my notebook. "And I committed a terrible sin. Something so awful."

"I'm sure it's not that bad, Papa *jahn*."

"It's worse."

On my path to manhood, I explained, I watched my family home descend into ashes. I wandered through the wastes of the Syrian Desert. I learned to coax a human voice out of a shepherds' flute. I became a slave. I lived as a monk by the seaside. I married a goddess under the glow of Orion. I had children named after ancient kings and queens, including Keran, the thirteeth-century lady. I became important. Then famous. And all along I was just a frightened seven-year-old boy. On the cliff's edge that my Great Crime would be discovered.

"Pa, but I still don't get why you didn't tell Mama after all those years. Didn't you think she would understand?"

"My exquisite child, not even God could love me if he really knew what I did."

"That's not true," Keran said but she seemed unsure.

* * *

It was the day of the big fire. April 24, 1915.

"Rupen, it takes courage to be a man. And today, you are a man. Tell the truth by Allah. Did you take my duduk?" The crooked nail on my father's thumb pressed against my shoulder blade. His clothes smelled of fresh cedar shavings.

"No, Papa!" I felt the instrument's smooth shaft under my shirt.

The squint of his eyes told me he knew I was lying. "Fine, son. Your word is good with me." He relaxed his grip and propelled me toward the hills to take care of the goats. He didn't trust me with his prized sheep yet.

"I'll show him I'm a man," I muttered to the goats as I forced them onto the narrow lane.

"Oh yeah?" they bleated back. "Then what's that thing under your shirt?" "Baaaa." How they mocked me. But at least it was in the key of D.

"What's this? A boy who talks to his goats?" A rough, amused voice asked.

I was so mad, I didn't even see the Ottoman soldiers turn from the centuries-old goat path and onto the winding dirt road that led to our village. I kept quiet as my father had instructed us kids, even as their leader ruffled my hair. There were a dozen of them. The soldiers, about the same age as my elder brother had he survived smallpox, shuffled behind their commander in dirty baggy pants. He had light gray eyes that looked right through me.

"Is this the way to the town?" he asked.

I nodded yes and looked away. "Where are you going, sir?" I asked after them.

"To take care of some very bad people," he replied.

"Criminals?"

He turned around and nodded. "Thieves. Be sure to keep quiet so you don't tip 'em off," he said with a wink.

"Here?" I asked in awe. A goat went missing the year before, but it had fallen down a well.

"So where do the people who worship on Sunday live, boy?"

"They're everywhere," I said, sealing the fate of the eighty people who lived in my village. "My father likes the carpet ladies who live over by the grove of olive trees." I pointed at our part of the valley. "The people who have the farm behind our house and the family that owns that land with the little stream. They build Christian mosques."

"What a smart young man you are," he said. I straightened my shoulders. "I'll make sure Enver Pasha gives you a medal for your service to the motherland." The soldiers snickered and marched off.

The goats baa'd. Key of E.

I couldn't wait to tell my father that I was promised a medal. Ha! I'd show him who the man was.

"Twenty-four hours later, I turned into somebody," I told Keran. "But not the man my father hoped for."

"Oh, Papa," she said and started crying into her hands.

"I killed everybody, *jahn*. Everybody."

Someone knocked on the door and we noticed it was 3 P.M. I was still in my pajamas, my body squeezed out like a dirty kitchen rag.

"Mr. R," Brian called out. "You in there? It's Thursday, right?" He asked more for his own benefit.

Keran grabbed her purse and jumped up to answer the door. She looked at her red eyes as she passed the mirror. The crack fractured her face.

"You should come home. You're sick," she said. I noticed she didn't say, "Come home, Pa."

I shook my head.

She stared at me for a minute and nodded. "I'll call you later." She walked out the door, the trench coat her bulletproof armor.

"Hey, Mr. R, nice outfit," Brian said.

"Thanks. From Targé."

* * *

I didn't leave my studio all week. I thought of my father and my daughter and mourned for the people who never met each other. I thought of the three little notes. I arranged them in the key of G. Too common. No wonder it's called the people's key. Half of the world's national anthems are in G, including the Armenian anthem. Then I tried C minor. Beethoven used C minor to express heroic struggle. But to me C minor had always sounded like recognition, heroic or not. I thought of snow and what it tasted like, of little creeks, their veins frozen by a fierce glance from winter and sliding on ice, fearlessly. How brave nursery rhymes are. I got up and turned on the heater.

The accountant's radio wafted up from the floor with the heat. Bill Clinton campaigned in Philadelphia, his voice hoarse for weariness and weather. *"Most Americans are struggling to make their voices heard every day."* I stood on the grate in my socks and undershorts, the warm air wafting up my balls, and listened. *"I believe, in the words of Thomas Wolfe, 'that we are lost here in*

*America, but I believe that we shall be found.' And this belief . . .
is for me—and I think for all of us—not only our own hope, but
America's everlasting, living dream."* I wrote three more notes on
the staff.

I walked around my 500 square feet. The only place I belonged. I opened cabinets and drawers. In the back of the old ice-
box, behind some tax returns, I found a very old duduk wrapped
in a piece of faded silk. I took it to the window to see it better. I
blew life into it. Then I cried.

Keran dropped by every day to bring me laundry, music and
books. She cooked my favorite foods, which I warmed up on
Armineh's hot plate but rarely ate. My daughter felt my feverish
skin and begged me to come home. I thought of the kids and was
too ashamed to face them.

"Remember when you wanted to move out during college?" I
reminded her. "I just need this time."

"Yes. But you didn't let me leave." She redid her hair in the
mirror, loosening tendrils onto her neck, pinching color into her
cheeks. She had discarded her sweats and was back to her glamor-
ous self in leather Prada.

"About that. I'm so sorry, I understand now," I said. She stuck
her tongue out at me. "How are the kids?"

"They'll be fine." Did she mean they'd be fine *after* I died?

"I forgot to give you this." She pulled a small purple box out
of her attaché case. It was from Bakery Opera. "Your friends are
wondering where you are. I told Armineh you were on a sabbatical."

"Was she impressed?" I cradled the box.

"She asked when you became a Jew."

I opened the box. It was filled with brownies and a folded
piece of paper smudged with chocolate. The note said: *These don't
have fennel seeds.* I lost my breath.

"I just can't right now," I said, pushing the breathlessness
below the surface.

"Do they suspect something?" Keran asked softly.

"No. Not that I'm a Turk. Armineh knows I'm dying, but no
one else."

"Okay, Pa." We stood by the mirror in silence, listening to the accountant coo at his birds.

"So what's new with you, *jahn?*" I asked. "Tell me something you've never told me."

"I'm seeing someone," she said after a pause, her cheeks rosy.

"Really?" A warmth crept over me. "So that's why you were sneaking out so much."

"You saw me?"

"When I was out with Haik."

"Oh. I'm sorry, Papa."

"I think we've transcended sorry, my *jahn*. In fact, sorry was two stops earlier."

She smiled.

"Do I know this Romeo?" I asked.

"He's not Armenian."

She was about to sigh, but I stopped her.

"It's okay."

"It's someone from work, so it's a little complicated."

"Who is it, Carter, Cooper or Klein?"

"Papa, those three are in their sixties! It's actually the new partner, Kraus."

"I hope no one has a stuttering problem in the office."

We both laughed.

"He's the new technology expert. But we met before he started to work at the firm."

"Really?"

"At a conference a couple years ago. I remember thinking he had a really nice smile. I felt guilty even thinking that. Then he started consulting at the firm a few months ago."

"Is it serious?"

She smiled again and shrugged.

"Do the kids know?"

"No. I don't know how to tell them." Her forehead wrinkled on its own accord.

"You'll figure it out. But if you want my opinion, you should tell them sooner than later," I said as she left for her date.

I rifled through the things Keran brought: a few records including Hovhaness' *Requiem and Resurrection*, some volumes of poetry. I opened the Kuchak, where I kept my mother's gold medallion with its graceful olive tree. I held it up to my lips and felt the letters against my chapped skin—*Wish well, be well.* I strung it on a shoelace and hung it around my neck. I wrote down three more notes.

CHAPTER THIRTY-NINE

On the seventh day, which was not the Sabbath, I left the building dressed in a dark blue sweatsuit Keran bought me. She didn't buy any sneakers, so I wore my brown Bruno Magli shoes. Ara would classify the look as "totally Armo." But my regular wardrobe, including the jeans and my favorite checked shirt, no longer fit.

It was the end of September and while it would be a warm day, something about the light reminded me that it was fall.

I walked across the street to the BMW and leaned against it to catch my breath. It looked like an abandoned animal. With a parking ticket. No matter. It growled with its usual vitality when I turned the key.

With the windows down, the morning breeze slapped my face awake. The weather had cooled during my seclusion. I turned on the seat warmer. I told myself I was driving aimlessly, but knew I was heading for a destination that was only half in my head. I drove to Westwood and sat in the parking garage of the Hammer Museum until it opened.

I was the first visitor of the day. The docent at the front desk said I must have really want to see this exhibit.

"Not really," I told her. "I was just in the neighborhood."

"Enjoy it anyway," she said. "You'll take something away for sure."

I walked through a labyrinth of white walls before being greeted by sea-blue letters morphed to look exotic: *Treasures of the Ottoman Empire.* Their form looked slightly dangerous, like they could leap off the wall if they didn't approve of the visitor.

Once past the maze, there were carpets, ceramics and miniatures. And one hundred Korans from five centuries—masterpieces of the illuminator's craft.

Although the human form can never be extolled in Islam, it reminded me of illuminations from the ancient Bibles we kept under lock and key on St. Lazarus. The calligraphy was intensely decorative to the point of abstraction. The designs hungered within itself, feeding on loveliness, curling inward and unfolding finally into patterns of gold and blue. Deep in the undulations, random snowflakes emerged. I borrowed a pen from the guard and wrote an ascending scale on the palm of my hand.

The Korans from the end of the Ottoman Empire, my childhood, stood out as the finale of a long tired life. Busy and overworked. Full of its own fading importance, grasping for beauty.

I returned the pen to the guard and got back in my car. I closed my eyes. Someone tapped on the glass. It was the parking attendant.

"Are you okay?" she mouthed.

I nodded and started the engine.

* * *

I parked the car under the balding jacaranda tree across from the studio. The afternoon clamor of birds reminded me I had a headache. When I slammed my car door, they startled into synchronized flight. Twenty or so lime-green birds with red tails burst out of the tree, falling into formation in the atmosphere. Showgirls. They announced their neon presence with flap and feather before flying west.

"So you really do exist!" I exclaimed out loud.

"Of course I exist," the accountant called out. He finished smoking his cigarette and went back inside to his caged parakeets.

I wondered how the parrots would survive winter.

* * *

Lucy was sitting on the top step, wrapped in a black wool sweater, when I climbed up to the studio. She held out her duduk, a dark instrument I'd made out of walnut rather than apricot.

"Hi, *Papik*. I'm here for my lesson," she said as if nothing had happened the week before. I scanned her face, taking in her dark eyes. "I've been waiting for you since 2 P.M. Mama asked me to give you your mail." She handed me a plastic bag.

"I'm sorry. I forgot you were coming." I hadn't forgotten. I just didn't think she would show up again.

"How are you, Grandpa?" she asked in English when we walked through the door. The studio looked like a mining camp. No offense to miners. Towels hung on chair backs, cups of old coffee piled up on the table, atop a river of used white paper that cascaded to the floor. "Your place needs a woman's touch." She cleared the dishes off the table and into the sink by the bathroom.

"What's all this?" She pointed to the paper.

"I'm writing something new." I hid the Moleskine notebook in a drawer.

"I thought you were finished with *The Crane's Lament*." She started making the bed. "Are you changing it?"

"No. It's something new." I leaned against the table, winded and nauseated from my trip.

"*Papik*, are you really going to die?" She struggled to stuff the bed in the closet.

"We all have to die," I said, closing the Murphy door from behind her. But I didn't believe it. I didn't want to go.

She turned around and hugged me, putting her head on my chest, a little girl again. The wetness of her tears saturated my sweatshirt to my soul. Would this be the last time I stroked her hair?

"*Papik*, you're giving me static electricity." She moved away.

"Come on then, young lady, you have work to do." She glanced at herself in the mirror as she moved the music stands near the window to catch the limp afternoon light. I suspected she'd done that countless times during the past few days.

"I feel generous today. Why don't you pick the music?" Lucy flipped through the tower on the floor, stopping at a worn booklet, passing it and then coming back. Without seeing, I knew what she had picked.

I Will Not Be Sad in This World, a piece based on a Sayat Nova composition. Written in the 1700s, its hold was strong enough to

---

cross the Caucasus, traverse the Atlantic and wind its way through tunnels and freeways to sit on our music stands centuries later. Sayat Nova was a royal musician who fell in love with a princess. Their love discovered, he was banished to the life of a wandering bard, unquenched.

"Oh, where did you get that wierd duduk?" she asked pointing with her chin at the instrument I unwrapped from its old silk. "It's so ugly."

"This?" I asked. I held out the scratched cylinder that I'd hidden for so long. It had a gash on one side. The finger holes were worn smooth like the middle of a staircase. A twist of darker-colored wood ran through the core, but it was sleek from the oil of so many hands.

"Yeah. Shouldn't you throw that away?" She picked up the trash can.

"Not yet," I said. "It was your great-grandfather's. You can throw it away when I'm gone."

"Oh." She sat back down. "Did he make it?" She shivered and buttoned up her sweater.

"Yes. It was the best he ever made." I turned up the thermostat. "He chose the wood from a dying tree. Something was eating it from the roots. But the branches were still strong. I remember he left it in the corner of his workshop for months to cure. Then one day, he sat under the old olive tree and started carving out the finger holes."

As Lucy and I played the first few notes, I remembered I hadn't picked up the duduk all week, the one thing that had always exonerated me. I sighed into the duduk, making it moan.

Brian, years before he became my student, had accidentally killed his young son with his car. He described the duduk as giving permission to let yourself go. To pour your soul into the murky depths of emotion and receive absolution. Once you get past that initial sad façade, there's a meditative quality in hearing the duduk. A breath from God. To play the duduk the way it's meant to sound, you must suffer first.

"Why do you think songs that tell you not to be sad, make you even sadder?" I asked Lucy, wondering what was going through her head.

"It's like cutting an onion, *Papik*," she balanced her duduk on her knee. "Even if it makes you cry, you feel better after. Clearer." Lucy understood music in a rare way. From the soul. Talented people can learn notes and technique, but knowing *how* to play the notes, that requires understanding the things that make us human. Just as the duduk couldn't be synthesized, the hard knocks needed to play this instrument couldn't be faked. In order to be the best duduk player, to be the maestro, I knew my Lucy would have to experience deep suffering. Was that what I wanted for her?

The piece was a little more than six minutes, but it was nightfall when we looked out the window.

"Mama said you don't want to come home," Lucy said as she put her duduk away. "Do you hate us?"

"How could I hate you? I'm so afraid you hate me."

"No. Never," she vowed. "I just don't understand myself anymore. Who am I, *Papik*?" She looked at herself in the mirror again, holding back her hair so only her face showed.

"You've always been you, Lucy."

She caught my eye in the mirror. She kissed me goodbye wordlessly.

I thought of three more notes.

CHAPTER FORTY

The phone rang as I sat to write. It was a collect call.
"Haik?"

He sobbed in response.

"What's wrong, my boy?" I asked. I didn't know if I'd ever hear from him. Not just because I thought he didn't want to talk to me. I just didn't think I'd be around to answer the phone.

"She left me."

"Oh. I am sorry." He didn't say anything more, so I finally asked him what happened. I leaned back with the cord curling around my elbow.

"I saw her in front of the hospital," he said barely above a whisper. "She had on a red party dress. It was low cut and her hair was down on her shoulders all curly and gold . . . she was getting into a brand new Porsche with some guy in a sharp suit."

"Was it a Versace?"

"I don't know what Versace looks like."

"Sorry. Go on, Haik *jahn*."

"She giggled at whatever stupid joke he made. You know that giggle when a girl plans to sleep with you later?"

"Oh, *that* giggle. What did you do then?"

"I told her I loved her and she shouldn't get in the car with fancysuit boy. And to come to the basement with me. That I'd made something just for her. My princess."

Haik grabbed her hand and pulled her toward the basement. The beautiful Christine in her red designer dress. Haik in his vomit-inducing green scrubs.

"Please," Haik begged Christine. "Just give me a chance."

She let him lead her through the side entrance, down the metal staircase. They walked past the laundry, took a right turn at the

226

morgue and proceeded behind the earsplitting generators. To his illicit cardboard collection. Christine's mouth fell open.

"It's for you, my darling," Haik said. "I did it all for you."

"What is this shit?" The boy in the Versace suit asked, snorting. He'd followed them. "Charmin boxes? Baby, we're going to be late for Cher. I have backstage passes."

Christine pulled away from Haik.

"Christine." Haik reached for her hand.

"Dude, step off." Versace boy pulled Christine behind him. "Stupid Armo."

Haik went silent.

"Hello," I said into the phone.

"I'm here," he replied.

"What happened next?"

"I punched him really hard. I think I broke his nose. She screamed. She called me a loser and said she never wanted to see me again."

"You're not a loser."

"Whatever," Haik said. We both listened to the static on the line. "I know you're dying."

"You know a lot more about me than that."

"I have to go now," he said after a minute.

"We can talk some more."

"No. My time is up." The line was quiet.

I wrote down three more notes.

* * *

"*Bari luis*, Rupen." The accountant knocked on my door in the morning.

"You're here early," I said.

"So you're living here now?"

"I'm on sabbatical," I said.

"Oh, that sounds important." He held a copy of *Asbarez*. "Isn't this one of your students? On page six was a picture of Haik—the surly photo from his work ID. The accountant patted his chest.

"Are you okay? Does your chest hurt?"

"What? No. I'm looking for my glasses."

I pointed to his head.

He leaned over the desk and read me the story, his early morning cigarette still on his breath.

Haik Bedrossian, 20, was sentenced to 30 days to be served out immediately at California Institute for Men in Chino, Calif., for assault, vandalism and intent to commit arson at Glendale General Hospital in Glendale, Calif.

According to sources, Bedrossian, originally from Yerevan, Armenia, constructed an elaborate 12-foot-high cardboard castle in the basement of the hospital for six months before officials discovered it.

"It had a set of arched gothic doors that opened to three rooms," said hospital electrician Armen Akelian, who dismantled it. "There were windows made from colored plastic, like stained glass and gargoyles on the corners. I'd never seen anything like it before."

Security personnel discovered the installation, near the construction site for an unfinished Proton treatment center, during an altercation between Bedrossian and a hospital visitor.

While officials couldn't prove any nefarious motives, they alleged a long rope had been attached to the castle and could double as a fuse.

According to the prosecution, Bedrossian was a troubled youth who could explode at any time, possibly setting the hospital on fire by burning the cardboard.

"There was no combustion vehicle," said Akelian. "It was just a nylon cord and some wires."

Bedrossian's court-appointed attorney said in defense of his client that the rope and wires were for a draw-bridge.

The jury sided with the prosecution and recommended a 150-day jail term, but the judge commuted the sentence to 30 days.

"The judge seemed impressed by the photos," said Akelian, who attended the one-day trial. "He told the young man to spend his 30 days thinking about a positive direction for his life."

Bedrossian was also fired from his job.

The accountant left the paper on my desk. Keran read it when she visited that evening.

"Papa, tell me something you've never told anyone." She warmed up tomato meatball soup on the hot plate.

"You're a glutton." I kept scribbling on the stack of white paper.

"No, really. Tell me something." She pulled out a white bowl with a faded gold rim from my small stack of housewares and rinsed it with hot water from the bathroom tap.

I put down my pencil. "Well, I can eat a box of Napoleons in one sitting."

"I know that already."

"I've *never* told anyone about my pastry prowess."

"I have a gift for observation. That came from Mama."

"Fine. What do you want to know?"

"What's your biggest regret?"

I traced the flaw with the rolled up newspaper.

"Well, Papa?" she asked looking up from the hot plate.

"Not telling your mother. And I had so many chances."

"Like when?" She sat on the striped bed, wooden spoon in hand.

"Remember when we lived in Paris?"

"Oh, Paris," she said with a smile.

"You sound like your mom. She loved it even if it snowed and we had no heat."

I told Keran about the day when white flurries whirled about us as we crossed the plaza in front of Notre Dame.

"Why do we have to leave Paris? We just got here." Artemis refused to hold my hand.

"It's warm in Los Angeles. There are palm trees and the ocean." I tried to entice her. I'd been a visiting instructor at the

Conservatoire when I got the call to play the duduk for a motion picture. "We won't ever move again," I promised.

"Snow crowned your mother's hair, creating a bright halo," I said. "But when she brushed the icy flecks off my coat, it was like she brushed the universe's dandruff off my shoulders."

"I might be able to find a dance studio here," Artemis had said, her arms folded across her chest.

"People dance in Los Angeles." I brushed her hair, trying to caress her shoulder.

"Are we living other people's lives?" she asked. I looked into her eyes and thought, Now's the time, Rupen. You missed your chance at the lake with the dying crane.

Rather than grasping the opportunity, I told Keran, I grew fearful and untrusting. *What had she found out about me? Did someone tell her something?*

Keran licked the spoon and stared out the window.

CHAPTER FORTY-ONE

I'd spent almost six weeks in exile when I finally called Armineh. "Do you want to go to the beach this weekend?" I asked.

"I don't go to the beach with strange men," she said.

"Sorry, my dove. I've been thinking of music."

"Are you sure that's all? Keran told me you were traveling but I didn't believe her. I'll be offended if I get a funeral invitation in the mail."

"I'll do my best to die in your lap."

"You romantic. Come over to the house at noon and we'll see." That was soft for Armineh.

She lived in a small bungalow at the very end of a cul-de-sac in Verdugo Canyon. She was flanked on either side by two of her daughters, who had tract mansions, the kind that were built up to within an inch of the property line. Double-parked cars lined the curve of the road when I pulled up. There were pink balloons tied to the mailbox in front of the giant house to the left of Armineh's. Dance music escaped each time someone opened the front door.

I sat in my car with the window down, immersed in the light mist that never quite lifted that day, wondering if I had the courage to knock on one of those doors. I didn't have to wait long. A warm, bony hand tickled my neck. It was Armineh. She wore a pink wool dress that brought out the sparkle in her eyes. She held out a wild sage plant in the other hand, its vibrant roots exposed to the air.

"I picked it for you," she said. The camphor smell filled the space between us. "It'll be nice on your big balcony."

More like fire escape. She didn't know I'd moved, of course. "What's going on here?" I asked, gesturing to the jam of cars.

"It's the baby's *agra hadig* today," Armineh said. "Can you believe Anoush is just four months old and she already has her first tooth?"

"She's smart just like her grandmother," I said, getting out of the car.

"Let's go have some cake." Armineh dropped the sage on her driveway and brushed the dirt from her hands.

"You can't just leave it there. It'll die," I said, bending to pick up the plant.

"Oh, it's strong. Look how thick its roots are." She tugged at my sleeve.

"No. It only looks strong." I helped her plant the herb in a cracked terracotta pot before we went next door. Water seeped slowly out the sides, but it would do until I took it home.

"Oh, Uncle Rupen, you've lost a lot of weight!" Alice opened the door for us. She had dyed her hair blond.

"Darling, there is no need to call me uncle," I reminded her. She blushed a little.

"When are you going back to Armenia?" I asked to change the questions in the air.

"At the end of the year." Alice closed the door behind us.

"Must you, my dear?" I asked.

"Will you miss me terribly?" She brushed up against my shoulder.

Armineh looked at us, her lips pursed the way they did when she worked on an American crossword puzzle.

"I'm just thinking of your safety, dear." I took Armineh's hand and we walked into the living room.

Inside, the women were split between a buffet table devoted only to sweets and dancing to music from the no-talent fluff band from The Black Sea. They were now a big hit.

"What a happy day," one of the dancing women said to Armineh, grabbing her arms and folding her into the swirl of perfume.

"It's a new beginning," another woman said.

One of the few men who were in attendance turned down the stereo as Armineh's youngest daughter, Arus, reclaimed her teething baby from the crowd. We piled into the dining room, where she sat with little Anoush in her lap. Someone covered the child's head with a cloth napkin and Armineh sprinkled some cooked wheat kernels on her head to summon a fruitful future, a ritual handed down from our pagan days. Then, they uncovered her head and placed a few objects on the dining room table. A daisy-shaped cookie cutter, a black plastic comb, a paintbrush, a pen, a twenty-dollar bill, a calculator, a wrench.

"A wrench?" Arus asked the gathering. "You think my daughter will install gas lines?"

"Why not?" Armineh asked. "There are too many bakers in the family."

They put the baby on the table and she lunged for her future.

"You can be anything, my dear," Armineh said.

The baby crawled to the comb.

"Oh, a hairstylist!" the balding father said.

But it was only a passing interest. She moved onto the twenty-dollar bill.

"She's going to be rich!" Arus said, clapping her hands. The thought of a lucrative future lit up her eyes.

The baby left that behind, too. She crawled to the cookie cutter and put it in her mouth. The crowd cheered.

"Well, she alone has chosen her future." Armineh grabbed the latest baker in the family and kissed her pudgy cheeks.

"Here, you hold her, Rupen," Armineh said, thrusting the warm, wriggling body into my chest.

I lifted Anoush up so her head touched my forehead. She giggled and her drool splashed into my open mouth.

"The ancients said swallowing the spittle of a baby is good luck," Armineh said.

"Which ancient said that?" I asked, wiping my mouth on Armineh's pink sleeve. Anoush nestled in the crook of my arm.

"I did," Armineh said.

* * *

After the teething ceremony, I invited Armineh for a drive along the ocean. I pretended to be generous and dangled the keys of the car in front of her face like a baby rattle. The truth was I could no longer handle long distances without my legs trembling and pain radiating from my gut to my back.

She whooped and changed from her heels into a pair of sturdy shoes that were leaning against the screen door of her porch. They were pink and sparkly. I picked up the sage in its cracked pot. Next to it was a climbing red rose a little past its bloom yet still fragrant. I snapped it from the trellis and tucked it in my pocket. I placed the sage in the backseat and opened the driver's side for Armineh.

"Oh, how chivalrous," she said. "Do you mind fastening my seat belt?" She shut her door before I could.

I climbed into the passenger side and closed my eyes. She drove. Fast.

Although it was the middle of October, it was still warm but the warmth was spiked with a knowing that a colder time was on its way. The sky, a pale shade of oyster, lent its hazy glow over the Malibu sand. We spread our towel on the powdery grains, light as filthy snow, and sat facing each other. Armineh opened her flask and poured out a generous cup of brandy.

"This will warm you right up," she said as I shivered against the sunny wind.

"What is it with you and brandy? Is it because you put it in all the cakes?"

"I like the smell. It reminds me of staying warm." She told me about the first bitter winter in Yerevan, when she and Levon lived next to the bakery hearth, the scent of burnt wood hanging heavy but not heating the flesh or dulling the brain the way the amber fire did. Those frigid days when they cut down trees in the central park near the opera to fire the ovens and baked bread from ground up tree bark. Sometimes they slept on the floor in front of the fire to stay warm. Their neighbor, the mechanic, distilled spirits from dried grapes, apricots and sometimes wood. Armineh still remembered the sweet aroma of dead fruit and the harsh burn that followed every time she took a drink. And then there was the lovely forgetting.

"Why did you tell me about your son?" I took a sip and passed the cup back to her. "Why not Robert or Hovannes or your daughters?"

She thought about it as the waves laced their way onto the shore. "I thought you would understand best."

"That's sweet. But what do you mean?" I still wondered if it was the aura of death that made me her confessor or did she have feelings that were more than friendly.

"You know me better than anyone."

"Even Levon?"

"Especially him."

"Do you wish you hadn't married him?"

"Wishing is an unaffordable luxury." Armineh kicked the sand with her toe.

"You've given up hope?" I nudged her with my elbow.

"Haven't you?"

"No. And I'm the one that's dying."

She made a face then said, "I wonder sometimes if doing your best is enough."

"Sweetheart, the best is all we can ever do," I said, taking her hand.

"Is that what death has taught you?"

"That's what life has taught me."

She leaned over and kissed my cheek. "Why are we talking about such gloomy things?"

"You're right," I said, taking the rose from my pocket. It was time for my grand gesture. The truth.

"What if I told you another secret?" I swatted her nose lightly with the fragrant rose.

"Did you steal that from my garden?"

"Would you still be my friend?"

"You mean if you told me a terrible secret or because you ravaged my yard?"

"Secret." I offered her the rose.

"I'm intrigued." She took the flower and it dropped a loose petal on the sand. The wind picked it up and tossed it closer to the waves. "Rupen Najarian, the most famous man, has more than one secret? Let me guess . . . you cheated on Artemis? I've seen the way some women look at you."

I hoped she wasn't thinking of her daughter. I shook my head.

"You're blushing! There is another woman." She poked my thin ribs.

"No." At least not yet.

"What then?"

"I cheated on myself."

"What does that mean?" She furrowed her brow.

"What if I'm not who you think I am?"

"You're not Rupen Najarian?" She snorted in disbelief.

"What if I were Rupen Marangoz?" I used the Turkish word for carpenter.

She didn't get it at first. I couldn't blame her for not remembering a language we'd left in the back of our mental closets, next to empty hangers that once held vibrant memories of true loves and high school physics. Then her eyes widened. She recoiled. She spat on the sand and crossed herself.

"Don't joke about things like that. It's not funny."

"I'm not joking." My hands trembled. I'm sure my eyes were earnest because she didn't laugh. "I need you to know."

"Why? Why do you want me to know something so awful?"

"I don't want to have secrets from you."

"How dare you tell me this now!" She dropped the rose and it skittered away until all the petals had blown in the wind.

"Because I love you."

"No. You don't." She struggled up from the towel. I had managed to shock her out of her sequined orthopedic shoes.

"Armineh *jahn*, what are you saying? You're everything to me." I was on all fours, trying to get up, looking like a donkey. "Don't you love me?"

"I can't love you," she screeched as her heels sank into the shifting ground. She turned toward the shore.

I tried to follow her. To reason with her. To stop her from twisting her ankle. She refused my presence.

"Please," I begged. "I'm not some marauding rapist. Look, I can't even get on my feet."

"Just go," she said shooing me with a hand as if I were some large shit fly. "I can't forgive you. Ever." Tears ran down her face as she pulled a brick of a cell phone out of her purse and punched

in Aram's phone number. He was dropping off a fare at LAX.
"Why?" I asked as I finally struggled to my feet. "Why can't
you forgive me?"

She faced me for the last time and I saw it in her eyes. I nodded.
"I've finally forgiven myself, dear friend. You have to forgive
yourself, too."

She ignored me and walked toward the lifeguard stand, looking
over her shoulder to make sure I wasn't following her. I couldn't
hear what she said to the lifeguard, but he jumped out of his seat
and asked me to stop following her.

I didn't leave. I waited by the BMW until the limousine pulled
up to the beach, sipping the brandy I somehow still held in my
hand. I left my hospital towel on the beach. I got in and drove
home behind them until they turned onto the freeway and I took
the streets.

It took me hours to get home. I stopped at a donut shop on
Venice Boulevard. The Cambodian donut maker suggested a maple cruller. I rested at Pico and Fairfax. The Ethiopian restaurant
owners burned frankincense to purify the air before the dinner
hour. I stayed until the haze cleared. I drove on. I stopped again in
Los Feliz by the white Moorish house, watching the painted door.
Something cracked and crunched behind my seat, stopping my
seat from reclining all the way. I drove home after a few minutes.

I parked the car in front of the studio and took my jacket from
the backseat. The sage Armineh planted for me had tipped over,
the pot, split in half, spilling dirt on the floor mat. I took the plant
to the road divider, uprooted a weed and placed the sage into the
hole. I had just enough energy to pack the dirt back in.

When I opened the studio door, a little brown bag rolled out
in front. It was a quarter of an ounce of something familiar. Purple
Kush. Someone was feeling very generous, but if Haik was in prison, who knew about my smoking? Suppose it was a trap?

Purple Kush always made me think of lofty snow-covered
peaks and fierce turbaned fighters. But the reality is so different.
It's a Northern California strain; a fuzzy sphere with a soft pine
bouquet and a sweet, fruit punch taste on a set of strong, earthy
legs. I was getting to be a marijuana gourmet.

My civic fear was thwarted by desire and I decided to smoke the weed. There was probably enough to make eight good joints. With the first bottomless inhale and the sweetness of the grape and cherry Skittles Lucy liked to eat, I wondered if I was worthy of love. I exhaled. The blinking lights on top of the mountains mocked me. They said, Rupen, you're not worthy of everyone's love. But you keep trying. Ha! I responded after the second inhale. What do you know, anyway? You're only blinking lights. I exhaled again.

* * *

The beach unclenched more than the series of three notes from the universe's tight fist. I couldn't stop the storm that poured from within as I worked in earnest on *Winter*. Up to this point, writing music had been a torturous practice. I could play anybody's compositions better than they could. But writing meant searching for the truth. I understood so late why *The Crane's Lament* had taken me fifty years to finish. And it wasn't that good.

Winter, on the other hand, took me three weeks. Notes and musical phrases moved from the inside out and back in again as if I were some permeable substance. At times the music gushed out, living blood out of a gaping wound. I was no longer afraid to lay myself bare. But I was just the universe's interpreter. Its mule. I lay bare so the truth could pass through me. Ah, to be alive!

Every few days, I'd find a small paper bag wedged under the door. My mysterious pharmacist. I questioned nothing and took everything as a gift.

I wrote and I wrote some more.

The first time I played the entire composition—all thirty minutes, I was reborn. I didn't hear the little knock on my door until I had finished the last note. My father's duduk was still on my tingling lips.

"*Papik?*" It was Lucy. "I want to play that," she whispered through the door.

I let her in and hugged her, holding the duduk against her spine, hoping to infuse her with what I'd just learned.

CHAPTER FORTY-TWO

"Mr. Najarian. I'm sorry. We've done everything we can, but nature, she is stronger than we are." Dr. Koslov looked uncomfortable, and not just because of the bad news. I had switched the cracked chair before he got there. His ass was getting pinched. "I'd like to recommend you see a colleague who helps people during this time of transition." As if I were moving from Glendale to Santa Monica.

"How long do I have?" I asked.

"Weeks, maybe." He responded in the special vagueness of doctors. "Shall I make an appointment for you?"

"That's okay. Thank you." But this time I wasn't thanking him for the news of my impending exit. I was just being polite.

Well, that was it. Death and I were on a first name basis. It was November 3, 10:09 A.M. to be exact. The Rolex might be ugly, but it keeps excellent time.

I could have ended my life in an avalanche of pastry cream and powdered sugar, but I had a couple things to do. First was a trip to St. Gregory's. Not to pray for my soul, but to end the reign of disorientation.

"Ah, Maestro Rupen," the priest greeted me. "May God lead you to vote for those who remain righteous."

"God doesn't give a damn about politics, Father," I said as I pulled the cloth firmly behind me. I prayed it wasn't his robe. I poked the holes, signed my name on the ballot and put it in the box. In return I was anointed with the sacrament of the sticker: I Voted.

The second item on my agenda required getting the BMW washed and waxed. All the delays forced me to take the freeway but I hesitated only for a moment before I pressed my foot to the accelerator, swerving onto the 210 East and a bit later, screeching to the right to catch the 71 Freeway. (In my defense, that is an ungodly connector.) Then I ran a red light at the Central Avenue exit before coming to a full stop in front of the gate.

I waited in the reception center, tired and parched, thumbing through a free copy of the Bible. King James Version. I turned to my favorite Psalm, the 88th. *"Are your wonders known in the place of darkness, or your righteous deeds in the land of oblivion?"*

"Hey," a raspy voice said. "Looking for absolution?"

"Sure," I replied. "Is it next to the bathroom?"

Haik smiled. "Thanks for insisting on picking me up. You shouldn't have."

"I'm glad you called."

"How're you doing?"

"Eh," I said.

He grimaced, taking in gaunt cheeks and a neck that shirts were now shy to embrace.

We walked toward the car. It had started to drizzle, dampening the guerilla nasal assault of the neighboring dairy farms.

"Have you been getting your stash?"

"Yes. But how?"

"I called your grandson."

"Ara knows I'm a drug addict?" My legs gave out.

"You're not a junkie." Haik held me steady.

"But still. I don't want him to think worse of me." I handed Haik the car keys.

"He didn't want you to suffer." Haik opened my door, helping me take off my jacket for the ride home. He fastened the seat belt across my lap.

"That's hard to believe. He still hasn't come to see me, you know."

"Have you called him?" Haik got into the driver's side. He adjusted the seat and the mirror.

"No," I said, closing my eyes.

"The car looks beautiful," he said after we passed the security checkpoint.

"It looked even better before it started to rain."

"Do you mind if I put down the window for just a few minutes?"

"Go ahead."

Haik drove with his arm out, his fingers outstretched, soaking his shirtsleeve to the shoulder.

"You should try the seat warmer," I said.

It rained harder as the front slammed into the San Gabriels near the freeway exit.

"What are you doing these days?" he asked.

"I'm writing something," I said.

"I thought that was over."

"So did I, but I guess I have something else to say."

He nodded.

"Have you heard anything from Christine?"

"Nothing."

"Women," I said.

"Yeah." But he didn't believe it, and neither did I.

"Do you think she would have loved me if I had money?"

I didn't say anything.

"Do you think your wife would've still loved you if she'd known?"

"I don't know. Maybe not. But I wish I'd told her."

Haik nodded. "It's better to know. Either way."

"What are you going to do now, Haik *jahn*?"

"I guess I'll finish the *khachkar*. Would you believe someone looked at it while I was away? A collector wants to buy it when it's done. For $50,000! She want to put it in a public garden." He shook his head in disbelief.

"My goodness," I said. "That's two blackmails worth."

"I'm sorry," Haik said.

"I forgive you," I said. "You're a wonderful artist, Haik *jahn*." I gave him what I'd denied him before. "Your *khachkar* is the most amazing piece of art I've ever seen."

"Thank you."

In all honesty, I didn't have anything to do with it after I showed Haik's *khachkar*/dolmen/obelisk/giant stone to Viktor. I can't take credit for his talent.

Haik parked in front of the studio and we waited for the rain to subside.

"Listen, I need you to go with me somewhere in a few weeks," I said, watching the droplets catapult down the windshield and puddle onto the hood. "*Inshallah*," I added just to irk him.

"Sure. Where?" he said with a blink.

"To the Turkish Consulate."

"What! Did they trace the bird shit envelopes back to you?" He sat up in his seat.

"No." I started to laugh so hard, my shoulders ached from the exertion. Haik never knew I sent those to the Armenian Consulate.

"They asked me to play at the Visit Turkey festival. I thought I'd go."

He sat still, examining his cuticles. He was about to bite the dry edges off and decided against it. "Yeah. Okay. I'll bring a big box of bird shit."

He opened a bottle of water and handed it to me. "You should hydrate. Take small sips."

I took the bottle from him and pretended to drink. Even water turned my stomach.

"Can I ask you something?" Haik said after a moment.

"Anything."

"Why did you stay an Armenian?"

I laughed. "For the perks."

"No, seriously."

I groaned. "I don't know. I'm tired, Haik *jahn*."

"You do. Tell me. Please." He put his hand on my shoulder, so warm and strong.

I nodded but didn't say anything for awhile.

"Did you do it for Artemis?"

I hesitated.

"Because you felt guilty for all the terrible things the soldiers did?"

I looked at the sheets of water sliding down my window.

"Rupen."

"I did it to play the duduk."

Haik drew in his breath.

"It was the only thing I had left."

We sat like that until the rain let up enough for me to get out.

242

"It's very bad weather. Why don't you take the car home?" I said.

He smiled and saluted. "Do you need help getting up?"

"No. Go home and surprise your family." I used a copy of *Asbarez* to shelter my head from the drizzle. I made it as far as the second floor before sitting on the stairs. The drizzle turned to rain, which then turned to hail. It came down hard, pleading to be let in. The accountant was holed up in his office, chirping to his parakeets. "Humans are idiots, my dears," he informed them. "Is it so hard to file the right papers?" As if his feathered family knew a Form 568 from a 565. His radio blared the weather report: Expect snow in Angeles Crest. I climbed up the rest of the way. Ara had left some pre-rolled joints under the door. My dinner.

CHAPTER FORTY-THREE

Thursday has always been my favorite day. Not because it signals the passing of the week so much as it brings the promise of Friday. My mother walked to the market in Sis every Thursday. It took her most of the day, but she saw friends and shopped or bartered to make an elaborate dish for the Friday meal. My father, who usually stayed behind, whistled in his workshop. I wore my favorite of the three shirts I had. Thursday was a day of anticipation.

When Haik came on that Thursday, Keran and Lucy were already at my studio. He stepped inside the door, then back into the hall and back in again, a gust of surprise buffeting him.

"Hello," Keran said in English. "You must be Haik." She kissed him on both cheeks when he crossed the threshold. "My father has told me everything about you."

He answered her formally in Armenian, "*Barev tzez, dkin,*" and tried not to recoil at the sight of Lucy. He blew on his hands to warm them up and to have something to do. "It's gotten very cold outside." He said to no one in particular. He looked around, presumably for Ara.

"Hi," Lucy said. "Sorry I hit you with the cactus."

Keran looked at her in surprise, but didn't say anything. I hadn't mentioned the kids had attacked him kung-fu style.

"That's okay. I healed up in prison," he said with a smile.

"They're coming with us to the consulate," I told Haik. "Lucy's playing the *dam.*"

"I don't know if I'm ready, *Papik,*" she said, tugging at the collar of her blouse.

"Of course you are. One day, you will be Maestro Lucy. You might as well start down that road tonight."

"Pa, are you well enough to do this?" Keran asked, taking my hand and chafing it between her palms.

"Well as I'll ever be." I squeezed out of her grasp and put on my beret. "Don't worry, we'll be okay."

We gathered our coats off the table. The flaw revealed itself in its imperfect glory. I caressed it with my knuckle. As we passed the mirror, we looked at ourselves in a brief moment of vanity, the crack turning us into a Picasso.

"My nose looks weird," Lucy said.

"Where's Ara?" Haik asked.

"He couldn't come," Keran said, touching up her lipstick.

Lucy snorted. "He didn't want to come."

"He sent *Papik* his best," Keran said, her voice trembling.

"I know Ara cares about me, my darling." I said. "That's what matters."

Keran linked her arm through mine as we walked down the stairs.

"Haven't seen you in a while, Maestro Rupen," the accountant called over the radio. "Are you hiding?"

"Not anymore, *Baron. Bari gisher*," I said.

* * *

"The freeway will be quicker," Haik argued when I asked him to drive through Hollywood. He turned up the heat and reversed down the length of the street.

"No. I want to see the city." I pressed back in my seat, feeling the heat radiate up my spine. My arm felt heavy with pain.

"Pa, you really don't look good." Keran said from the back. She held Lucy's hand. "Let's cancel."

"Don't make excuses because you're in the mood to cuddle with someone," I said. Lucy shot her mother a sideways glance.

"Now I know you're really sick," Keran said. "Let's go home."

"No." I refused.

Haik turned on the radio. "Bundle up, Angelenos, it's cold enough to snow in L.A. tonight." The DJ read the weather report. "The last time that happened in Downtown was in 1962. But before you get out your skis, it was less than half an inch. And how about a song to keep you warm tonight? Here's Smokey Robinson with *Baby Come Close.*"

Keran hummed along, her eyes closing for a second. Lucy shot me a questioning look through the mirror. I gave her a wink.

"Haik?"

"Yes, Maestro?"

"The car is yours."

"No. You don't have to give it to me. I don't need it anymore."

"I know. But one thing."

"Yeah?"

"You have to call it Aralez."

"Thanks." Haik drove past the mini mansions on Los Feliz Blvd. The walled Moorish house sat desolate, shorn of its riotous bougainvillea scarf. He cut across Koreatown. A drunken group of boys exited a karaoke bar, singing. Badly. They rushed back in when they realized the temperature had dropped. When we got to Hancock Park, Haik stopped so I could throw up in the gutter. The edges of my vomit froze.

"Let's go back, please," Keran begged as she wiped my mouth. Puffs of condensation punctuated her words.

"No. It's okay. I'm just making room for the reception food." She didn't laugh. I rinsed my mouth with bottled water. "And look. There couldn't be a more comfortable neighborhood to throw up in."

* * *

The Turkish Consulate, on Wilshire Boulevard, has a view of Carthay Circle, which isn't a circle at all but a parallelogram. When they first built the neighborhood, they disconnected it from all the major streets, creating a society unto itself. Haik got trapped inside the parallelogram and it took a few minutes to free ourselves. We were late.

The festival coordinator ushered us into the small auditorium on the ground floor. A large bank of windows looked out onto San Vicente Boulevard. He introduced us to a trio of folk singers and a *tanbur* player. Their eyes widened with recognition when they saw me. I was famous among the Turkish people. Well, at least their musicians. Either that or they were surprised that Armenians were invited to their concert.

"Maestro, would you like to go backstage to prepare?" the coordinator asked. "We'll start the program in a few minutes, at 8 P.M. sharp."

Lucy carried our duduk cases as we followed him behind the curtain.

"You know, I had an Armenian classmate in Istanbul," he said as he showed us to a table. "He was so smart."

Lucy groaned in my ear.

"He's trying," I said in Armenian.

We shared the space with a man preparing hors d'oeuvres. It was the chef from The Bosphorus. He nodded and continued to mix his pepper dip.

"It's so strange being with these people," Lucy whispered. "I don't like it."

"I'll give you a gold star for your efforts when we go home."

"Okay, *Papik*." She squeezed my shoulder. "Do you want one of these *paneer boregs*?" She asked, pointing to mini cheese turnovers sprinkled with caraway seeds. "I wonder if they're any good."

"Try one." I channeled Haik. "It will be your secret revenge to eat their snacks before they wish it."

"Not bad," she said, offering me a bite. We could hear the audience starting to file in.

"*Che, merci*. I don't feel like eating." Lucy drifted off toward the heavy drapes that separated us from the rest.

"The *tanbur* player is starting to play," she said, peeking through the gap. "Her butt looks like it's holding up a circus tent. She shouldn't have worn a pleated skirt. Oh, it looks like they're recording our performance tonight."

Lucy provided a running commentary while my mind wandered to snow. I imagined it engulfing my body, filling every crevice. Preserving me in its objectivity. My eyelids closed. Resting.

* * *

"*Papik*, it's time," Lucy says, helping me from the chair. She straightens my vest and smoothes her hair. She smells like lilacs and feta.

On stage, the coordinator introduces me in English. "It's our honor to present tonight the great Armenian duduk master, Rupen Najarian."

I brace myself on Lucy's shoulder as we walk toward the light. They're giving me a standing ovation. A horde of dust particles fly in the spotlight's beam.

Move, I tell them telepathically. It's my moment.

"*Merhaba*," I greet the audience in Turkish.

The label on my shirt scratches my neck. Someone hisses. Others drown him out with their applause. I wait until they quiet to say that Lucy and I are about to play an original piece of music that has roots in Anatolia. I say they are the first to hear it. A murmur threads through the crowd. Everybody loves an exclusive.

We sit quietly on pine chairs as the lights dim. Robert is on Keran's right side, a purple pastry box on his lap. He raises two fingers in greeting. Or is it the peace sign? Haik is on the left, looking like he's sitting on the cracked plastic chair from the doctor's office. The red-headed journalist from the *Times* sits behind him—without her notebook. Viktor stands at the back next to the coordinator.

Lucy takes a deep breath only I can hear and starts the *dam*. I lift my father's duduk to my lips. It doesn't play well anymore, so I'll have to try harder. We play without reading music. Sparse. Cold.

The snow inside me starts to fall. It is the first little flakes of the season. Light and beautiful. It drifts, soft as goose down, to frost ponds and decorate pines. It tantalizes us into its elegant frozen arms with the hope of something clean and new. The anticipation of change. It is a gift.

I play the second movement. The snow is steady. The lengths of white that block the horizon. The slush we trudge through on our way to a thankless job. The kind we curse because it's always there. The sort that taunts and teases and makes us slip and break our bones. Predictable. Dirty. Invasive. It covers our world in numbing monotony.

It's now the third movement. This is the snow of danger.

Avalanche. Blizzard. The moment where land and air become one big white nothing. The drift that consumes, destroys, that steals everything from us but reminds us that we are vital. It invites us to fight it. To rail. To scratch and claw through it. Only if we want to live. And when we do, we're grateful for the experience. How else do we know we're alive? It is exciting. This, too, is a gift.

The ground trembles. I hear a thud. The duduk slips from my hand and rolls toward the window. It's not an earthquake like at my birth. It's just me. I'm lying on the stage floor, soft as snowy down.

"*Papik!*" I hear my Lucy's voice as if she's in another room. My dearest, darling successor.

"Someone call an ambulance!" Keran screams. For some reason, she's holding the pastry box.

"Rupen," I hear the quiet urgency in Haik's voice. "Are you leaving?" He climbs up on the stage and places my head on his lap.

I don't want to go yet. I want to tell Haik this, but all I say is, "Don't forget to turn the coffin three times."

"Shhh," he says. "Rest." He strokes my temple.

"Make sure."

"I promise." There's a crack in his voice.

I turn my head to the bank of windows. Specks of white fluff float slowly toward the earth. They disappear before touching the sidewalk.

Out of the shadows, a young man walks toward me. He wears a simple white homespun shirt and a green wool cap. He stands smiling in the flurry, as if snow could never touch him. I know him so well. I smell the sweet smoke of wood shavings. He comes closer and I see his face. It's so clear. *How could I have forgotten my Ara looks just like him?* Small bits of ice streak past my father. He reaches me and tries to shelter me from the cold as the snowflakes drift onto my cheeks, their crystalline edges prickling my skin.

"I stole the duduk," I tell him.

"It was always yours," he says.

ACKNOWLEDGEMENTS

The Musician's Secret is a work of fiction. All the characters; some of the locations (Glendale General Hospital); a few details (cell phones with specialty music rings in 1992), are imagined. While I've tried to keep Rupen's journey within a historical timeline, it's by no means completely accurate. Any resemblance to real people isn't intentional. I've made every attempt to verify myths and traditions but I apologize if there are any mistakes.

I'm grateful to a number of duduk players: Djivan Gasparian, whom I had the pleasure of interviewing in 2005 for a *Los Angeles Times* story on the duduk. Writing that story planted the seed that became this book. I also interviewed Bear McCreary, Pedro Eustache and Jon Ehrlich. Bear was kind enough to share his thoughts on composing for the duduk. I'm also grateful to have met and interviewed the great duduk maker Karlen Matevosyan Smbati.

I'd like to thank my tribe, the Mathew family, for always being there: My mother Rachel; my sisters, Sue and Reny and their families; and my father, Mathew.

My thanks to my in-laws Shake and Vahan Khosrovian for sharing their stories; and my sister in-law, Vartouhe Khosrovian and her husband, Robert Issagholian. I'd also like to thank the extended Issagholian and Khosrovian families for the friendship and insight into a lovely culture. Special thanks to Hasmik Issagholian for her kindness and recipes. And to my husband, Melkon, to whom I've dedicated this book. He makes each day fun.

I'm grateful also to Zara and Robert Assarian for their friendship and stories. I was inspired by Robert's education on St. Lazarus to model Rupen's time there.

Thanks to David Hochman who put me firmly on the path to writing and all my friends on UPOD. To Al Watt and my friends at the 90-day novel workshop. Yes, you can write a first draft in ninety days. It's the second, third and fourth drafts...

I'm indebted to my readers and good friends, some who've survived several drafts: First and foremost my dearest friend, Gloria Mattioni. Thanks also to Sandra Tsing Loh, Frier McCollister and Ronnie Keller. Stephen Krcmar, Alfred Eisaian, Lusi Mkhitaryan, Jasmine Aslanyan, Anush Amiryants, Laura Agajanian, Judy Walker (who also designed the cover), Janet Durnford, Kaumudi Marathe, Ruth Kennison, Leslie Pollock and Reny Mathew. Thank you!

Thanks also to Clair Lamb, Wendy Lee, Jennifer Pooley and Karen Stedman for their editorial help. To Jay Wilson for his keen eye. And a very special acknowledgement to Shea "Sheram" A.J. Comfort whose photo is on the cover. (Thanks to his brother, Sage Leitson, for taking that amazing carbon print). The photo of the duduk on the back cover is by Shea.

And lastly to my hometown, Glendale, California: With its plethora of bakeries, thanks for being such an interesting place.

Photo by Thomas Mathew

Litty Mathew is a former journalist. She has written for *Saveur*, *Readers Digest* and the *Los Angeles Times*. She is also a full time spirits maker. She and her husband run Greenbar Craft Distillery, L.A.'s first distillery since Prohibition. She lives in Glendale, Calif., with her husband. *The Musician's Secret* is her first novel.

Made in the USA
San Bernardino, CA
24 April 2015